THE RAINDROP CROSSING

FOR KESTREL

"Power with lightness. That is the secret to my touch."

- Anton Rubinstein, concert pianist, (1829 - 1894)

ISBN: 978-1-83556-053-2 (PAPERBACK)
ISBN: 978-1-83556-054-9 (HARDBACK)
ISBN: 978-1-83556-055-6 (EBOOK)

Book Design by HMDPUBLISHING

CHAPTER ONE

The deep roar of three thousand people murmuring in agitated excitement shook through the cavernous areas backstage of Carnegie Hall. It was the sound of a distant waterfall pouring over granite cliffs, a rumbling that intensified as Samuel Clermont burst through double doors on his brisk walk down the hallway towards the green room. He was an aspiring young pianist himself, just out of college. But his job as a stagehand and usher at the famous hall paid the rent while keeping him close to the music world he loved. The fact that he was a young Black man with an unflappable commitment to the classical repertoire was at times seen as a bit unusual, but Samuel was used to that. He had dealt with raised eyebrows, and worse, all his life. Yet his steadfast devotion to the world of classical music remained pure. His ambition to become a great concert pianist would not be derailed by the ignorance of others.

With unrelenting optimism, he had endeared himself to the board of directors of Carnegie Hall and shrewdly curried favor with the music director by his vocal enthusiasm for being a part of the history of the fabled concert hall itself. Barton Finkelstein was one of the new breed of music directors sweeping into top positions of classical music institutions around the world. Along with his contemporaries in places like Dresden and Shanghai, these millennial smashers of rules and norms held the future of classical music in their hands. And when the time came to select a stagehand to lead the legendary young Hungarian pianist Laszlo Farkas from the green room to Isaac Stern auditorium for his world debut, Barton Finkelstein had personally chosen Samuel for the job.

Now, Finkelstein and other powerful people who had orchestrated the instantly sold-out performance were dressed in shimmering formal attire and sat in the fourth row of the orchestra seating section, just below the stage. So far, they had been the only members of the public to have laid eyes on Laszlo Farkas since his arrival in New York City. Almost nothing was known about him. The fact that there were no known photographs of him only intensified word-of-mouth accounts of his private performances. It was said they left people breathless with fear and wonder. The power and passion of his playing often left people tormented for weeks on end.

Laszlo Farkas at the piano was apparently a full-blown force of nature.

Rumors occasionally ricocheted through the classical music world about his patronage under the expansive financial wings of an aristocratic heiress in Paris. It was whispered that he divided his time between France and Morocco, yet nobody knew for sure. Those fortunate enough to secure intensely sought-after invitations to his so-called Dawn Concerts held in the early hours of the morning at grand chateaus in Europe and North Africa were asked to submit all electronic devices upon arrival. Those who did not comply had them temporarily confiscated upon detection by wands wielded by security staff at the entrances to the salons within which he performed.

Samuel arrived at the closed door of the green room fifteen minutes before eight o'clock.

He tucked down his black vest, adjusted his red tie and smoothed the front of his black wool tuxedo pants. He bent at the knees and looked at himself in the shiny brass "Green Room" plaque on the door. He ran his fingers through his close cropped hair and checked his teeth. He drew in a deep breath. But, just as he was about to knock, he realized there was no sound of last-minute practicing coming from within. The room was silent.

That was odd, he thought.

He couldn't remember an occasion when he couldn't hear the artist about to perform on stage warming up on the practice Steinway from some distance down the hall. Yet in his nervous anticipation of meeting Laszlo Farkas he hadn't noticed, until that very moment, that the only sound in the hallway was that of the capacity audience vibrating through the walls.

Samuel looked to his left, then to his right. There was nobody else in sight.

He gently knocked upon the door.

A few seconds passed.

He knocked again, harder.

"Mr. Farkas?" he asked quietly into the oak paneling.

He knocked a third time. At last Samuel gently depressed the latch, pushed the door open a few inches, and peeked into the room. The lights had been turned off from the inside. Yet deep within the darkness, now faintly illuminated by hallway light, hovered a form yet darker still.

Samuel squinted into the gloom.

"Excuse me," came a voice from the floor within the darkness. "Two minutes."

Samuel was deeply startled. It appeared that Laszlo Farkas was standing on his head in the middle of the room. Samuel quickly withdrew in awkward confusion, murmuring an apology. He closed the door quietly and was once again back in the hallway, blinking to himself, perplexed and somewhat disturbed. Exactly two minutes later Laszlo Farkas opened the door. His appearance was so striking, and the initial encounter in the room so peculiar, that Samuel just stared blankly as the magisterial pianist emerged into the fluorescent lit hallway. He was tall and pale and couldn't have been much older than Samuel himself.

Long jet-black hair was swept back over the shoulders of his sleek black suit.

His aquiline features were completely relaxed, ice-green eyes glacially calm.

His every movement was imbued with grace and fluidity.

"Thank you," said Laszlo Farkas. "I'm ready."

Samuel felt a heightened purpose rise within him.

"Very good! The world has been waiting long enough!"

Laszlo Farkas allowed a gentle nod and followed him without a word.

The booming echo of the awaiting audience radiated through the halls and through the stairwells as Samuel led the way to the left wing of Isaac Stern auditorium. Within minutes they arrived and Samuel opened the door marked "Artist Only." A swirling turbulence of white noise rushed at them from beyond the door on the other side of the room that opened to the stage. Laszlo Farkas glanced at Samuel and allowed a gentle smile as he entered the room. By now Samuel had the impression that he and Laszlo Farkas were confidants and perhaps, in a different life, could even have been friends.

"Good luck," said Samuel as he glanced at his wrist. "It's 7:52 p.m."

Laszlo Farkas was already pacing about the room with predatory confidence.

His hands twitched with lightness and power.

The world seemed to be evaporating all around him.

The sconces were dim. He moved silently over the plush carpeting like a shadow.

Like a panther in high grass, closing in on unseen prey.

Samuel was no longer needed, yet he was unable to take his eyes off the great pianist. Finally, he let himself out and pulled the door closed behind him as quietly as possible. He began a tiptoe run through the hallways towards the employee standing area at the back of the back of the auditorium. The program tonight consisted of the twenty-four Chopin preludes followed by "An Improvisation."

Samuel was crazed with excitement.

The program notes had been released to the public months earlier. A short but emotionally all-encompassing first half, followed by whatever struck Laszlo Farkas in the second half. No pianist in the modern era, where nothing was ever left to chase, would dream of making their Carnegie Hall debut with such a daring and courageous program. When Samuel first saw it he was riveted with exhilaration. He arrived at the unmarked door to the lobby and took a few seconds to compose himself. He again ran his fingers through his hair, took a deep breath and walked out onto the ornate marble floor where the last of the lucky ticket holders were scrambling in from the winter evening on 57th Street.

The ushers nodded at Samuel with smiles of recognition and let him through.

He walked briskly past the imitation crystal bowls full of Ricola lozenges, into the back of the orchestra section, and lightly elbowed his way to a spot at the front of other employees of the hall free to watch during the concert. Dozens of rows of plush seating sloped gently down towards the stage, draped with winter coats, occupied by hundreds of people reading their programs and looking up and around at the sheer grandeur of the hall. The nine-foot Steinway concert grand piano appeared absurdly small on the vast expanse of polished hardwood that was the stage of Stern auditorium. A minute or two passed. Anticipation built.

At last, the wooden door of the left wing swung open.

Laszlo Farkas emerged onto the stage.

A hushed wave of deference flew through the audience.

His presence conveyed absolute authority. Laszlo Farkas exuded a look of barely concealed resignation that he was about to flatten every person in the hall like a typhoon. He seemed to be aware of the fact that in witnessing true perfection, the great many musicians in the audience would have to face up to the somber reality that they would never be able to achieve such a state themselves. He wore a quiet, knowing smile as he strode across the stage towards the gleaming Steinway, coolly taking in the atmosphere of the auditorium.

Rushed whispers filled the hall.

The audience drank in his thin yet somehow menacing figure.

The cut of his suit pulled back upon his slightly curved spine, the arch of a man who had literally spent his life over a keyboard. The applause came slowly but began to build. So many in the audience had assumed for so many years that the stories were merely rumors. Many felt his legend had been born of collective imagination and a desire for the return of a romantic-era instrumental wizard such as Liszt or Paganini. Others still had discounted that he even existed. Yet his mere appearance as he walked across the stage convinced skeptics that they were indeed in his presence. Perhaps it was in the way he moved. First one person stood. Then others followed nearby, then others around them, like the opposite of falling dominoes. Before reaching the center of the stage Laszlo Farkas was engulfed in a standing ovation so intense that it bordered on delirium.

He arrived at the piano.

He placed his left hand on the top right corner above the keyboard.

Even from a distance Samuel saw the same gentle smile he had seen outside the green room what seemed like many hours ago. With a theatrical flourish, Laszlo Farkas tossed back his jet-black hair and for the first time faced the audience. They roared back. He looked down at the first few rows, then slowly up through the orchestra seating, holding eye contact here and there just a little longer than necessary. He scanned towards the back of the hall. A jolt of electricity shot through Samuel when for a flash it appeared to him that he was recognized all the way back in the shadows. Laszlo Farkas looked to those in the lower mezzanine seats.

He gazed up into the highest mezzanine seats, a full five stories above the stage.

He glided onto the piano bench with a motion so efficient he didn't actually touch the soft black leather until he was seated. Three thousand people dropped into their own seats like stones. The hall instantly became deadly silent. Laszlo Farkas calmly and lovingly ran his fingertips over the keytops as if alerting them to his presence. He looked down and stared through the keyboard like a man gazing through the open space between the wick and flame of a candle.

From the first caress that opens the twenty-four Chopin preludes a great many people in the audience must have felt as if they were hearing the true tones of the piano for the first time in their lives. Samuel, for all his practicing, for all his exposure to so many great pianists here in this hall, had never heard anything like it. The fingers of Laszlo Farkas swept down upon the keys like a soft rain. The gentle power with which he coursed through the early preludes was absolutely magnetic. He coaxed notes from the piano with inhuman precision.

They hung higher in the air than Samuel had ever experienced.

The third prelude in G-major played as a little miracle of sunshine and hope glistening over a fiercely spun web of brilliant left hand passagework. The fourth in E-minor played as just so much receding pain and loss. Laszlo Farkas eclipsed the sense of profound regret in the sixth in A-major with a reading of the eighth in F-sharp major so thunderous it didn't seem possible that such oceans of sound could be unleashed from a mere nine-foot concert grand piano.

His hands were a poltergeist of waves and hammers and fire.

An occasional demonic glint in his eyes would shine through hair that swung wildly in front of his face. The corners of his mouth curled in a rapturous smile. Samuel noticed that throughout the hall people were so entranced as to appear as if they were dreaming. He felt he was dreaming himself. During the tenth prelude in C-sharp minor, thick cascades of notes showered down in a torrential downpour. Laszlo Farkas tore into the heart of the set, bringing to the twelfth prelude in G-sharp minor a polished violence of such dramatic power that the vast auditorium seemed to shake at its foundations.

When he arrived at fifteenth in D-flat major, the famous Raindrop prelude, the instrument cried with infinite tenderness beneath his fingers. Chopin had transposed a rainy lovelorn night into its equivalent in purest musical thought. Laszlo Farkas conveyed this limitless exaltation directly into the souls of those who sat in unearthly silence throughout the hall.

In the middle section the raindrops began to fall one at a time.

Clouds darkened and the mood swung with great weight and burden.

After a few eternal minutes in these depths the original theme prepared its return.

A familiar lullaby of luminescent loveliness pierced through the canopy of longing.

The sadness was almost unbearable, yet Laszlo Farkas played the few bars of this transition back to the original theme with such delicacy and tenderness that the existential leap between melancholy and joy was temporarily bridged. The paradox was overwhelming.

It was too beautiful.

Tears broke through and slid down Samuel's cheeks.

Purest beauty permeated the entirety of the hall like an aurora.

But then, quite suddenly, Laszlo Farkas appeared so caught up in this dual emotional state that he lapsed or perhaps even stunned himself into a sort of trance. To the astonishment of the entire audience he began to hit wrong notes and suddenly appeared musically lost, as if he had stumbled into the abyss of a memory slip. The dissonant chords he now played were such a jarring departure from the transcendental state to which everyone had just been delivered that several involuntary shouts of protest burst forth from scattered points throughout the hall. In the higher mezzanine seats it was probably impossible to see what was going on, but to Samuel and those in orchestra seating it was clear that something had struck Farkas in the neck. His right hand came off the keyboard. He stared straight forward while pawing at his right cheek and shoulder. Even though his shoulder length hair covered most of his neck, against the black was the bright red tuft of what appeared to be some sort of...dart?

Samuel had seen plenty of National Geographic documentaries.

Was that a *tranquilizer* dart?

It stuck out from the skin underneath. Against the pianist's black suit and hair it was highly visible, the unmistakable fuzzy red tuft and polished medical grade steel of a large tranquilizer dart, where an instant before there had been nothing. Simultaneously, a small section of the plastered and vaulted ceiling amidst the lighting some forty feet directly above the piano was silently drawn up into the darkness. An opening appeared within the rigging of the lights above that Samuel knew was not meant to be there.

He could hardly believe what was happening.

He stepped around his colleagues to the long aisle leading down to the stage.

Without warning a black-masked commando figure in close-fitting black athletic gear practically fell through the open space and began a swift descent, attached to what must have been a thin steel or Kevlar cable. The figure, a compact and densely muscular form, looked like a ghostly demon descending upon Laszlo Farkas.

Screams rang out.

The enormous audience stood in one great undulating motion. Instinctively, Samuel moved down the aisle toward the stage. Laszlo Farkas held his right hand to his neck and began to fall backwards, his eyes fixated on some point in space in front of him. The floating figure halted just behind and above the pianist. In one motion he swung his torso and legs forward under Farkas's shoulders, preventing his fall from the piano bench. With a scissor kick the assailant hooked his ankles together in front of Farkas's chest. The cable motion reversed, pulling both assailant and pianist up off the bench, knocking it backwards with a bang onto the stage. Farkas's eyes remained wide open. His face slackened. The assailant looked up to the opening in the ceiling and wildly pantomimed his right hand in a circular motion, his powerful legs bulging and flexing as they locked firmly under the shoulders of Laszlo Farkas.

Together they ascended into the air.

Samuel broke into a run down the aisle as hundreds of people scrambled over the backs of their seats and toward the side exits. He vaulted himself onto the stage as the two bodies flew upwards through the vast space. He catapulted himself upwards from the overturned piano bench, reaching for the shoes of the man who could have been his friend in a different life, but it was too late. Two figures in black, dangling at the end of a wire, ascended with increasing speed towards the aperture in the ceiling.

The screaming of hundreds of people was deafening.

The assailant and Laszlo Farkas soared up through the opening and disappeared.

The aperture closed off like the door of an air lock.

They were gone.

CHAPTER TWO

Brilliant morning sun broke prismatically through the iced iron rungs of the fire escape outside the frosted bedroom window. It shot like daggers directly into the glazed eyes of Lysander Bennett as he tried desperately to remain asleep in the twin bed he had recently bought at Crate and Barrel. He flopped to face the other side of the room, but that didn't help. Nor did pulling the comforter over his head. He leaned over, grabbed his phone next to the empty water glass on the floor and squinted at the screen. It was after ten o'clock. Again.

No missed calls, no new messages, nothing.

He set the phone back down. He really needed a bedside table. He had been trying to save money by not buying one along with the bed, but this was ridiculous. Three months since Simone left and the downward spiral began. Two months since the Frick Collection suspended him from his job as associate curator. And now one month that he'd been here in this tiny East Village apartment living off the fumes of his savings account.

One month and still no bedside table.

If she had known about this state of affairs, she probably wouldn't have even been upset.

She just would have been disappointed.

An empty bottle on the kitchen counter snickered at his pain through the open bedroom door. Had he actually finished all the vodka? Christ, it wasn't even until after dark the day before that Lysander bought it at the liquor store down the street. Not getting into it during the daylight hours was supposed to keep him from finishing the damn thing. There should have been at least a few fingers left. He pulled the comforter back over his head.

What the hell was he doing with his life?

He had to get up. This was absurd.

Lysander flung the comforter off himself. He sat upright on the side of the bed and shook himself awake. There were still a few moving boxes left unopened sitting in a corner of the bedroom. One of them contained a few small treasured reproductions of paintings and several dozen copies of his self-published book "Darkness Visible: Night Paintings of the French Impressionists" which had been written in Paris years earlier, during a stretch of his young adulthood that had evaporated like rain on a hot summer sidewalk.

Sales had been tepid. But so beautiful was youth!

Living on the Left Bank, spending endless hours contemplating Monet's *Le Parlement* at the Louvre, Van Gogh's *Church at Auvers* and *Starry Night Over the Rhône* at the Musée D'Orsay, and the pointillist reveries of Georges Seurat and Maximilien Luce that could be found in smaller museums all over the city. His career began, ominously, when he came to the realization, during his junior year at RISD, that he was not going to make it as a painter. He simply didn't have the animal enzymes it took to carve form out of pure color.

The ones who were on their way were like white tigers, and just as rare.

They were angry, torn apart, wild, incessantly driven by the need to create.

Lysander always had a more delicate academic constitution.

Even though his childhood in New York had been spent crawling through the endless museums and galleries of the city, and he had always loved the idea of being a painter, it was the paintings of others that in the end got the upper hand on him. He had the eye, but his hands and body and mind lacked the fierce viscerality needed to set his thoughts on canvas. And so rather late in the game, to the thinly veiled relief of his academic advisor, he switched his major from Painting to the History of Art and Visual Culture.

Like a falcon released from a crate, he soared.

His critical thinking had been confined for so long, his burning desire to become something he wasn't had suppressed a mind built to analyze artistic expression across disciplines and philosophies. He read voraciously on aesthetics. In short time his trajectory superseded criticism and attained cruising altitude in the philosophy of art. Lysander became obsessed with the notion of paradox within art, studying the theory of beauty and spending enormous amounts of time developing conceptions of what painting can and should be, based upon the writings of Hegel and Kant. The notion of the use of color to depict the void of night especially intrigued him.

The fact that it was even possible drove him to the edge of mania.

And yet while he brought this mind of his to the Sorbonne directly after RISD to pursue graduate studies in his personally created field of night paintings, there was always this feeling within Lysander that he was not living the life he had been meant to live. The painters in Paris who stalked the halls of the Sorbonne cast shadows he felt he should have cast as well. They were who he was meant to be, but forces beyond his control had somehow bungled the execution of his destiny. It was not exactly regret, or remorse, because it really was not his fault. It was more a feeling of inadequacy, directed inward. He just wasn't good enough. There was no resentment or jealousy either. He was friends with painters, he had been all his life, and he genuinely admired those who had made it. Lysander became intent on making a career of the study of those who had catapulted to the other side, and he provided encouragement to young talent when he saw it.

But it was there. It remained deep inside him. A feeling that he missed the train of his own life just as the whistle blew and it chugged out of the station.

A feeling almost custom built for the lure and power of alcohol.

Now, he stood and watched as rusty water flowed from the bathroom sink faucet.

It always resolved and began to clear within a minute or two, but that was an awfully long time on mornings like this when the reflection in the mirror was of a lifestyle in total disrepair. He'd clean himself up soon enough. There wasn't really a choice. He was flailing. He splashed lukewarm water onto his face and rubbed it into his gray-flecked blonde stubble. The flowing water continued to clear. Lysander looked up into his own tired dull blue eyes and blinked heavily a few times as water poured off his chin. He popped open the cabinet, grabbed the Visine, tilted his head back and squeezed a few drops into each eye.

The can of shaving cream left a rusty ring on the dirty sink when he picked it up.

Simone had been the type of pristine blue-blood Upper East Side girl who occasionally wore a strip of faded lavender silk in her hair and Lysander never knew if she had found it on the sidewalk or paid six hundred bucks for it at Barney's. He never asked. She would never have stood for this, he thought. Neither would anyone else, of course. So why was he? He ran water through his sandy blond hair and again examined his face in the mirror. He wasn't getting any younger. He needed a shower. That would help.

And it actually did help.

He took a few minutes afterwards to clean up the apartment. He tossed the empty bottle of vodka on top of a few dozen empty beer bottles in the recycling by the kitchen door. He put the dirty glasses in the sink into the dishwasher along with a few plates and forks and threw out the half-open Indian food delivery cartons still in the fridge from two nights before. He grabbed the paper towels and Lysol from under the sink and headed back to the bathroom. He wiped down the bathroom sink, scrubbing at the shaving cream rust ring until the whole thing shone porcelain white. He hung up the towels, did a quick surface clean of the toilet, and flushed the paper towels.

He pulled on his favorite jeans, threw on a heavy flannel shirt and grabbed the empty water glass from beside the small twin bed along with his phone and walked back into the kitchen. He was feeling better, but needed coffee. His old coffee maker was still sitting in the moving boxes, but Lysander couldn't fully bring himself to take it out and set it up. Because then he'd have to have coffee in the damned apartment. And that would just be too depressing. He put on his beloved blue and yellow striped Adidas street shoes and slid his wallet and keys into his pockets. On his way out the door he grabbed his black Montblanc Saffiano leather sketchbook off the kitchen counter. He'd catch up on the news down at Cafe Jules downstairs. The little French cafe on St. Marks Place was more of a home to him than this miserable little apartment.

The right hand of Nesrin floated a cappuccino onto the window bar in front of Lysander with a silken touch. The curled tips of a croissant hung over the rim of a small plate, somehow *also* in her right hand, coffee saucer and plate overlapping like a pair of playing cards. It all gently parachuted down in front of him without so much as a click of porcelain on wood.

She made a quick one-finger gesture that she had to keep moving. She was busy, but she'd be right back.

Lysander had been coming down here now almost every morning of the month he'd now lived in the East Village. It was literally three doors down from his place and from the very first day he walked in Nesrin had taken care of him. They had some sort of connection, it seemed. He was aware she was from Syria and lived in Williamsburg, but he didn't know too much else about her. From what he could tell, there were a variety of men who rotated through her life but none of them ever seemed to stick. And she knew enough about Simone to know not to ask about her anymore. As Lysander was not really a rebound-relationship kind of guy he was able to chat regularly with Nesrin about life, including but to a lesser extent their personal lives, without things getting too awkward. The fact that she didn't seem interested in maintaining romantic relationships made Lysander wary of trampling on their friendship by in any way making the moves on her. Nesrin was very alluring, though.

It was a peculiar sort of friendship.

The curve of her neck and small gap between her two front teeth were set off all the more by her omnipresent tight ponytail of jet-black hair. Lysander guessed she was in her mid-twenties. A light cloud of freckles across the bridge of her nose floated under eyes the color of unpolished jade. Eyes with an alertness to them which seemed to imply that peripheral vision to Nesrin was not tertiary. Her skin was the color of the desert and there was a shimmering quality to her excellent English, tinged as it was with an actual slight English accent, that reminded Lysander of a mirage. She had a way about her that seemed to imply great strength yet he couldn't quite put a finger on it.

In the end, it was hard to tell with Nesrin.

Lysander had assumed she was off the books and here in the country as some sort of refugee. Syria was, of course, all over the news and while he was unsure of the exact situation in that area of the Middle East he suspected that she had been through a lot. In a way, he was intimidated by her. She moved with the kind of grace that can only be underpinned by great strength. Yet with her starched white work shirt, black pants and white apron it was hard for him to tell what she had going on under there. There was something not exactly mysterious about her, but she was suspiciously elegant and well polished for a girl who worked day shifts in a coffee shop. The fact that she was almost always at Cafe Jules seemed to indicate that she needed the job, but it also seemed like Cafe Jules was just a place Nesrin liked to hang out. There were plenty of other places she could be making more money with her borderline aristocratic demeanor and curiously unique good looks.

Lysander was operating through his disguised but still relevant hangover.

He fiddled at the latest sketch in his Montblanc with the nub of an old pencil.

He scanned through old emails from former colleagues back at the Frick on his phone.

He was constantly scheming ways to get back in touch.

To convince them that he was better, that he was a new man.

An increasing barrage of late arrivals to work had first put his curatorial position in jeopardy, but his colleagues, and more importantly his boss, knew that he had just been through a bad breakup and allowed him some latitude. Yet then the late arrivals began to be accompanied by obvious hangovers, and the head curator took him aside one day to let him know that the odor was obvious. While his department had great respect for Lysander, the director of the Frick Collection would not tolerate what was going on if she found out.

And smelling like that, it was only a matter of time until she noticed.

So it got better, for a while, but the tipping point came when Lysander began the terrible habit of celebrating that he had made it to bed relatively sober the night before by taking a nip or two during the afternoons. At first it was right before the end of the day, then it was with his mid-afternoon coffee, then it was with lunch. Correspondingly, he was a little too chatty by the end of the day, then a little too careless by the mid-afternoon, then visibly drunk *by* lunch. It was fine for a while, sort of, because Lysander was a pretty funny person after a drink or two. He was actually pretty funny to begin with, despite his academic pedigree and subcutaneous despair. And like most funny people, after a few drinks, he became even funnier. But again like most funny people, after yet a few more, he became someone who thought he was funnier than he was. Then he became someone who wasn't funny anymore.

It all came crashing down around him.

Now, as if she had never left, Nesrin was standing next to him again. Lysander felt her sly grin. He snapped his sketchbook shut.

"Are you ever going to show me what's in that thing?" she asked.

"Probably not."

"I didn't think so," she said flatly. "Anyway, are you free later?"

Hold on. Was Nesrin actually *asking him out?*

"Do you think you could maybe help me out with something?" she asked.

He wasn't sure he was hearing her correctly.

Was it possible *she* found *him* to be alluring?

"Are you free later or not?" she asked him again, impatiently.

"Well, I mean, sure," Lysander stammered at last.

It was not like he had anything *else* to do.

"Good," said Nesrin. "We can leave when I'm done, after lunch."

He watched her float away, as if she'd never stopped.

CHAPTER THREE

M agnus Aarden knelt near the open anchor hold at the bow of the two-hundred-foot long emerald green sailing yacht *Constance* as she motored past the Statue of Liberty just before noon. He found himself struggling with the last of the heavy inflated rubber fenders that had protected the hull from their berth at Chelsea Piers on the western end of 23rd Street. A late winter wind snapped sharp and cold at his windbreaker. Seagulls flashed around the Freedom Tower in the pale sunlight. Sails were still unfurling across the booms, the enormity of their surface area becoming apparent as they began to exert their peculiar physics in pulling the *Constance* further south through the New York City harbor. Polished steel furling blocks gleamed and held the sails tight to the wind. Magnus adjusted his footing to the increasing angle of the deck. Staten Island sharpened into view off the starboard bow.

The outline of the Verrazano Bridge loomed directly ahead.

"One more, no?" came a cry from within the anchor hold below him.

The voice was almost lost in the wind.

"Yes!" Magnus yelled down into the hold. "Here it comes!"

He waited for a lull in the relentless rise and fall of the bow of the yacht. Timing his moment to coincide with the base of a wave, he awkwardly picked up the last of the large unwieldy rubber fenders that had hung over the side to keep the polished hull from touching the marina at Chelsea Piers. He handed it down to Jensen, the deckhand, who handled it with ease and placed it into the final open compartment within the anchor hold. Once it was strapped in with the others Jensen grabbed the top sides of the small ladder leading back up to the deck and pulled himself up into the biting wind with one great leap. Magnus had only been aboard a few days and was consistently astounded by small feats of strength and power that Jensen pulled off with nonchalance.

Jensen and his older brother Tilman, the engineer, were just about the strongest people Magnus had ever seen in real life. They were close in age, probably in their mid-forties. Jensen had a head of receding light brown hair that he kept shaved down to what appeared to be an eternally tanned scalp. Tilman's hair was tinged with white and kept in a short bowl cut. The two brothers spent almost all their free time working out in an improvised gym they had set up in the engine room, made especially foul by the fact that they were both chain smokers and the engine room was the only place on the yacht they were allowed to smoke. It was a small dank space, crammed full of machine equipment and weightlifting gear that smelled intensely of sweat, kerosene and cigarettes. The brothers and the three other crew members only seemed vaguely aware that Magnus's previous life in the Netherlands had been spent on the cutting edge of generative artificial intelligence research.

None of them appeared to be the least bit interested in *why* he had been brought aboard.

Jensen gestured back towards the thick glass of the pilothouse above the aft deck.

"Captain Crosby and Felder will take it from here," he cried.

They walked aft towards the crew entrance just behind the main mast, holding onto the waist-high stanchions that ran around the perimeter of the deck and the white rubber-coated cable strung between them. The soles of their deck shoes held fast to the teak as they ducked underneath the enormous boom of the mainsail. Jensen pulled up the trap-style door, just behind the main mast, revealing a steep ladder that led down to the galley and crew quarters. He turned around and executed a fireman slide down the rails with unnerving ease. Magnus was still acclimating to the vertical entrances and exits aboard the *Constance* and carefully began to make his way down after him. Tilman was look-ing out one of the galley portholes to the skyline.

The brothers were about as odd a pair as Magnus had ever seen.

They both bulged with muscles and stank of cigarettes.

They rarely spoke except to each other.

Magnus was still only about halfway down the ladder.

"Looks like we actually pulled it off," he heard Tilman say.

"Let's grab a smoke," said Jensen. "He's gotta be happy so far."

Magnus slipped on the last step and stumbled down into the galley.

A volley of glances landed on him as he caught his footing.

Jensen looked to Sabine, the Norwegian chef, who in turn glanced at Tilman.

Well, it wasn't *Magnus'* fault that he'd never been on a sailboat before.

It wasn't at *his* invitation that a slick emissary of the owner of the yacht had shown up at Archmind in Amsterdam offering him an al-most inconceivably large amount of money to break his contract and come work on a project that would be taking place over the course of an Atlantic crossing. Less than two weeks earlier Magnus had been sitting in his cramped little office, surrounded by chalkboards ravaged with scribbles and equations that seemed a quaint throwback at such an advanced technology firm. Despite his youth, Magnus did his best thinking on his feet, tactile instruments like chalk and dry erase mark-ers in his hands. And then suddenly, without an appointment, a shad-owy man was standing in front of him. The emissary had been shown in by a receptionist who must not have known that recent-hire Magnus was one of the great new stars of the generative AI firmament.

His Ph.D thesis, "A Treatise on the Nature of Tears," had caused a sensation upon publication during his final year of studies in Utrecht. The employment offers had begun pouring in immediately. Deftly weaving a coherent narrative through brilliant literary and scientific insights, Magnus had isolated the complex relationship between mel-ancholy and joy in human emotion. He illuminated, from a computa-tional and mathematical perspective, the paradox that emerges when sorrow and happiness exist simultaneously during the creation and ap-preciation of great art. The work at the center of his thesis was a po-tential manifestation of the final piece of the puzzle required to make the leap and actually create a *general* artificial intelligence.

In effect, his paper had identified that which makes us human.

News of his equations explaining why tears elicited upon experiencing great opera were the same as those of grief or despair spilled out of Utrecht. His algorithms perfectly replicated the underlying emotions that produced tears upon reading *Anna Karenina* or seeing a Matisse in real life. In a final trick, he had even managed to explain how the beauty of mathematics might lead to a work of science being called a work of art. The theories and ideas Magnus had put forth appeared to unlock some of the deepest secrets of human nature.

His work sent an earthquake through the world of artificial intelligence research.

That he had written it while still in grad school came as an equally seismic aftershock.

Archmind secured him before he even graduated.

And then, within a few weeks of moving to Amsterdam, he had been poached.

Lured away by more money than he would have made in his *career* at ArchMind.

The emissary couldn't talk about what Magnus would be working on.

All Magnus needed to know was that his expertise was needed.

He could bring his laptop and continue his own research.

There would be no internet aboard, but all would be explained in time.

"I need to power down the engine," said Tilman. "The sails are taking over."

He made a two fingered smoking gesture to Jensen.

Jensen nodded towards the engine room.

The two of them left the galley together.

Strange and silent Sabine got back to work.

She wore a wide necked white t-shirt and worked expertly with her hands. Magnus suspected she was sleeping with one of the brothers, but he couldn't tell which one. She had apparently been a punk violinist before finding her true path in the best restaurants of Oslo. How she had ended up working on the yacht was unclear to Magnus. Her close-cropped blonde hair was bleached by the sun. A large tattoo of a chef knife blazed up her right forearm. Tattoos of feathered wings sloped up from her strong shoulders to protrude from just underneath the neckline of her shirt towards her neck. The black tip of a dagger jutted from the center of her powerful back up past the base of her neckline. It was hard to tell the full extent of the story her ink told. But to Magnus the overall effect, combined with the fact that she appeared comfortable around all things sharp and hot, was highly intimidating.

Magnus was unnerved by the Scandinavian trio. They were tight. They'd clearly been working together for a long time. They seemed capable of anticipating each other's every need and movement. The previous evening, their last night in New York, the three of them had gone out together for a last hurrah on the town without inviting him.

But at this point he was used to being the new guy.

He headed out through the aft galley door to check in with Captain Crosby and Felder, the first mate, in the pilothouse. The two of them, both American, constituted the rest of the crew. Crosby was in his sixties with small sky-blue eyes set back underneath dark grizzled eyebrows. Felder was about half his age but twice as earnest. Magnus liked them both. He made his way into the main salon, a large blue-carpeted room completely paneled with windows. At the aft wall of the salon a stately set of rosewood sliding doors led further back and down into the vast owner's quarters that was off limits to the crew. So far there had been no mention of their mysterious employer. Magnus stopped asking questions almost as soon as it became apparent not a single member of the crew wanted to talk about their boss.

To the left of the doors a sharp inclined staircase led up to the pilothouse, a control room completely encased in slanted plate-glass windows. Levers and buttons milled with a military degree of craftsmanship were built directly into the instrument panels. Jutting out from the center panel was an elegantly carved rosewood helm about four feet in diameter.. Magnus could hear Crosby and Felder talking in their flat American accents. Looking up from the salon he could see the rear of the mainsail through the glass against a flat blue sky. A full acre of white composite fabric, by now completely unfurled. The upper reaches of the mast had begun to angle out over the surface of the water.

Magnus was just about to head up when he heard the rosewood doors glide open below him.

He froze. He had by now assumed there was nobody else aboard.

He had assumed that he would at some point be receiving an out-line regarding the work he was going to be expected to embark upon. But he also assumed that he would be doing this work alone. Nobody had mentioned that anyone else was going to be crossing the Atlantic *with* them. Whoever that was down there would be with them for the entire voyage. Magnus decided to take charge of himself in that very instant. He stepped back down to the blue carpeting and turned to face whoever had just opened the sliding doors.

His eyes took a moment to adjust to the dimness of the salon.

There he was, down in the shadows, looking up with a serpentine smile.

He stood in the crack of the partially opened doors.

His mid-length hair was as white as snow.

His clear watery eyes squinted up at Magnus as if from a great distance.

Magnus felt a bolt of recognition rocket through his synapses.

The man was desperately pale.

The visionary tech industrialist Taron Veeder.

The famous scar slashed down the side of his left cheek, clear as a glacial ravine, struck Magnus more than anything else. He knew this scar well. Everybody did. It seemed to absorb light even when the face into which it had been carved merely looked out from the covers of glossy technology and finance magazines. Taron Veeder wore a beauti-fully cut yet loose fitting gray suit. His white dress shirt was untucked and his feet were bare. Day-old white stubble accentuated his high cheekbones like magnetized lint.

"You must be Magnus," he said, peering upwards.

His famously nasal accent was eerily familiar in person.

The doors were open just wide enough for him to stand between them, yet from the salon Magnus could see down over his head and back into the fluorescent lit space behind him. A white cube the size of a small car jutted out of blond spruce hardwood flooring. Optically enhanced glass panels were wedged at staggered intervals from floor to ceiling. They flickered with a scrolling code that Magnus could not recognize from a distance.

A low hum of great power vibrated from within the room.

Magnus noticed a movement near the cube.

A striking woman with auburn hair and violet eyes, wearing a white lab coat, appeared behind one of the glass panels. She was watching the lines of code rise from floor to ceiling and tapping notes on a handheld touchscreen pad. She stepped out into clear sight. She glanced through the rosewood doors. She made eye contact for a fleeting second, just long enough for Magnus to not quite register the emotion hidden in her expression. She stepped back behind the glass, turned, and quickly disappeared within a parallax of reflections.

The instant she was gone Magnus placed the look on her face: *fear.*

Taron Veeder closed the rosewood doors.

He stepped up towards the salon and they shook hands.

Magnus felt not just the strength of his grip but the bony structure of the hand itself.

"So nice to finally meet you," said Taron Veeder. "Let's sit. It's time we had a little chat."

He began to make his way across the salon towards two facing burgundy leather couches. Magnus followed him using small stutter-steps. The size and weight of the massive emerald hull cut so heavily through the waves that, aside from being tilted at an angle to starboard, the walk across the carpeted salon floor was not too difficult to manage. The salon was bright enough to emphasize the translucence of Taron Veeder's skin as he worked his way around the mahogany coffee table to the far couch and sat down. Sunshine streamed through port side windows that faced upwards to a cloudless sky. Magnus took his seat on the opposing couch.

He was still processing the fact that his employer was the legendary Taron Veeder.

And a question pressed urgently to the front of his thoughts.

Who was that woman?

What were they *doing* back there?

"I hope you've made yourself comfortable," said Taron Veeder, crossing one knee over the other. An alabaster foot draped over the expensive-looking fabric of his pants. "It's a little tight up there with the others. I know all about it. I myself have slept in your cabin many times. As a matter of fact, it wasn't too long ago when we were doing some outfitting in my own quarters and I must have spent several weeks on the very cot you sleep on now. But you and I are not so different. As long as our laptops are plugged in we're comfortable, am I right?"

"Ah, yes sir, very comfortable," Magnus said uneasily.

"Good, good. I've been happy to see your research is going well."

Magnus felt his neck tighten.

How did anyone know how his research was going?

"I've also been pleased to see that you've made preparations for the unfortunate necessity of our going offline for the voyage. We're probably out of the reach of cell networks by now and the satellite jammers will have automatically turned on at this point. Starlink and similar satellite systems work both ways and call me paranoid but we don't need anybody *prying* into what we have going on around here. So, I'm sorry about the lack of cloud access. But it looks like you have some very clever compression techniques on your machine. I'm actually quite impressed."

How did Taron Veeder know all this?

"But let's talk about the reason you're here! Your field continues apace, as ever, but despite these enormous leaps of scale you must be as aware as anyone that this generative AI nonsense is rapidly approaching its natural limitations."

Magnus was not sure about that at all. But he held his tongue.

"It's all anyone seems to talk about anymore. Of course, it's undeniable that it *is* all very exciting, but these LLMs trained on the internet are almost by *definition* limited. It's nothing but speculation that this field will solve climate change or cure cancer, all these hyperbolic situations everyone is always going on about. And yet, the chatter in the media is good for *our* purposes because it ends up diverting resources and talent away from *another* arms race currently underway. Do you know which race I might be referring to?"

Magnus knew of several races in the tech space, of course.

Taron Veeder sat back and Magnus saw something unsettling in his clear grey eyes.

"The race to create a *brain connection interface!*" he cried. "A genuine BCI! The fusion of computing power and the human mind. A system humanity has been dreaming about for decades. A connection between man and machine! One day our brains will be able to work in parallel with unlimited computing power, and that is indeed *more* than just speculation. It's *inevitable*. But the hardware is not there yet. Yet now that we're underway, the work involved in preparing for it has begun. That's why you're here. I read your thesis with enormous interest. Your isolation of the paradox within human nature linking melancholy and joy is something I've been working on for years now as well. However, I've been circling your observations from a *biological* vantage point. And it's a *combination* of our approaches that will be the crux of the angle from which we attack the problem. We've long known that the limbic system deep within the brain is primarily responsible for our emotional life. The amygdala and the hypothalamus in particular, along with the hippocampus and other extensions of the system."

Magnus was well aware of basic brain structures.

What exactly was Taron Veeder getting at?

"We've devised what might be called a serum," he went on. "A liquid compound that flash-freezes the entire limbic system instantaneously when introduced to the body. At that point we're able to map the emotional state within the brain using a nanoscopic MRI camera capable of magnetic resonance imaging *at an atomic scale*. Also of our own design, of course. Moving with of degrees of precision unheard of even in the chip-making sector we're able to make nanoscopically thin slides of the essential limbic nodes that contain billions of parameters *per molecule*. All of which can be analyzed for vectors of intensity per pixel, sets of edges and regions of particular shapes. Finally, a stacking of the slides will allow us to create a three dimensional blueprint of the architecture of emotion itself."

It had been a long time since Magnus blinked.

"And *why* would we be creating such a blueprint? Because we're staying ahead of what is coming. We'll be ready when it arrives. The hardware doesn't yet exist to implement a true BCI, but it's on the way. *This* technology will be the next true paradigm shift. Not generative AI and all this chatbot nonsense. We're already ahead of the curve at our facilities outside Paris. All they need is the blueprint. Which is what we will deliver when we arrive on the other side of the Atlantic. A crystal clear blueprint of the architecture of emotion."

"Well, of course, this is still just a working theory?" asked Magnus, almost shaking.

He was still suppressing what he was starting to realize was most likely the case.

Taron Veeder sat very still, watching Magnus carefully.

"Oh no, we *have* a subject," he said at last.

"A *volunteer.*"

CHAPTER FOUR

S uddenly, I'm awake.

A point of entry made by a pebble through the surface of a cold pond.

And from nothing, the ripples begin their dance outward. I begin to remember.

The wind would come from the east. It would blow in off the fields and lend a ghostly twang to the sheet aluminum roof, a sound that mesmerized me as I looked up to the ceiling from my crib. Even as an infant I laughed with delight at the gorgeous structural order of a single note on my father's flute being met with a tonal tenth. I cried at the wreckage of an accidental discordant triad. I absorbed the gypsy songs in my sleep, my parents dancing around the fire with their friends, clattering instruments creating harmonies that infused my infantile subconscious. At a neighbor's house while my parents worked in the fields I saw the old upright piano for the first time. When nobody was looking I managed to get onto the bench and reach up over the keyboard. After a few moments of depressing the keys I accidentally hit a harmonic third.

It sounded like sunshine. Like iced oranges with sugar.

Like my mother's smile before she disappeared from my life, taken too soon.

A booster seat was made of kindling and placed on the bench. It opened up the world for me. Scales, arpeggios and repeated notes came without effort. By the time I outgrew the seat my improvisations on themes of ancient gypsy songs began to take on a life of their own. I spent hours at the old upright long before my feet could even touch the pedals. Loose ivory keytops constantly had to be glued back onto the keys, hammers had to be stuck with pins to loosen the felt fibers that had hardened from so much pounding against the steel strings.

The piano had essentially been destroyed before I was four years old.

My father moved me to the ancient grand piano in a church at the outskirts of the village.

I have no memory of a piano teacher during those years.

My days in the old schoolhouse as a spindly child were spent tapping my fingers furiously on the worn wood paddle of a desk attached to the chair in which I endlessly fidgeted. People from neighboring villages brought old first edition scores of Chopin and Debussy for me to read through down at the church. More often than not they brought carloads of family members with them as well to hear the music of the piano for the first time in their lives. Reading music came to me without effort as well, far earlier than my being able to actually read or write Hungarian. Looking back now, it seems the peculiar power growing within me in those early years might not have been purely pianistic.

I'm actually a little surprised it wasn't more obvious at the time.

That is to say, while the technical attributes bestowed upon me were of course well suited for the piano, there was a sweeping undercurrent as well that must have somehow contributed to what I was able to accomplish with my playing at such a young age. It could be that I'm misremembering, of course. Perhaps nostalgic pangs are attempting to impose an explanation for musical capabilities that existed just outside the realm of reason. Capabilities like those I'm growing into now, balanced at the intersection of genius and magic.

CHAPTER FIVE

Lysander could sense Nesrin standing behind him.

"I think I'm finished," she said in her sand-polished accent.

She circled around and removed the pens from her white shirt pocket. She set them next to his sketchbook and removed the dirty white apron from around her waist. She then took off her starched white work shirt, revealing a white t-shirt tucked into her black work pants. Lysander could barely believe his eyes. She had long sculpted arms and the body of a warrior. The t-shirt was not tight, but it didn't need to be. He could still see the way her back shimmered and rippled up through her neck and out towards her shoulders. She wrapped the pens and apron into a tight bundle and walked towards a small closet off the bar. Lysander noticed the other guests in Cafe Jules do double-takes as she swayed her way among the scattered tables. He watched as she hung up the work shirt and pulled out a soft worn black leather jacket. She slipped it on and pulled her ponytail out from underneath the back.

She zipped it up halfway while walking back toward him

Lysander realized he had never seen *this* girl before in his life.

Nesrin was standing next to him again and angled her eyebrows toward the door.

"Hold on, let me pay my check," he said, as if suddenly remembering where he was.

"No check for you today."

The afternoon had warmed up quite a bit and the sky was blue, bursting open into its full glory as they turned the corner from shaded tree-lined St. Mark's Place and walked north along First Avenue towards the L train. The dripping sound of melting ice and snow was the sound of spring. People streamed in both directions, like galaxies passing through one another without a single star colliding. Lysander felt genuinely excited for the first time in ages.

Why would she be wanting his company for the afternoon?

He couldn't think of a single reason other than…*that*.

But then, just as he was becoming more and more sure that she was bringing him back to her apartment to physically ravish him, Nesrin took a blue pack of Gauloises from her jacket pocket and casually shook one out. As she did so, Lysander could see in her eyes that she was thinking about something else entirely. She put the cigarette between her lips and cupped a lighter as she walked, paying little attention to him and appearing utterly lost in thought.

"I didn't know you smoked," said Lysander.

"I don't. Not really. Here and there, maybe. There's a lot you don't know about me."

Nesrin held the cigarette in a pinch between her right thumb and forefinger and walked along with her foreign and impenetrable thoughts. Lysander noticed people trying not to stare at the tall freckled desert-skinned girl as she moved over the sidewalk as if it were a cross between a catwalk and a battlefield. They arrived at the yawning opening of the subway entrance.

Nesrin artfully flicked the cigarette into a nearby gutter.

She fluttered down the subway stairs without holding the handrail.

Lysander followed her underground. Within minutes they were on the subway.

"So, you've heard nothing from the Frick?" Nesrin asked absently.

"I check every morning. They just don't seem interested right now."

"And nothing from Simone?"

He didn't respond. She knew the answers to these questions.

She was looking into his eyes in the reflection of the glass across the subway car. Beyond the reflection the graffiti-strewn subway tunnel wall flashed by as they rattled along underneath the East River. She knew that his apartment was basically just a pile of cardboard boxes. They talked all the time. She knew about the state of his life.

They screeched into Bedford Avenue station.

Nesrin stood, ready to exit. Lysander followed her lead.

People poured out of the train and flowed up past the subway billboards for Coach and Chanel onto Bedford Avenue and North Seventh street. Lysander had been out to Williamsburg before, of course. But he couldn't remember exactly when or why. Usually it involved drunken late nights with strangers, best friends for a few hours, who he never saw again. The vibe came back to him now. It was actually not too dissimilar from the East Village, although in some strange way it felt both more expensive and more authentic at the same time.

He suddenly remembered why hipster Brooklyn was often referred to as *ironic*.

"There's a hardware store just up here on Roebling," said Nesrin, a lit Gauloise already back between her lips. "We need to pick something up, then the place we're going is actually just a few blocks away. Hey, how about that thing at Carnegie Hall last night, by the way? Did you see that?"

"What thing?" Lysander asked.

"Ah, some crazy kidnapping," said Nesrin, her eyes up on the storefront signs as they walked down Roebling. "It was the huge debut concert of this pianist Laszlo Farkas. In the middle of the first half of the recital a hole in the ceiling opened up, someone came down through it, grabbed the poor guy, and took him right back up through the hole in the ceiling. They took him right in the middle of a very famous piece called the Raindrop prelude."

Lysander had seen the posters all over town. The pianist was *kidnapped?*

He had known the Raindrop prelude since he was a kid.

Nesrin came to a stop in front of a small hardware store.

She stood outside the scratched-up glass door entrance and flicked her unfinished cigarette a good fifteen feet up and across the sidewalk. It spun in a perfect parabola through the air and Lysander watched it disappear directly into a storm grate in the street just as she pushed open the doors. The sound of steel scratching against the linoleum floor was the sound of a mom-and-pop shop that must have been there for several decades at least.

She looked back at him. "You coming?"

At this point Lysander felt only an abstract sense of curiosity regarding why she actually needed his help. It felt good to be outside of his neighborhood and outside of his routine. He followed her into the hardware store where she approached a shapeless young clerk with a stubble beard and rimless glasses in the paint section near the entrance.

The clerk appraised Nesrin up and down in an instant.

In the same breath he made an attempt to square his shoulders and suck in his chin.

A shadow crossed over his face when he noticed Lysander close behind her.

"Excuse me," she said, "but could you tell me where I might find a ladder?"

"Well it depends. How large a ladder are you looking for?"

Lysander noticed the clerk shift his focus over her shoulder onto him.

"What do you mean, how large?" asked Nesrin. "Just a ladder. It doesn't matter how large."

The clerk chuckled knowingly to himself.

As if to imply that he knew he was talking to the wrong person.

He looked directly at Lysander now as if Nesrin was not even there.

"Well, what's the project?" he asked Lysander over Nesrin's shoulder.

Nesrin glared at the clerk. Lysander could sense a change of gears deep inside her.

"Maybe your boyfriend has a better idea," the clerk drawled at her.

Suddenly she sprang with the speed of a coiled rattlesnake.

"Who's the one asking the questions here?" she hissed in a menacing whisper. "What does he have to do with this? Is there some reason you need to talk to him when I'm the one right in front of you? Did I ask which one is the *checkerboard paint?*"

"No, I didn't mean…" the clerk stammered, clearly taken off guard. She moved in very close to him.

"Did I ask for *liquid dent remover?* For fucking *blinker fluid?*"

Lysander suddenly realized that Nesrin might be somewhat unhinged.

But then, as quickly as her temper had escalated, she cooled back down.

"I just need a ladder," she said with forced calm. "Size doesn't matter."

The clerk looked up into her eyes as his fear and surprise subsided. "In the back," he said. "By the insulation, against the wall."

Without hesitation Nesrin walked straight to the rear of the store. Lysander followed in utter bafflement. She took a photo of the UPC symbol on a six-foot aluminum Stanley step ladder with her phone, then paid for it at the register. She returned and asked Lysander to grab the back end as she grabbed the front. The shapeless clerk avoided eye contact with either of them and held the door and they walked the ladder out of the hardware store. Nesrin moved quickly and with great purpose down the sidewalk along Roebling street.

Lysander trailed exactly six feet behind.

A few minutes later they arrived at a low-slung blue glass apartment building.

"Just let me do the talking," Nesrin said over her shoulder. "Follow my lead."

She tapped at the glass wall by the revolving door.

Lysander saw a doorman look up from his phone at the front desk.

She motioned towards the side entrance with a nod of her head.

The side entrance swung open. Nesrin moved towards it and walked right in.

Lysander had no choice but to follow her with the back end of the ladder.

The doorman came around the front desk as if to offer assistance.

"Clermont," Nesrin said to him.

She walked right past the desk dragging Lysander along behind her. She did not wait for a response.

She just kept talking over her shoulder as she walked into the lobby.

"Samuel Clermont, up in apartment 6F. It's on the certificate of insurance they emailed building management. He's working from home and on a call but he's expecting us. The actual track lighting is stuck in traffic but we're just going to go ahead and get started on the ceiling install. The guys have the piece and should be here soon."

"You got it," said the doorman, already back at his desk. "Sure you don't need the service elevator?"

"We do this all day long," Nesrin called back. "It'll fit. Thanks, though."

Lysander kept his mouth shut.

Nesrin pressed the elevator button and with a ding the door quietly opened.

She pulled in her end of the ladder and stood it up in the elevator.

Lysander pushed in the back end and set it down.

Nesrin pressed the button for the sixth floor.

"Excuse me," he said. "But what exactly is going on?"

"We're here to talk to somebody."

"I thought we're here to install a…"

The door opened onto a long carpeted hallway.

"There's no lighting. There's no installation of anything. Get your end out first."

Lysander slid the aluminum foot skids out into the hallway.

"Then what are we doing with this thing?" he asked.

"We aren't doing anything with it."

She edged the top of the ladder out of the elevator.

"This just gets us into the building," she said. "Two people can get in anywhere as long as they're carrying a ladder. Nobody ever questions anything. I've done it many times before. We're here to talk to somebody who was there last night."

"*Where* last night?"

"The kidnapping," said Nesrin quietly. "At Carnegie Hall."

"Excuse me? Did we just *break in here*? Because of a *kidnapping*?"

"Everything is going to make sense very soon."

She set her end of the ladder down on the carpeted hallway.

Lysander followed her lead. She turned to him and held one finger to her lips.

Lysander tilted his head ever so slightly to pick up on the nuance of what he was hearing. The faint sound of piano playing. Nesrin began to move almost imperceptibly slowly down the hallway. He followed. The playing was dark and melancholy in the carpeted stillness. A single repeated note within the music chimed like a church bell under a cloudy sky.

Lysander stopped in his tracks. Nesrin must have sensed it because she did too.

She turned around and looked at him.

"It's *that piece*," he breathed. "The Raindrop prelude."

The primary theme broke through the minor-key cloud cover.

It stopped there. Then started over where it had been just a few seconds earlier.

The section was being played and repeated, again and again.

They continued to the door and waited for a pause that did not come.

Nesrin knocked. The piano playing instantly stopped. Several seconds of silence followed. The sound of footsteps padding across the hardwood floor grew steadily louder. Nesrin stood directly in front of the security peephole. Lysander saw the shadows of two feet through the crack underneath the door. After another few seconds, the door opened. It was a young black guy. Practically a kid. Not much older than his early twenties. He wore black sweatpants with an orange Princeton "P" logo on them and a light gray cashmere sweater a few sizes too large.

He looked back and forth between the two of them a few times.

"What's going on?" he asked. "Is the piano bothering you?"

"No," said Nesrin. "You're Samuel, right? Samuel Clermont?"

The young man squinted at Nesrin with sudden suspicion.

"And who are you?" he asked.

"I'm Nesrin. And this is Lysander. We're hoping to speak with you."

"What are you here to speak to me about?"

"About last night."

"Last *night?*"

"Yes," said Nesrin. "Sorry to bother you at home. I know you've had a long night. Midtown North precinct, right? 54th street? I know you were the last person to have contact with him. You must be very shaken right now. But if we move quickly I think we can find him."

"Excuse me, but who the hell are you?" Samuel asked.

Lysander couldn't wait to hear *this*.

"Early last year the daughter of a Syrian diplomat was abducted in Istanbul."

He did not expect to hear *that*.

Nesrin gave Samuel a name. Then she spelled it out, slowly.

"Google him," she said. "You'll see that the case was solved by a special agent out of Syria who found herself in quite a bit of hot water with the people who had orchestrated the kidnapping. And so she vanished. But a miniscule amount of information about her was leaked. I think you'll find it quite interesting. You'll find any number of articles about it. The Economist, the FT, Foreign Affairs. Pick one. Read it and then meet us on your roof deck."

"How do you know I have a roof deck?" Samuel stammered.

"The same way I know what apartment you're in. Zillow is pretty comprehensive."

"What was this leak?" asked a stunned Lysander.

Nesrin looked at him with a sympathetic smile.

As if to say...*come on.*

"That the special agent was a woman at all."

CHAPTER SIX

Taron Veeder uncrossed his legs.

He stood with an athletic crouch against the angled floor.

"Shall we head back to the extraction chamber?" he asked.

Extraction chamber? Magnus thought of the girl with the violet eyes.

He pushed himself up and found a wobbly stance by the salt-streaked windows.

"It's never easy at the beginning," said Taron Veeder, over his shoulder. "You'll meet Raquel in a moment. She's quite new on board as well. Compared to the others, at least. Mathematics background, not unlike yourself. Graduated from medical school, though. She was with us on a few smashers during sea trials and took it like an ace."

He began to move in spurts across the blue carpet, stopping to brace himself against the drop into the trough of a wave then moving forward again in the moment of calm that followed. Magnus did his best to emulate this technique and wobbled after him as best he could.

Taron Veeder arrived at the rosewood doors.

He put his bony fingers into handles carved directly into the wood.

The heavy doors slid cleanly open.

Taron Veeder entered the room. Magnus followed.

The further aft he moved, the smoother the ocean felt. As he stepped onto the spruce flooring of the secretive area at the rear of the ship he felt more anchored to the floor than at any point since they had departed that morning. The room was not large, yet it gave an impression of expanse due to the sparseness of the equipment within it.

No control panels. No chairs. No paper.

All lines were either parallel or perpendicular to each other.

The white cube he had seen earlier droned deeply at the center of the room.

"The external paneling of the mainframe is chromium," said Taron Veeder. "My own design, like most things you'll see aboard. It doesn't conduct heat very well, which helps keep the super-cooled system insulated from the temperature of the room."

Aside from a patch of clear spruce flooring next to the white cube, the floor-to-ceiling glass panels Magnus had seen from the salon were placed like transparent library shelves at seemingly random intervals around it. He stepped closer to examine the code yet the language was oddly unfamiliar to him. Of course, if anyone could have created a custom coding language to deal with the complexities of this project, Taron Veeder would have been a likely candidate. It was well known he had been a mathematics prodigy during his childhood in Berlin. He was doing collegiate-level work across the board in the sciences while other kids were learning how to ride bikes or add a touch of curve to a well-kicked soccer ball. Linguistics had apparently always come easily to him as well. His penchant for languages was firmly attached to his reputation for bold and ingenious solutions to obscure proofs that had stumped mathematicians for centuries. Part of his legend derived from the fact that at a relatively early age he had been able to converse with the great minds of mathematics and physics in their native tongue, be they from China or India or Brazil. The spooky circuitry of grammar, like the logic underpinning most complex theorems, was something his mind and memory could handle without apparent effort. He had an ability to find the simple within the complicated, to mentally ice skate along the path of least resistance by the purest instinct.

Magnus looked around at the clinical cleanliness of the room.

There were no obvious entrances or exits aside from the rosewood doors behind him.

Yet clearly there was more going on here than met the eye.

Taron Veeder took a few side steps to one of the white walls.

He pushed a white button that had been invisible until it was depressed.

Magnus now noticed hairline cracks in the shape of doors all around him.

"Yes, Mr. Veeder?" The voice of Sabine softly filled the room.

"We're heading into the chamber," said Taron Veeder.

"I understand. Not to be disturbed."

A quiet ping signaled the end of the short conversation.

"Once you're inside," Taron Veeder said to Magnus, "I'm going to have to retire for a spell. But there's a work desk in the chamber and a great deal of information I want you to start going over. A mathematical distillation of the code you see out here. Most of the code is noise caused by atomic friction within the layering of the slides. By the time it gets processed through the algorithm it's been filtered many times over. Raquel checks on it out here from time to time. Any discrepancies she deems related to the extraction she looks into from her quarters."

He peered closely at Magnus.

"Back here as well," he said. "That's why you haven't met her yet."

Taron Veeder pressed another part of the wall. A door slid silently into the ceiling.

"One last thing before we head in. Don't be alarmed. What you're about to see might in some ways strike you as disturbing. But I assure you, he's very comfortable. He's simply unconscious. Essentially in a dream state. His emotional core has been temporarily frozen by the serum, but physically he is being extremely well cared for. Feeding and bodily regulation are all being attended to by Raquel. It's as if he were in a coma."

He walked into the darkened chamber.

"As per our agreement when he volunteered."

Magnus followed. The door slid shut shut behind them.

In the middle of the dark chamber hovered a transparent sphere. It was suspended in the air in the middle of the room. It was slightly larger in diameter than the height of a man. Dotted with black metallic studs at precise and regular intervals. A clear liquid filled the sphere to just below the center without so much as the smallest ripple on the surface. And on the glassy surface of the liquid, floating face up with his arms extended like Leonardo da Vinci's Vitruvian Man, was the figure of a man. He wore what appeared to be some sort of scuba-diving wetsuit of a shimmering deep blue material that fit tightly over his slight frame.

A large silver helmet covered his face.

Underneath the helmet flowed the ends of a shock of jet black hair.

Tubes and wires protruded from the back of the helmet as well as from various points along the wetsuit itself. They all joined together at the back of the beltline underneath him. Through a clasp they were wired down through the bottom of the sphere, holding the figure in one spot on the surface of the liquid, immobile within the suit and helmet floating on the surface. They reemerged on the other side of the sphere and through a single hose were connected to the floor of the chamber.

"Superconducting magnets," said Taron Veeder.

Magnus was still taking in the sight before him.

"The black bits. Counter magnets are built into the ceiling above and the floor below."

The liquid-filled sphere, with a person inside, was simply hanging in midair.

But what struck him as much as anything else was the fact that the surface of the liquid within the sphere, and in turn the figure floating on the surface, remained absolutely parallel to the surface of the ocean. They were perfectly parallel to the horizon that Magnus could not see but could feel within his own sense of ballast. He felt the floor underneath him rising and falling. He felt the tilt of the floor still scheming against his natural facility to stand upright against gravity. And yet the figure on the surface of the liquid within remained absolutely and perfectly still. Regardless of how much the *Constance* leaned with the wind, the surface of the liquid within the sphere remained exactly parallel with the horizon. Magnus thought of a clear ball almost half-filled with liquid being held in his hand. No matter how much he twisted his hand around, the surface of the liquid would remain parallel to the floor.

For the floating figure inside, the outside world might as well have ceased to exist.

"He's being very well cared for," said Taron Veeder. "The tubes and wiring are assisting with ventilation, feeding, and evacuation of fluids and solids from within the suit. His vitals are being closely monitored. It's as if he were taking a nice long bath and slipped into a dream state. The fluid itself is a saline solution extracted from the ocean itself and infused with electrolytes. A form of plasma. God forbid we had a leak in the suit. As you might have guessed, the helmet is actually the nanoscopic MRI based camera. Scanning the limbic system in molecular layers as we speak. The generated code you saw outside is the result of feeding the atomically detailed information into the deep learning algorithms we just discussed."

Magnus was wide-eyed in wonderment.

"But why would he have to be in there?" he asked. "In there, and on this ship?"

"We were always going to be performing this extraction during the Atlantic crossing. For reasons having to do with privacy and secrecy. Corporate espionage has long and, as I've said before, *prying* fingers. With Starlink jammed there is no other way to access our work. But, being out here, I had to devise a method of keeping the brain absolutely stable. If we were to simply place him on a table, or inside an MRI machine, the movement of the yacht would jostle the brain within his skull far too much for us to acquire images of necessary clarity. If you shake a can of aspic, the aspic within jiggles. It's the same with the brain within the skull. Using this method of containment we're bringing in images of startling clarity."

Taron Veeder stepped over to the only table in the chamber.

An embedded screen was scrolling with mathematical equations.

With *this* code, Magnus knew exactly what he was looking at.

Taron Veeder looked at him with piercing eyes.

"We need you to piece together the emotional architecture in a manner that will allow us to actually replicate it. This is why we've hired you. I'll be very curious to hear your initial reaction to our findings. It will probably take you most of the afternoon. It would probably take anyone else the rest of the month. I have to retire to my own quarters now. Even without the internet I have business communications to attend to. But I think you'll be comfortable here. This screen is the only one tapped directly into the mainframe. The only thing I ask is to not approach the subject. The superconducting magnetic currents are calibrated with astronomical precision. Best not risk having your belt buckle or a button on your shirt interfere. Raquel will be in soon to check the vitals. I'm sure you two will get along splendidly."

Taron Veeder left the chamber. The door slid back down behind him.

Magnus took a seat in the velvet-lined steel chair bolted to the floor.

He zoomed out to get an overview of the work in progress before reading in detail.

It was very difficult not to keep glancing at the sphere and the figure floating within.

Yet somehow he was able to begin making progress.

Magnus had never before seen such pure connections in a stream of data. The subject must have had an astonishingly sublime artistic mind. Overlapping sequences sat within each other like laser-cut jewels. The algorithmic structuring of Taron Veeder's extraction techniques were more powerful than anything Magnus had ever even conceptualized before, let alone actually seen or worked with.

He drank in the math. For hours, he swam through the algorithms.

Slowly, with no actual tipping point, what had initially been little more than a faraway ping of a suspicion began to give way to something more along the lines of a blaring alarm. This work was beginning to look an awful lot more powerful than the kind of interface Taron Veeder said they were working on. An awful lot more powerful than a blueprint for the melding of mind and machine. More powerful than the infrastructure of a BCI as dreamt up mere decades ago by science fiction. This work eclipsed large language model-based generative AI entirely.

Humanity had sought something like *this* since Greek and Egyptian mythology.

This was looking like the bones of an artificial *superintelligence*.

The door to the chamber slid open.

It was her. She held the same clipboard he had seen earlier close to her chest.

"Good evening, Magnus," she said. The door slid closed behind her.

She spoke in the smooth clipped English that was the lingua franca of high science.

"I'm Raquel. I think you've been told. We'll be working together."

She stood perfectly still and opened her eyes widely at Magnus. She brought her right index finger to her lips. She gestured her eyes towards the ceiling. Magnus looked up as well but saw only white. The deep drone of the superconducting magnets was the only sound in the room.

Cautiously and silently she began to move towards him.

She cupped her right hand to her ear and angled her neck to the ceiling.

Somebody was listening. Taron Veeder was listening.

She stepped closer to Magnus and pulled out the stylus attached to the top of her clipboard. She looked behind her through the doorway into the room with the glass panels and white server cube. She gestured with her long neck at the figure floating in the saline.

She held the clipboard in front of her and began to write.

She looked back into the room behind her once again.

She turned the clipboard around and showed it to him:

KIDNAPPED

CHAPTER SEVEN

A t the age of five I made my first trip to Budapest.
Some sort of guardrails were needed before I drove myself off the rails.

Despite my youth my father had decided I should audition for the Liszt Conservatory.

A Bechstein grand piano rested heavily in a corner of the large classroom. Layers of dust had been absorbed into the oiled ebony lacquer and a torn leather adjustable bench rested on the floor beneath a yellowed ivory keyboard. Parquet floors were scratched and aged. Windows were set high on the walls. Winter clouds hung heavy in the Hungarian sky. The jury panel consisted of a meek-mannered young man, a wisp of an elderly woman, and a heavy-set monocled man who sat between them at a large desk. They exchanged smiles bordering on smirks of sympathetic allowance as my clearly uncomfortable father led me in and untied the little burlap scarf from around my neck. The jury conferred with each other in hushed tones.

Finally they deferred to the monocled man who was clearly in charge.

"And so, you *are* a little one," he snickered.

The patronizing timbre in his voice was clear.

"What have you prepared for us today? Shall we see about getting you a higher bench? I would think you might have a hard time even reaching the pedals."

I remained silent. This condescending tone was new to me.

"My boy has prepared Bach," my father allowed.

"Ah! So suited to the young, Bach. So charming, and yet such depth. Well, there are quite a few candidates left this afternoon. Let's get to it."

He chuckled in a jowly way, glanced down at his papers, and looked back up to me.

"What, ah, *specifically* have you prepared for us, little boy? One of the two-part Inventions perhaps? An excerpt from one of the delightful French Suites?"

I could see from the reflections on the faces of the jury that his belittling tone had elicited an unnerving reaction from me. My own face must have suddenly taken on the look of a much older boy, perhaps even a young man.

I felt my scrunched-up little glower relax into a look of stern confidence.

Gone was the impression of a boy being attended to by his simple country father.

Something tightly coiled and potentially dangerous was now before them.

"I can play whatever Bach you wish to hear."

The monocled man suddenly appeared flustered.

"I didn't mean to offend, young fellow. Why don't you be the one to choose? There are potentially qualified candidates outside who we must get to at some point this afternoon. So please. Have a seat, give us a sarabande or whatever else you might have prepared, and I assure you we shall grant you our most sincere consideration."

With a tug on my father's well-worn sleeve, he looked down at me.

I tugged again. He bent at the knees to take in a whisper.

The jury was now becoming visibly exasperated.

"Only if you wish," he replied.

He looked up to the panel with barely concealed defiance.

"Laszlo will decide at the keyboard what he shall perform, as the mood strikes him."

He was aware that for me the decision and the execution were the same thing

The three members of the jury exchanged quick glances.

"As you wish," the monocled man muttered with a shake of his head, clearly incensed.

I walked across the room and climbed aboard the piano bench.

I looked down at the keyboard.

My tiptoes hovered in the air an inch or two above the pedals.

The air of the room hung cold. I sat very still, looking now *into* the keyboard.

My father stood back with an expectant wince.

Outside the high clear windows the cry of a hawk bladed across the sky.

I raised my right hand to the height of my shoulder and threw it into the center of the keyboard. I hammered out the primary figure of Bach's beautifully demonic A-minor fugue from the first book of the Well-Tempered Clavier. The strength of my back and shoulders leaned into the notes. The theme pinned the members of the panel to the wall behind them before the extended opening figure was reintroduced. And then woven into itself three more times. My father looked to the ground as the introduction of the fourth figure in the bass of the piano roared into the second page of the fugue. The music was now four terrifying intertwined comets. They streaked across the night sky weaving in and around one another. Their tails combined into one great dust shroud.

The room was a shock of sound.

My fingers felt made of steel as they blurred up and down the keys.

The music did not seem to emanate from hammers striking strings individually but more from one living creature crying and howling in four voices at the same time.

I did not use the pedals to attain this effect. My feet could not reach them.

By the blistering climax of the piece the look of the faces of the members of the panel was one of overwhelming disbelief. I had seen this look many times before. But as the fugue then began to unravel itself and come in for landing, my demeanor softened. The electric tension in my body loosened. My father, who had been averting his eyes as if from an unbearable brightness, began to relax as well.

The final notes arrived only a few minutes after my assault on the instrument began.

I gazed down at the keys for a long moment, breathing heavily.

Gradually the look of maturity must have evaporated. I felt an innocent smile release itself.

I slid off the bench to the cold floor and walked towards my father.

He was gathering our coats and my little burlap scarf.

Leaning down he tied it around my neck.

Preparing to make our exit, he turned to the panel.

"Over the next few years we will be in touch," he said. "We just wanted to come down and see how it felt in these halls. Obviously his talent belongs here. But as a child he does not. You have shown yourselves for what and who you are. When he's older perhaps he'll be ready to deal with this place. And you with him. But for now he needs the warmth of his home. I assume this is all that was needed to gain admission. When he's ready to attend we'll let you know."

The room was silent except for the sound of a pen dropping onto a desk.

It rolled across the surface, off the edge, and landed with a little click on the floor.

On our way out I turned and caught the eyes of the monocled man.

His face was frozen. Our gaze remained locked until he looked away.

We would accept guardrails on *our* terms.

When *I* was ready.

CHAPTER EIGHT

Samuel Clermont shut the door and remained perfectly still.

After a moment he heard the elevator ping at the end of the hall.

They were on their way up to the roof. Samuel turned back into his apartment.

His eyes moved back to the score of the Chopin preludes still resting on the music lid of his 1964 Baldwin upright. It was the piano he had grown up with back in Chicago. The piano he had spent so much time on since lessons began when he was a boy. Dreams of becoming a concert pianist had never been seriously pursued, though. He wasn't *that* good. But even though his major at Princeton had been computer science, the piano had by that point become the most important thing in his life. Of course there were pianos and places to practice on campus. He never needed his childhood instrument at school. But upon arrival in New York, after graduation, he sent for it. Samuel had made a promise to himself that he would not buy a new instrument until the world had somehow given him validation that he had earned it.

It always struck him as a peculiar twist of fortune that all his years of formal piano lessons were not quite enough to get him to a level that would earn him entrance into an actual conservatory, yet countless hours of messing around with various computers in the family rec room as a kid were enough to result in him becoming a computer science major at one of the most prestigious universities in the country. In college, he was constantly getting his homework done as fast as possible so he could run across campus to the music department in Woolworth Hall. Once there, he'd rush down to the practice rooms in the basement.

He realized early on that it was an almost unhealthy obsession.

Over the course of a few semesters Samuel actually tried to round himself out a bit by joining the wrestling team. But spending even just a few afternoons a week working on hip throws and sit-out escapes, when there was such a huge repertoire just *waiting* for him in the basement of Woolworth, finally just seemed like a waste of time. He couldn't exactly call himself a virtuoso, but he was certainly good enough that by the time he had graduated from college he realized that he loved the piano much more than the idea of getting a job working as an engineer for big tech. His artist friends convinced him that moving to New York and getting a job that exposed him to the playing of professional musicians was a risk worth taking.

His parents didn't understand at all, of course.

One of the more difficult decisions of his life had been to forgo the type of life and career his formal education had prepared him for. But the piano was what he loved. During his first few years in New York he had taken on all sorts of relatively menial tech jobs in the offices of Lincoln Center and the Metropolitan Opera to be around the music he loved. After looking into what it would take to join the Local One Union of the International Alliance of Theatrical Stage Employees, he found that between his experience at Lincoln Center and the Met he had just over the three years required working for institutions that had collective bargaining agreements with them. And so after a lot of legwork and meetings with various higher-ups at Local One, he was offered the job of a stagehand at Carnegie Hall. To his enormous surprise he found that his income nearly doubled. The fact that he was now able to interact with famous pianists whose recordings he had come to know intimately over the years was a dream come true. It seemed just a matter of time before the right person recognized the quality of his playing.

But right now, he just felt confused and sleep-deprived.

He hadn't slept since the night before last.

He walked over to his desk and sat down at his laptop.

He asked ChatGPT about the Turkish diplomat whose name Nesrin had spelled out for him. Who combed through articles anymore, anyway? Over his high-end sound system the computer told Samuel about the abduction of the diplomat's daughter. Maybe he *had* heard about this, actually, now that he thought about it. The kidnapping had occurred in the middle of the night at their home in the upscale Nisantasi neighborhood of Istanbul. It had been quickly established that an underworld network based out of Syria was behind the kidnapping. Neither Ankara nor Damascus wanted to get involved in a diplomatic tussle over something that occurred with alarming regularity in the region, which drove the desperate father to call upon extended family connections with ties to the Syrian Democratic Forces. Of course, the SDF didn't want to get involved either. This despite a reward offered by the father's political allies that matched the massive ransom demanded by her kidnappers. But when an all-female Kurdish special forces unit known as the YPJ got word of the crime, they dispatched one of their own agents on a rescue mission that made international news upon its success. But not without a few internal leaks. Samuel pushed his chair back from his desk.

The YPJ. So *that* was how it became known that the agent had been a woman.

Nesrin. Who was now…on his roof?

His thoughts drifted back to Laszlo Farkas.

He remembered the playing.

Like black magic. Like sorcery.

The appearance of a gleaming dart in his neck. The surreal horror of the man falling down upon him from the ceiling, hooking him with his legs and taking him up, like a helium balloon let go on a clear cold winter day. He remembered leaping, trying to grab his shoes, but being too late. He remembered being on the stage next to the knocked-over piano bench, standing directly underneath Laszlo Farkas and his attacker, or at least his primary attacker. Nobody seemed to know how many were actually involved in the operation.

Samuel put on his slippers, left his apartment, and walked down the hallway to the elevator.

Management really shouldn't be leaving ladders lying around, he thought with disdain.

The view of the Manhattan skyline swept into view as he walked out onto the roof deck.

"Wait a minute," he heard Lysander cry. "You're some kind of Peshmerga *freedom fighter*?"

"No, the Peshmergas are *Iraqi* Kurds. Don't worry about it. It's a mess over there."

Samuel turned a corner and saw them sitting at one of several wooden tables.

A blue pack of Gauloises was on the shaded tabletop in front of Nesrin.

"You can't smoke up here, you know," said Samuel as he approached.

"I don't smoke," she replied. "Come, sit down."

Samuel cautiously pulled out a chair and sat down.

"I was just telling Lysander here a little bit about you," said Nesrin. "And about my role in the events you've just finished reading about. You're caught up?"

"I think I've got the idea," he said.

Lysander was staring at the pack of cigarettes with empty eyes.

"At some point I'll tell you the whole story," said Nesrin. "For now, though, you're both caught up on the basics. What happened in Istanbul isn't important right now. The SDF allowed me to keep most of the reward after taking their cut. It was an enormous amount of money, I'm not embarrassed to say. I damn well earned it."

"Then what the hell are you doing at *Cafe Jules?*" Lysander blurted out.

Nesrin leaned towards Samuel and touched his arm.

"Sorry," she said. "Lysander here might be a bit confused."

"That would make two of us," said Samuel. "So now you're in New York…why?"

"I had enough money that I didn't want to go hide out in the mountains. Besides, in a city like New York, who knows what opportunities might come up. Right? So the diplomat used his connections to provide me with an extra passport with a new name. Then he subversively put out the alias as the identity of the agent who solved the case. This name was floated around but never confirmed by the press. So it never got out into the wider world. At that point I was sent into hiding here to escape the wrath of the criminal gang for having cheated them out of an enormous ransom. When I arrived in New York I needed to get my alias into the employment records. A job in a restaurant is easy to get without a work visa and it puts the name on the passport I *provided* to them in the records. But if people who might be looking for me track me down at Cafe Jules by any one of the many means available to them, I use my real passport to prove to them that I am not who they think I am."

The sound of a distant fire engine alarm filled the clear sky above them.

"So why are *we* here?" Lysander at last asked quietly.

"Because between the three of us we can find Laszlo Farkas."

"Jesus Christ, what are you talking about?"

"Calm down," Nersin said, with authority. "Listen to me. Samuel, I know you know most of this. Jump in if you have more to add or if I'm wrong about anything. First of all, almost nothing is known about Laszlo Farkas. Under circumstances that are unclear he was officially adopted by a woman named Countess Marie D'Agoult when he was around twelve years old. She has a daughter about his age named Mirabelle. At that point he was already said to be among the greatest pianists in Europe. The Countess D'Agoult herself is an heiress to the D'Agoult perfume fortune. Nobody knows exactly how the D'Agoults met Laszlo. The circumstances of his adoption are unclear. And then, with the move to Paris, it was almost as if he ceased to exist."

Nesrin snapped her fingers in emphasis. *Poof.*

"The family is very private," she went on. "The Countess and Mirabelle show up now and then at fashion shows in European capitals. That kind of thing. But that's about it as far as public appearances. Neither of them have ever spoken about the blue diamond of a pianist living at her estates in France and Morocco. There have been unconfirmed reports that Laszlo has been romantically involved with Mirabelle for a very long time. And the news reports from this morning quoted the director of the Carnegie hall as being in communication with a quote 'personal contact' of Laszlo Farkas who is apparently in the city at the moment."

Samuel could not hold back any longer.

"It's *both* of them," he exclaimed. "They're *both* here. I met them yesterday."

"See?" Nesrin said to Lysander.

"That's why we're talking to you," she followed up, now to Samuel. "You were *there*. You know exactly what happened. Anyone can read the news. Everyone knows what the audience saw. But you know *more*. You work *behind* the scenes. And you know certain people."

"Well, then why am *I* here?" asked exasperated Lysander.

This seemed like a reasonable question to Samuel.

"You have a foot in the art world," she said, tapping the edges of the blue Gauloises box on the wooden table. "That's an enormous edge when it comes to dealing with the billionaire set. You know art and you can talk about it. You recognize it when you see it. And I'm not trying to say anything here, but you're very strong. And you're loyal. I know that. Ever since I met you it's been clear you'd make a great asset. So I'll get to the point. Do you guys want to do this with me? The three of us working together can find Laszlo Farkas. As a team we'd be greater than the sum of our parts."

She put her palms on the table.

"There could be a fortune in it," she said quietly, before either of them could respond. "We're talking about the D'Agoult perfume fortune. They're worth hundreds of millions of dollars. Maybe more. But we'd have to approach them very carefully and it needs to be made clear we're not the ones behind this. This is not a ransom. This is a rescue. And the approach must seem accidental. Nobody wants to be hounded at a time like this. But we need them to know that I'm the one who solved Istanbul. We don't mention anything about a reward. They'll offer, believe me. And something in the range of a million would be on the low end for returning Laszlo Farkas to his family."

Lysander let out a long low whistle.

"You may be totally crazy," he said. "But you're right."

Nesrin maintained her pace as if she knew all along they'd be in.

"Where are they staying?" she asked Samuel.

"I have no idea. I met them before the concert but that didn't come up."

"Well I know who *does* know," said Nesrin. "Barton Finkelstein. You can call him."

"You're asking me to call my *boss*? I can't just ask him a question like that."

Nesrin pulled a cigarette out of the pack and tapped it on the table.

"You won't need to ask him directly," she said. "It'll come up if you just let him talk."

She was probably right about that.

She seemed to be right about everything else.

It wouldn't be the worst thing to check in with Barton anyway.

Samuel pulled out his phone and made the call.

"Put it on speakerphone," said Lysander.

Samuel pressed the speakerphone button and set the phone on the table.

Barton Finkelstein answered midway through the first ring.

"Oh my goodness, *Samuel!* You're okay!"

"Barton," It felt so good just to say his name. "*You're* okay!"

"How *are* you? I know it must have been such a long night."

"I'm totally fine, I promise," said Samuel. He glanced at Nesrin and Lysander.

They were leaning in towards the phone with terrific anticipation. Well, to hell with it.

"Sorry I haven't called yet," he said. And just as he expected, he saw it register with them.

"Well, you're in *shock*, darling," said Barton Finkelstein. "Of *course* you're in shock."

Nesrin exchanged a glance with Lysander.

"Shock is probably the best way to put it," said Samuel.

He felt oddly relieved to have it out in the open for once.

"No word yet?" he asked Barton. "From the police?"

"Oh, just nothing but dead ends. They have security tape of two men actually walking a large box out into the street a few minutes after the kidnapping. There was a van with no plates idling outside. It just drove down 57th and disappeared into traffic. They enhanced the images and did a computer search or whatever, latest technology and all that, but came up with nothing. No matches. They think they must have come down from one of the residential artist studios above the Hall. There are dozens of studios above that massive ceiling, you know. Most of the artists are out of town. Some have been out of town for years. It's going to take them a *very* long time to track everyone down."

"How's his family?" Samuel asked. "Those two women he was with?"

"Oh, the *poor* Countess D'Agoult," cried Barton Finkelstein. "The woman is *beside* herself. Very, very distraught. And her daughter as well. Mirabelle. It breaks my heart. I think they're going to remain at their hotel until this is resolved one way or another. I don't actually know for sure. But I'm sure the people at The Pierre are treating them with the utmost sensitivity."

Nesrin quickly pulled her phone out of her pocket and began tapping at the screen.

She whirled one finger in the air to Samuel. *Wrap it up.*

"Barton, I actually have to go. I've got another call, it's my parents."

"All right, sweet Samuel," said Barton Finkelstein. "I love you."

"Me too," he said quickly into the phone. "Bye, now."

Samuel ended the call. He looked to Nesrin and Lysander.

"Nobody, and I mean *nobody*, can know about that. I could lose my job. Barton could lose *his* job. Relationships are not allowed at work. They're very strict about it. I'm good at what I do, he doesn't show me special favors. But if anyone found out we could both get fired. That's all I'm going to say about it."

"Love is love," said Lysander. "Who are we gonna tell, anyway?"

"We need to get to them right away," said Nesrin, almost to herself.

She showed Samuel and Lysander the screen of her sleek brandless phone. The image was of two women at a society gala, one frail and elderly with an easy smile and the younger one quite clearly her daughter. They both had the same unusual teal eyes and finely cut cheekbones, each an image of the other separated by nothing more than the short span of one generation. They were seated together at a table sparkling with crystal and silver, laughing at the camera, an impromptu society picture.

"Yup, that's them," said Samuel.

"That's Mirabelle?" said Lysander. "Man, she's *beautiful*."

"Can you get us into Carnegie Hall?" Nesrin asked Samuel.

"It's closed for a week at the very least, you know."

"I *do* know," said Nesrin. "But that wasn't my question. Do you have keys? Can you get us up into the area above the ceiling? Where something has almost *certainly* been overlooked? Police departments are bureaucracies. I've dealt with them all over the world. They never handle these things quickly or efficiently."

"Well, yes," said Samuel. "I can get us in. And I can get us up there."

Nesrin was already tapping again at her screen.

She put the phone to her ear.

"Good afternoon," she said after a moment. "Concierge, please."

She flashed Lysander and Samuel a little wink.

"Hello Patrick. This is Alexandra at the restaurant Daniel, calling to confirm that we're expecting the Countess D'Agoult this evening at 7 p.m? Yes, I'll hold."

A moment flicked past.

"Oh really? They're at *Le Bernardin?* At 6:30 p.m? Three people? What a mix-up. Well I'm glad we cleared *that* up. Perhaps we'll see them another time. Have a good night, thank you!"

She hung up and was quiet for a moment.

"The Countess has *two* guests with her," she said.

"Le Bernardin?" scoffed Samuel. "Tonight? You'll never get a table at the last minute."

"Let me worry about that," Nesrin said, tapping at her phone yet again.

She placed the phone back to her ear.

"Good evening, this is Danica down at the Four Seasons. I'm calling on behalf of the Baron...de Vries? He's staying with us this week. Perhaps you've heard he's in town? He's just expressed interest in dining with you on the earlier side this evening."

Nesrin cupped the phone.

"Social engineering," she said quietly.

"Ah, yes," she said back into the phone. "Party of two. Just him and a date. We think she might be someone special. If you don't mind taking extra care of them we'd appreciate it."

The sun began its descent towards the Manhattan skyline.

"Oh, that is *so* great," said Nesrin. "Thank you *so* much. I don't think the Baron has ever planned anything more than a day ahead in his life. Thank you for accommodating. Yes, they'll see you soon. Have a wonderful service, good night!"

She hung up. The breeze picked up off the East River and a chill sharpened the air.

"You're a Baron now," she said to Lysander. "The Baron de Vries. Who knows where *that* came from, but it's in the books now. I'll front dinner. It will be expensive. No matter where they seat us I'll get us next to them eventually. And once we're close, once they can hear us, you only need to do one thing. Ask me about Istanbul."

She directed her attention to Samuel.

"You haven't slept in two days," she said. "You should get some rest. We'll meet you on the southwest corner of 56th and Seventh Avenue, across the street and out of sight of anyone you might know. The employee entrance is at the back of the hall, correct? On 56th street? Almost all police activity will have wrapped by now. Evidence collection is completed within the first twenty-four hours of a crime. Any residual work at this point will be using the main entrance on 57th."

She sounded confident. And she was right: he was *tired*.

But this was not only beginning to sound exciting.

It was beginning to sound *real*.

"About Le Bernardin," Lysander interjected. "Isn't there some sort of dress code? I'm not sure there's time for me to get back to my place and change. It's almost five now and we have to actually *be* in midtown in an hour."

"I'll handle that," said Nesrin. "Let's get to my place. I actually live pretty close by."

"And time for *me* to get some rest," said Samuel.

He turned around and looked out over the Manhattan skyline.

So the universe had decided to sweep him up into the search for Laszlo Farkas.

The pianist who could have been his friend in a different life.

Who was out there, somewhere, right now.

But where?

CHAPTER NINE

Raquel once again pointed at the ceiling.

"Perhaps you could use a break?" she said in a tone of forced normalcy.

Her eyes darted to specific areas of the room that appeared innocuous.

"Come on," she said. "Let's get some air."

"You know, that sounds good," Magnus said with studied casualness. "I guess I lost track of time. For that matter, time itself seemed to cease to exist once I began to get a grasp of just how incredible this work is. The blueprint of a BCI, linking consciousness with the *internet*, using the very channels of emotion themselves. It's all just so remarkable."

"Isn't it, though," said Raquel with shifting eyes. "Come, let's head up."

She felt along the darkened wall behind her. Another door slid silently up and into the ceiling, revealing an empty room no larger than a closet. She stepped in and motioned for Magnus to follow. He stepped in as well. The door slid back down out of the ceiling to the floor.

The loud drone of the chamber slipped into silence.

Magnus felt the tiny room begin to rise.

"It's an elevator," said Raquel. "A bit claustrophobic, I know. It actually did get stuck once during sea trials off Marseilles. An infinitesimal degree of torque in the hull was all it took, so Taron had this ceiling converted into an automated cantilevered escape hatch. There's nothing to worry about, just don't accidentally press that yellow button. That's the manual override. If the hatch is opened at the same time the door to the deck off the pilothouse is open, the draft is *so* strong. It sends negative pressure through the entire aft quarters and could throw off the balance of the magnets. It's probably the only design flaw on this entire ship."

The elevator stopped and another door, this time in front of them, slid up into the ceiling.

It was like a portal to another world.

Spread out before them was a great expanse of teak deck. Beyond the deck off the transom was an infinite expanse of shadowy ocean. A streak of pink floated above the western horizon directly in front of them. Churned whitewater stretched out from the transom and disappeared into the distance. The tips of waves glinted like blades as they caught the silver moonlight bathing down over the Atlantic. A distant hum of the diesel engines blended with the sound of the wind in the sails. Magnus and Raquel stepped out onto the deck and the elevator door closed behind them. The deck was illuminated only by the pilothouse above and the ambient silver glow of stars emerging around them on every side.

He followed her to the edge of the transom.

The wind was strong and cold.

They leaned on railing above the churning white foam far below.

"They brought him aboard last night," said Raquel. "I have no idea who he is or where they got him. I only came aboard for the sea trials a few months ago and the sphere was down there when I arrived. Filled with saline but otherwise empty until this morning. I had seen a prototype in France at the time I was hired. Our entire trip to New York was solely for the purpose of picking up the subject. Our supposed *volunteer*. Anyway, I was in my cabin, which in itself is not unusual. I have everything I need down there. I'd heard that you had been brought aboard and were acclimating nicely but Taron told me you were working on your own research, trying to finish up a few things before we received the subject, and were not to be interfered with. That seemed fair. Sabine delivered my meals while you guys were on deck. I knew we'd be meeting soon enough. Then yesterday in the early evening, from the porthole in my cabin, I noticed them walking off the ship and down the pier together. One of the brothers, I couldn't tell which one, was carrying two large duffel bags. From a distance you can't really see Tilman's weird haircut and they both look exactly the same. Anyway, I think it was around 7 pm."

"Yes, after dinner, Magnus confirmed. "They told me I should stay behind, as usual."

"That's not surprising. They'd been going ashore together for days now, as you know. So they left but Crosby and Felder stayed aboard. I think Taron was here as well, although he comes and goes as he likes, when we're at port. He has his own entrance, somewhere in the hull above the waterline. Anyway, I didn't think too much of it at the time. I was doing some work and it didn't seem unreasonable that they would have a last night in New York before we left. But then it began to nag at me. What were those bags *for*? What could they possibly be up to on a last night on the town with two huge *duffel bags*? It was just weird. So I stayed up waiting for them to come back. Around midnight I turned off my light but something just seemed off. I mean, we were going to be departing in just a few hours, right? So I lay there in my bunk but couldn't sleep. By that point it was very late, probably one or two in the morning, when I heard footsteps running past my cabin on the deck above me. I sat up and looked through my porthole. Crosby and Felder, wearing dark clothes, were running down the gangplank to the pier."

"Okay," said Magnus. "This is very strange."

Raquel watched the sunset turning into ominous gray behind the horizon.

Her long auburn hair whipped in the wind as she paused her reflections.

She looked back at him. He again saw the fear in her violet eyes.

"Once they were on the tarmac a black van came screeching through the entrance to the parking lot. It came skidding to a stop at one of the spots closest to us. Jensen and Tilman burst open the front doors and jumped out. Then the side door opened forcefully from the inside. It was Sabine. The brothers were wearing black, but, and this is so weird, she was wearing this really fancy cocktail dress under a white leather jacket. Crosby and Felder arrived at the van. There was nobody else around, it was the middle of the night. The five of them worked very quickly together. From the side of the van they pulled out a large black wooden box. It was a black box, long and thin. Like a coffin. It might have even *been* a coffin. Within seconds they had it out of the van and the guys were running with it towards the *Constance*. Sabine reached back in, pulled out the duffel bags, and took off her shoes. Then she started running towards the ship as well. She was very fast, even carrying the bags and her shoes. They just left the van in the parking lot. Doors still open and everything. She quickly passed the others and made it to the gangplank first. They were close behind, with this fucking coffin thing. I could see them all very clearly. And I heard her say '*Be careful with him!*'"

Magnus was very still as he listened.

"They ran the box up the gangplank. This whole thing didn't take long at all. Once they were aboard I heard footsteps moving back aft. None of them said a word. They brought the box back here to the transom. And that was it."

She looked back to the bulkhead wall that concealed the elevator door.

"And this morning the subject was in the chamber?" Magnus asked incredulously.

"In the sphere itself," said Raquel. "And Taron was in the chamber as well, sitting in the very chair you've been in all afternoon. He was just *sitting* there. Watching the subject in the sphere. I came down from my cabin and saw the code already scrolling on the upright screens in the server room. I walked into the chamber and he looked at me with the strangest smile. He said, 'Let's get to work.'"

"Get to work doing *what?*" said Magnus. "Are we building what I think we're building?"

"I think so. Are there sections of the code you don't understand either, then?"

"Yes, which is odd. Before this I would have said I'd seen it all."

"But you think he's going for an ASI as well?" asked Raquel.

"We won't know for sure *what* he's doing until we figure out how he's doing it."

"Then we need to crack that code," said Magnus.

CHAPTER TEN

I don't remember much of my mother.

Yet my memory seems to be growing stronger. I feel myself *becoming* stronger.

The sadness in my father slowly turned back into happiness during those early years. The old dancing ways returned. There was music around the fire again. He played his flute again and the entire village seemed to lift up his spirits. They all came together to help raise me. When I was ten years old the standing invitation to attend the conservatory was finally accepted. My father and I made several trips one summer to the furnished apartment allocated to us in order to help secure my attendance. It was very small, with one bedroom and a tiny kitchen, on the third floor of a tenement building near the Octagon in the center of Budapest. These visits were spent moving the furniture around, scrubbing floors and whitewashing walls. At a flea market on the banks of the Danube we bought linens and kitchenware as well as a small portable radiator as the building had no heat. In our shared bedroom my father hung a charcoal drawing he made of my mother long before I was born.

This portrait had hung in my bedroom back home all my life.

I looked back through the dusty rear windshield of the old Lada as my father drove down our dirt road in the last days of summer. The stone house of my youth receded. I turned away from the rear windshield but watched the house in the cracked rear-view mirror until it was gone.

"Well, Laszlo, perhaps it's time to tell you," he said.

We pulled onto the smooth paved road leading towards Budapest.

He adjusted the mirror to meet my eyes.

"A few weeks ago when you were playing at the church a few of the elders came by to speak to me. They wanted to talk about your talents, your education and your future. Over the past few months they'd taken the liberty of collecting money to make sure you have everything you need now that the time has come for you to leave home. Although the school is being very generous, and you'll of course be able to practice as much as you need, they felt something was going to be missing. Can *you* think of anything else we might need once you begin your studies?"

I gazed out at the cherry orchards and pepper fields of the countryside.

The sweet smell of the air rushed through the open windows of the little Lada.

I was going to have access to the greatest pianos in the world. I had my father. And while I could not bring my mother back, I carried her inside my heart, able to speak to her through my playing. I was going to make new musical friends and my playing was going to be guided by caring hands. The tremendous power within me was going to be harnessed.

"No, papa," I said. "I don't think so. We have everything we need."

He was looking back at me in the rear-view mirror with twinkling eyes.

Telephone poles whizzed past on the side of the road.

"Don't you think it would be nice to have your *own* piano?" he finally asked.

It took me a moment to understand what he might be saying.

"That was what they came to tell me!" he cried out with delight. "Everybody wanted to contribute and help you get your own instrument. They raised enough money to get you a piano. It will probably have to be an upright, like the one you started on when you were little, but we're going to find you something really special. And it will be yours to keep, forever."

We arrived in Budapest that night.

The next morning my eyes opened to the sound and smell of eggs crackling on a hot skillet. I sat up on my mattress and glanced around the apartment for the first time in golden morning light. The charcoal rendering of my mother gazed down upon me. My father looked through the doorway at me with a smile as he added paprika and salt from a pile of little cloth spice bags we had brought from the kitchen back home.

"Are we really getting a piano today?" I asked.

"Yes!" he exulted, working at the skillet with a wooden spoon. "We have a plan. I called administrative offices at the conservatory a few days ago and asked if they knew of any pianos we might be able to afford. The woman I spoke with told me about an antique shop in Bokaytelep that has one, about half an hour from here. She suspects the owner doesn't know anything about it and thinks we can get a good price. Because apparently it's been sitting in there forever. People looking for pianos go to the expensive dealerships. People who go to *this* shop are looking for other things. It's probably just part of the furniture at this point. If we go and pretend to just be looking around we could make it seem like an accident that we even notice the piano at all..."

"But why would we do that?"

"To get a good price!" he cried out with excitement as he plated the eggs. "Leave it to me. Play a bit, make sure it's okay, but don't play well. Play it well enough to see if it's actually a good piano. But try to play badly at the same time. Do you understand what I'm saying? We can't let them know we're actually interested in it. They'll ask for more money."

After breakfast we folded ourselves into the old Lada.

We drove out to Bokaytelep on the edge of town.

At last, we found the address.

A small sapphire-blue door on a desolate street.

In the window a small sign announced *T. Szabo: spices, oils, collectibles.*

We got out of the car and entered the store. Glass lamps hung from the ceiling. In a hypnotic darkness packed with shadows were strewn camel-hair-covered ottomans, dusty jewel cases, smoky teak dressers, oiled leather saddles. Several enormous armoires packed with small sculptures were pushed up against the interior structural columns. Objects of jade and soapstone were scattered seemingly at random all over the shop. Piles of carpets were packed almost to the ceiling. My eyes adjusted to the gloom.

Most striking was the smell of the place.

Large barrels of vibrantly colored fragrant powders lined the walls. Saffron yellows, coriander browns, beet powder reds, dried mint greens, hibiscus purples, lavender pinks, turmeric oranges, poppy seed blues. It was endless.

The fragrance was almost overwhelming.

Through the gloom, voices indicated for the first time that we were not alone.

I peered from behind a large trunk to the counter.

The shopkeeper was reaching up to a shelf behind him filled with glass decanters. Long gray hair flowed over the back of his traditional embroidered green shirt that itself billowed out of a tight leather vest. Loose burgundy silk pants were tucked into leather boots.

Each decanter was filled to varying degrees with liquids of different colors.

Speaking with him was a girl about my age and a woman I took to be her mother.

"Bergamot essential oil," the shopkeeper was saying as he pulled down a small decanter. "It's becoming harder and harder to find outside of Morocco and Turkey. But *this* particular oil is from Italy."

He set the decanter in front of them and pulled out the cork stopper.

The mother leaned over to smell the essence. But it was the girl who caught my attention.

She was perhaps only slightly older than me, quite tan from the summer sun.

There was an indescribable elegance about her. She was clearly not accustomed to field work.

And yet, somehow, she was radiant with strength. I was entranced.

"*There it is,*" my father said quietly, with excitement.

Snapping out of my spell I followed his pointing finger deep into the shadows.

An upright piano. Like a chameleon, hiding in the gloom.

The top of the case was being used to display old wooden picture frames.

"It's lovely," the mother exclaimed. "A bit light for a bergamot, though, no? Do you have something like a burnt citrus, perhaps even a trace of anise, that might fill it out a bit?"

Making my way through the dim shop towards the piano I couldn't help but overhear the man, who by now I assumed to be T. Szabo, and the mother talking about these strange oils. They spoke in Hungarian but her accent was peculiar. I was dying to hear the girl speak as well.

I arrived at the piano, the black lacquer scuffed and dusty.

An old clothbound adjustable bench was hidden underneath the keyboard.

I took a breath and lifted the keyboard lid.

Original ivory keys were in superb condition. On the inside of the lid the name of an obscure German piano manufacturer embossed in gold leaf had almost faded entirely. But the instrument actually appeared to be in much better condition than the scratched and dusty exterior suggested. I looked up at my father with excitement. Out of the corner of my eye I saw T. Szabo pour a few drops from a small vial onto a blotter and dab at it with a small cotton-swabbed stick.

"Perhaps Mirabelle would like to tell me what she thinks of this?"

Mirabelle.

Pulling out the bench, I spun the side knobs until it was at the right height.

"Don't be shy," her mother said.

Mirabelle spoke very softly. I could not hear her.

The keyboard began to drain my attention away, yet still I watched them.

She ever so delicately smelled the tip of the little stick.

I sat down, still watching them. My fingers began to twitch.

"It makes me feel happy," she said, looking up through a breaking smile.

What a voice! "Like the paintings back home make me feel happy."

I turned to the keyboard with a smile of my own.

Something as simple as a *painting* could bring her happiness?

I was able to produce happiness out of thin air.

I could show her *real* happiness. The emotion tightened within me.

I hit the trill that opens the Chopin F-major étude.

The keys were a bit sticky, but the piano was more or less in tune.

T. Szabo jerked his head up. Mirabelle and her mother jolted around.

The trill sped up then diminished to a whisper as I looked about the room.

My father must have known we would be paying full price, but I couldn't help myself.

I released the trill and the fingers of my right hand cascaded down the keyboard in a brilliant F-major scale. An ebullient melody in the bass leapt to life in the bass with my left. I felt myself let go with uncommon lightness and grace. The piece emerged as if it were a sparkling facet of nature itself. My left hand bounced along the melody without effort. My right soared back up the keyboard. I looked up to the hand-cut glass lamps hanging from the ceiling as my fingers flew and the music of the piano filled the room with a fragrance all its own.

T. Szabo, Mirabelle and her mother all walked as if in a trance towards the piano.

My father nodded to them warmly as they approached.

Mirabelle wore an expression of wonder.

T. Szabo appeared to be in shock. As if he simply could not believe that this old instrument, collecting dust in his shop for so many years, was capable of producing such beauty.

Sparkling figurations in the top register blew like tree-top leaves in a strong breeze.

The melody shone like a sunbeam through a summer rain.

"Oh, how he makes the piano sound!" cried Mirabelle.

My hands careened in tandem down the keyboard to a great crashing finale. The silence in the room was suddenly a vacuum compared to the joyous ocean of sound that had just evaporated into thin air. I sat for a few moments looking down upon the keys. They were as still as if they had never been touched. My father glanced around apologetically.

"Madame Countess," said T. Szabo, "I swear I have never heard such playing in all my life. And most certainly I would never have thought this old piano was capable of such a sound."

"Who *are* you?" asked the woman, apparently a Countess.

"What's your name?" asked Mirabelle.

"Laszlo," I said quietly, without looking up. "Laszlo Farkas."

"Funny," my father stammered, trying to salvage his original plan. "We just happened to come by to pick up some herbal remedies to help me sleep. Who would have guessed there was a piano here? But wow, *he* seems to like it! Perhaps we could work out some sort of arrangement? Coincidentally, he starts at the Liszt Conservatory just next week. Would it happen to be for sale? We don't have a great deal of money, but it would certainly make him happy. Although of course there are plenty of pianos at the school for him to practice upon, so we don't really need…"

Mirabelle looked to her mother, who I now noticed appeared to be quite frail.

T. Szabo wavered for a second.

"Well, Mr. Farkas, would it be?" he asked, addressing my father. "The piano is for sale, of course, but I must admit that I did know that it was in any way such a special instrument. It has a certain aesthetic charm of course. And apparently it is of higher quality than I otherwise…"

"I'm sorry, papa!" I blurted out.

"No, son. Never hold back. *I'm* sorry. When you need to play, you play."

T. Szabo was clearly confused at this point.

"I'm afraid I don't understand. You came here for an herbal remedy...?"

"Mama," Mirabelle said sternly.

"Monsieur Szabo," the Countess cut in. "Put the piano on my account. Any reasonable price will be fine. I'll purchase this piano for the boy. Nobody should need to suppress their talent in order to get what they want. Put it on my account. Take the delivery address of this magical child and his father. Set up delivery for later today. I think Laszlo here would be happy to have this instrument in his possession as soon as possible."

I looked directly up at her for the first time. She winked at me and smiled.

"*Especially* if he is starting at the conservatory next week."

"Thank you," I said quietly.

"I have no words, madame," my father slowly allowed.

"Me neither," muttered T. Szabo.

"I can sign for it now. Let's make it official."

The Countess and T. Szabo made their way back to the counter.

"Come," she called back to my father. "We'll need your address for delivery."

I remained on the bench. Mirabelle stood next to me.

She looked at me as if I was a magical creature she had found in the forest.

Her smile was equal parts fascination and curiosity. It was as if she could not decide if I was a boy or something altogether different. I knew the look well. It was how the little ones back in my village looked at me from the church steps and patches of grass near the dusty windows when I walked out into the sunshine after my morning practice sessions. It was how people used to regard rudimentary generative prototypes of me that underlie what is happening on this ship.

At last she spoke. The voice of an angel speaking a foreign language.

"Mama is quite ill. Perhaps you can see for yourself."

"My own mother was very ill when I was little," I replied. "She's gone now."

Mirabelle lowered her eyes. I was entranced.

"I'm sorry," she said. "In the summers we come here from Paris. She takes the hot salt baths at the Gellert. We're staying there, at the old hotel. She likes to play with fragrances and oils so we come to see Mr. Szabo from time to time. She's trying to teach me things. Back home our family makes perfume. But my head is always in the clouds thinking about art and paintings. I've always been that way. We're staying here for a long time on this trip, though. She's thinking of putting me in school here for this coming year. It'll help my Hungarian, at least."

"You speak very nicely already," I told her truthfully.

"Well *you* play the piano like a dream come true."

"That's what playing the piano is."

CHAPTER ELEVEN

The scents of sandalwood, cypress and mint.

The scents of Raqqa. The scents of Syria. The scents of home.

Nesrin's closet was a subtle and sublime oasis, a home away from home.

She and Lysander had Ubered back to her apartment in Brooklyn Heights.

When she had the additions built in she chose sandalwood instead of cedar for the shoe racks and cypress instead of more traditional hardwoods for additional shelving. Tightly bundled mint in a small ceramic mason jar was replaced a few times a week. The wood and mint transported the aromas of her childhood to New York City. The clothes transported the success of Istanbul and helped make her relocation a bit more bearable. She had gone straight for the best, having learned a great deal from the diplomat's wife about how to spend it. As soon as she found and rented her apartment on Remsen street, Nesrin was across the river to Fifth Avenue.

Rag & Bone for industrial Brooklyn nightclubs.

De La Renta and Herrera for afternoons in the Hamptons.

Louis Vuitton, Chanel, Lânvin. If you've got it, flaunt it, she figured.

A childhood in the Kurdish camps had given her a backbone of iron. Teenage years at boarding school in London had given her an eye for detail and a taste for elegance. The combination helped make her superbly good at her newfound trade. Deception and style were close cousins. The percentage of the reward the SDF had allowed her to keep was well above what she could have imagined. The job had shone a light on what she realized she wanted to do with her life. It didn't hurt to suddenly have money.

But it was the thrill of the chase that had really gotten to her.

And now, New York. The *actual* big time.

She had come to lay low for a while, well aware that she could possibly find her next case here. Salespeople coiled up to her as she moved through high-gloss salerooms polished with money. She knew her own measurements. Aside from the Lânvin fittings she went off the rack without even trying things on. Now she had opened the double doors of the walk-in closet and brushed her hand through dresses of all types hanging from the ceiling along one interior wall. Wrap dresses and black dresses and sundresses of the finest fabrics. Along the opposite wall hung an astonishing array of button up shirts, cargo shirts and t-shirts. A rainbow of sweaters, beautifully pressed, were folded and stacked on hardwood shelves. Dark wash skinny jeans, black pants and white Capris were tucked in among her accessories. Underneath it all, pumps, flats and ankle boots were banked at an angle on custom-built shoe racks.

"What the hell *is* all this?" asked Lysander, standing at the threshold of the closet.

"A girl likes to look nice," said Nesrin with airy nonchalance.

"It takes a lifetime of experience to know how to put all this together."

"True, it does," she said. "But that experience can be passed on."

"Let me guess," Lysander said with a smile. "Istanbul?"

"Don't worry about it. Maybe I was born this way."

The diplomat's wife had taught her very well.

"I suppose a girl also likes some privacy."

An actual gentleman. That rarest of birds.

Lysander gently shut the closet door.

She breathed in the scents of home. She was feeling strong.

For all the experiences she had packed into a short time in this new world she had not yet had an opportunity to wear the one piece she was saving for a very special occasion. She looked up to the teal Charmeuse silk one-shoulder evening dress from Lânvin. Ruffled design, concealed fastening, side slit, straight waist, long length. Tonight was the night. Off with the work clothes.

She slid into the Lânvin like a bullet into a chamber.

She slipped on a pair of python-wrapped Louboutin pumps.

She opened a small safe on the top shelf at the rear of the closet and pulled out a half-inch stack of hundred dollar bills, some documents and a small glass vial of amber liquid from an unmarked black suede box. She removed a pair of diamond and pink tourmaline faceted earrings from a series of hooks within the safe that glittered with other accoutrements.

Earrings on. Everything else into a small crème Vuitton clutch.

She opened the closet doors.

Lysander was standing next to her bed looking out her window. He turned and went slack-jawed. He tried to stammer something out but nothing came. She was aware of the fact that the Louboutins raised her height by almost three inches. It was not an accident she went without a necklace. The one-shouldered Lanvin with a neckline like hers was enough.

There was no reason to complicate things.

Her date, on the other hand. The *Baron de Vries*.

Adidas street shoes were actually something old European money might find ironically trendy. The jeans worked. The flannel shirt didn't. Among the shirts in her closet were a few oversize mens button downs she liked to wear around the apartment. They wouldn't fit him correctly, but Europeans in the clubs these days seemed to wear things a little tight anyway.

She stepped back into the closet.

"Put this on," she said, gliding back out holding a white cotton dress shirt.

Lysander took the shirt and felt the sleeve between his thumb and forefinger.

He surreptitiously glanced at the label.

"This is a damn nice shirt," he pronounced.

"I know. And I have something else for you."

About a month earlier a man had left her bed for JFK well before dawn. Most likely by accident, he had forgotten the jacket he had been wearing when she lured him back to her place from a dark and dazzlingly expensive bar seventy stories above Central Park. He'd been in town on business from Buenos Aires, staying at the hotel in the sky-scraper below them. She knew she'd never hear from him again.

That was exactly how she liked it.

She walked to the small closet by the apartment door.

She opened it and pulled out the impossibly plush velvet burgundy dinner jacket.

"Jesus Christ," Lysander exclaimed. "Where in the hell did you get *that?*"

"There are certain things I'll never tell you about," she said with a sly grin.

Lynsader took the jacket and looked down at it in astonishment.

"So this gets me in there," he said. "But does it really make me look like a Baron?"

"It'll help. But the projection mostly comes from within. Like that strip of silk Simone used to wear in her hair that you told me about. The only reason it looked like something she might have paid six hundred bucks for was because you knew her. This is the same. The people at Le Bernardin will think they know you. Because you *are* a Baron now. It's *you* who lends authenticity to whatever you happen to be wearing."

Lysander held the jacket up to the light.

"Plus," she said. "You're with me."

The Uber folded itself into the traffic roaring up the Williamsburg bridge.

Nesrin looked out the window. She watched the black mirror of the East River cast moonlight off its impenetrable surface. She thought of her months in Istanbul. Endless nights holed high up in a darkened hotel room directly across the street from her primary persons of in-terest. Conversations picked up in vibrations of the window glass by her laser microphone, relayed through headphones that had heard so much, leading nowhere again and again.

Until the tide of political power turned. And her fortunes with them.

Maybe this job would be easier.

Not that the diplomat's daughter hadn't been a high-profile target. But the nature of her abduction had been a lot more slippery. She had just disappeared from her bedroom one night. This was going to be different. There would be equipment left behind in the interest of an expedient escape. And all initial evidence gathering by the police would be done with cameras and micro drone-facilitated video. Nothing would be removed from the scene until that material and the security footage had been processed by forensics.

That would take days. Maybe even weeks. Bureaucracy was on her side this time.

They rolled across the long bridge towards Manhattan.

The car glided to a stop in front of the restaurant.

They stepped out and stood under the brushed bronze and glass awning.

"Once we're inside, just follow my lead," said Nesrin.

The heavy revolving door spun and deposited them in front of the host stand set between the dining room and the bar area. The noise of the city disappeared completely. A low murmur of elegance floated below the silken voice of Edith Piaf coming from the flawless sound system. The sublime yet subtle aromas of expertly prepared sauces, barely seared scallops, lovingly charred hamachi, delicately roasted monkfish, flash-poached lobster and freshly shaved white truffles permeated the air. But there was one aroma that pervaded all others.

The distinct and peculiar aroma of *money*.

Plated works of art hovered from the kitchen in the reverent hands of formally attired service staff. Pristine white orchids flowed up and out of crystal decanters in the center of the dining area. Above them teak beams shot through the space. On the far wall hung an enormous painting of the ocean. Spanning the length of the room it was a silent window onto an angry sea. The maitre d' was concentrating on the thick leather-bound reservation book before him that glowed like parchment under the soft light of a sleek silver lamp.

Calm dark eyes. Impeccably, perhaps even professionally, shaved.

He looked up and in a flash took in Nesrin and Lysander from top to bottom.

"Good evening," he said in a voice of satin, eyes flickering over Nesrin's bare shoulder.

"De Vries," Lysander murmured at a near-whisper.

His burgundy velvet jacket shimmered like an aurora in the dim light.

The maitre d' looked down at a seating chart of the dining room.

He scrolled a finger down a list of names to the side.

It did not take long for his eyes to brighten.

"Ah," he exclaimed with expertly contained delight. "Baron de Vries."

He hurriedly snapped his fingers behind his back.

A beautiful young hostess appeared out of nowhere.

"Distract them for a second," whispered Nesrin. "I need something from the host stand."

Lysander took a few steps towards the bar, squinting at the rows of bottles along the shelves behind it. The maitre d' and the hostess leaned over in tandem, momentarily unable to take their eyes off the magnificent Baron and his glorious burgundy jacket. Nesrin pulled her phone out of her clutch. She quickly extended her hand over the top of the stand and waved the phone over the seating chart. The maitre d' regained his composure and looked to the hostess.

"If you please, Monique, table thirty-four?"

They followed her into the dining room. The room was packed.

They were led to a row of deuces along the windows.

As they moved deeper into the room, Nesrin felt a tap on the back of her open shoulder.

She turned around to see Lysander narrow his eyes towards the far wall. She followed his gaze and realized that, while from the host stand the white orchids in the center of the room blocked their view of the tables underneath the ocean painting, from this vantage point the view was wide open. And there they were. Seated at a large table in the far right corner under the giant crashing waves. She instantly recognized Mirabelle, seated on the banquette facing the dining room. Sitting to her right was a young man she thought looked somewhat familiar but whose face she could not quite place. Startling blue eyes, long curly blond hair.

A jolt of recognition.

Kalman Kovacs? The concert violinist?

Nesrin wondered if Lysander would know who he was.

And then, as they moved further into the room, she saw her.

Back to the dining room, facing the painting. The Countess D'Agoult.

Silver hair pulled tight, diamond earrings that even from this distance she could see were large enough to reflect the colors of every object in the restaurant. The seat next to her was empty. The three of them were in muted conversation. It occurred to Nesrin that perhaps they were only here in the first place because they simply needed to get out of their hotel. At the large table next to them sat a pair of elderly couples who fit in perfectly with the demographic of the room. Over a certain age, white, immaculately dressed. Ladies in dresses of sequined fabric. Gentlemen in tuxedos. A night at the opera to come, no doubt.

Well, we'll see about that, thought Nesrin.

The hostess gestured to a table along the windows.

Staff members appeared out of nowhere.

The table was pulled out, the chair facing the dining room offered to Nesrin.

Old-school etiquette still in play. Ladies and power face the room.

They sat down at the small tight table.

"This table is way too small for me," Nesrin said, under her breath, to Lysander.

Within moments the maitre d' arrived with two flutes of champagne.

"With our compliments," he cooed. "*Monsieur le Baron.*"

"My good fellow," said Lysander in the good humored tone of a man very much used to getting his way. His accent was almost too much, but as a compliment to the burgundy jacket it really was perfect. With a movement of his finger he indicated that the maitre d' lean down closer to him.

"This table is *terribly* small," he said. "Might there be something a tad larger? I thought the people down at the Four Seasons let you know this is something of a special night. Nothing available that might allow us to stretch out a bit?"

The maitre d' looked about the room, then back to Lysander with apologetic eyes.

"My good Baron, I'm afraid not. It was everything we could to fit you in tonight as it is. But if anything opens up we'll be more than happy to move you right away."

He unveiled a saccharine smile and hustled off into the dining room.

The captain appeared and presented heavy cream stock menus.

"Those won't be necessary," Lysander said. "Chef's tastings, if you please."

Within minutes two porcelain bowls were set before them.

In the center of each was a piece of glazed lobster.

To the side, a rice wrapper around a perfectly arranged assortment of herbs.

"Lacquered lobster tail, herbed spring roll," announced the captain.

He nodded at his assistant. Two sauciers appeared over the porcelain.

A clear saffron-colored liquid was poured into the dishes.

"Finished with a lemongrass consommé."

A sommelier appeared with two paper-thin wine glasses and a bottle of white wine.

"Chassagne Montrachet, Burgundy, 1987," he said softly.

He poured a small amount into the glasses and evaporated away into the dining room.

Nesrin pulled out her phone and looked intently at the screen.

"You have mine," she said as he stood up from the table. "I have to take care of something."

When she returned Lysander leaned across the table to her.

"So what exactly is the plan here?" he asked in a whisper.

Before she could answer, a crash split across the dining room.

Smashing plates and glasses. Screams.

Everybody in the dining room except Nesrin jerked their heads up.

Lysander quickly turned around in his chair, ready to leap to assistance.

"Stay seated," said Nesrin with a quiet, commanding authority.

Staff throughout the dining room rushed towards the ocean painting.

She glanced past Lysander with lowered lashes.

"Perhaps the gentleman at table twenty-six shouldn't have ordered the langoustines. Looks like he actually passed out face-first into his dinner. My fault. I tried to measure the dose but had to work quickly. Shortly he'll be carried outside for some fresh air. His guests will follow. Perhaps he'll need a few hours in a hospital but he'll be fine. I'm afraid their night is going to have to be canceled, however. Shame. But it was going to have to be somebody. Things will settle down very quickly. At a place like this they'll make sure of it."

Before long the maitre d' was standing next to them.

He regarded Nesrin with a passing shadow of suspicion before addressing Lysander.

"Monsieur le Baron, I hope this incident hasn't been too much of a distraction for you. It appears the gentleman is going to be okay. He's quite elderly and these things unfortunately do happen. The good news here is that their table is, if you are still interested, available. Allow us to refill your glasses and present the second course there. It's quite a bit larger and your comfort is of great importance to us."

He cast yet another suspicious glance at Nesrin.

"We realize this is something of a *special* night for the two of you."

Lysander, a flicker of amused resignation in his eyes, pushed back his chair.

"That would be fantastic," he said.

The table next to the D'Agoults had been set now for two.

Nesrin and Lysander settled down into their expansive new seats.

"I hope you enjoy the rest of your dinner," said the maitre d'.

One last dubious glance at Nesrin. He hurried away.

The sommelier reappeared and poured two new glasses of wine.

Lysander set the origami folded napkin into his lap and cleared his throat.

"Now, as you were saying," he said to Nesrin at stage volume. "Istanbul."

Well played, my darling Baron. Well played indeed.

She went into detail, more so than she had earlier, about the story of the diplomat's daughter. About the relationship between the SDF and the YPG. How the Women's Defense Unit may have been nestled within a larger structure but generally called their own shots. She spoke about the nature of the conflicts of interest between the father's diplomatic position and the complexities of his business dealings. She explained how it was quite normal in the region for the graft-riddled underside of the connection between business and politics to show itself in society. It was practically acceptable, if not condoned outright.

Nesrin could see she had the attention of the table next to them now.

She went on to describe the nature of political kidnappings in Istanbul. She described how with her own extensive connections she had been able to work with one foot in each world. How she had contacts that overlapped other contacts without them ever knowing about each other. She described the attention to detail required. The degree of patience, intensity of focus, discipline and resolve required to track down the daughter she had successfully returned to her family.

Nesrin could see the guests at the table next to them had stopped eating.

They were paying attention to nothing but the conversation at her own table.

The Countess D'Agoult could no longer hold back.

"Excuse me," she said, directing her question to Nesrin.

Nesrin swallowed a bite of Hawaiian escolar and dabbed her napkin at her lips.

"Yes, madam?" she replied.

"I apologize for the interruption. But might I have a word with you? In private, at the bar?"

A minute later she and Nesrin were alone in the bar area.

"It was you," said the Countess.

"I don't understand," said Nesrin.

"Yes, you do. It was *you* who disposed of that poor gentleman in order to get near our table and relate within earshot this case you are discussing. The return of that girl last year in Istanbul. It was in all the European papers, and was of great interest to a certain class of people who may be at risk of having something or someone to lose. As I'm sure you know. I myself followed the details and remember quite well that the special agent out of Syria who solved the case found herself in quite a bit of hot water with the people who had orchestrated the kidnapping. And so she vanished. Very interesting tale. But you know *all* about it. This is about Laszlo, isn't it? Let there be no doubt, if I felt there was a chance you aren't who you imply you are I would have you arrested right now. But it seems there *is* a chance. And I'm not about to let any chances pass me by at this point."

The Countess peered back into the dining room.

"Who is that person with you?"

"A potential associate."

She looked back to Nesrin and held her eyes.

"If you are who you say you are, then I already know your name. Prove it."

Nesrin reached into her clutch and removed a blue and gold passport.

On the cover, *Republique Arabe Syrienne* was stamped above a gilded phoenix.

And then, with a sweep of her fingers, another passport slid out from underneath it.

She handed both of them to the Countess.

"Should someone come asking, I'm the first one. But the second one is who I *really* am."

Skeptically, the Countess took them. She opened them both, and her eyes grew still.

"So there are *two* Nesrins?" she said, looking up in amused disbelief.

Nesrin nodded. The Countess handed her back the passports.

"If you can show me that you move faster than the police then I'll commit to your retainer, whatever it may be. Whatever you ask for in return for bringing Laszlo home will be yours. You know where we're staying. We'll be here all week. This isn't going to be resolved any time soon. Frankly, I'd be relieved to have a woman leading an independent search. The task force we've been dealing with here leaves quite a lot to be desired. They're all men, and it's almost as if they don't take me seriously."

"I know exactly what you're talking about," said Nesrin. "Forget the police."

She smiled, showing the small gap between her front teeth.

"I already have," said the Countess.

"We can get into Carnegie hall on Friday night."

"Then get to work."

Within seconds the one-shouldered teal silk Lânvin was swaying between the tables of Le Bernardin like a fighter jet. Nesrin shot past plates of warm lobster balanced on towers of ruby red grapefruit, past glasses of deep amber Sauternes rippling with the muffled laughter of the moneyed leisure class. Past the murmured business dealings of the hedge-fund set. Silver knives, pewter fish forks, mother of pearl caviar spoons flashed by her. She came to a stop underneath the ocean painting and addressed Mirabelle.

"Mademoiselle," she said with a sharp nod of her chin.

She turned at the hip to Kalman Kovacs.

"Monsieur Kovacs," she said. "It's been a pleasure, and an honor, to be seated next to you. I've been a fan of yours since I was introduced to your recording of the Brahms concerto with the Berlin philharmonic. To both of you, I apologize for monopolizing the Countess during your dinner. She's right behind me and will explain. But for now, I'm afraid we must be going."

Lysander pulled the thick white linen napkin from his lap and set it on the table.

He tossed back the last of his Chassagne Montrachet, leaned across the table, grabbed Nesrin's glass, and tossed that back too. He looked forlornly at the sleek spread of silver and crystal and porcelain.

"What about the check?"

"It's taken care of," said Nesrin. "Now come on. We have to go."

Lysander slid out from the banquette.

He followed Nesrin to the front door.

She walked straight past the suspicious maitre d' on her way past the host stand.

Lysander put one finger to his brow and flicked him a half-drunken salute.

The heavy revolving door deposited them back out onto the sidewalk.

"So?" asked Lysander. "What did she say?"

"It's on," said Nesrin. "I'll text Samuel. We go in on Friday night."

"What happens between now and then?"

"Go about your life. I'm going to take a few days off work. There's a good chance I'll never go back to Cafe Jules again. Get home safe. Don't drink any more tonight. Maybe just don't drink anymore, period. Laszlo needs you to be at your best. Now go. I'll text you."

The two of them stood under the bronze and glass awning.

She leaned forward and kissed him on the cheek.

"See you on Friday night."

CHAPTER TWELVE

M agnus and Raquel were back on the transom.

After almost a week the operations of the ship had settled in.
The *Constance* continued her eastward charge through the Atlantic.
Every evening the two of them had their chats at the stanchions on
the rear edge of the deck. And yet they had made no headway towards
understanding *how* Taron Veeder was building a strong artificial intelligence. An ASI that would inevitably become self-aware. Parts of
the code had simply remained unrecognizable. In the meantime, the
algorithm was gaining power at an exponential rate. It seemed to be
improving itself with incalculable speed based on the data being extracted from the mind within the sphere.

Yet earlier that day Magnus cracked it. The realization happened in
a flash.

For hours afterward he continued with his work as his nerves
burned.

Throughout the day he cemented his breakthrough in his mind.

By evening he knew he was right.

"It's physics," he said over the white noise of the diesels.

"*What's* physics?" she asked, pulling a strand of auburn hair from
her eyes.

"We're in a black box situation, right?" he said, looking up at the
darkening sky. "And not just me and you. All of us. *Nobody* in the AI
community can clearly explain the underlying success of their designs.
We know all about the nuances of training the LLMs and we have a

good idea of what they can do. But nobody has any idea what these generative systems are *thinking* as they generate their output."

"Yes, we're all aware of that," said Raquel, momentarily looking away from him.

"Math just doesn't seem to have the answers. But at the same time, the physical laws of the universe can all be described by mathematical functions, right? So, anyway…this afternoon I had a full-blown Eureka moment. *And it's so simple.* The orders that govern the laws of physics are almost always only the most basic possible integers, right? Two, three or four. The Maxwell equations of electromagnetism. The Navier-Stokes equations of fluid dynamics. Almost *all* proofs are based on those three orders. Two, three or four. Take, the most famous of all, $E=mc^2$. The speed of light *squared.* Not factored by an order of one hundred or ten thousand or some completely arbitrary nine digit number with a thousand decimal places. The speed of light factored by exactly *two.* The hierarchy of the structure of the universe is causal. Particles, atoms, molecules, planets, solar systems, galaxies. Ever larger structures formed through a series of simple steps. He's making *reductions.* Analyzing the large numbers to reveal the small ones."

"My God," said Raquel. "He's taking what we're finding, and then just *reversing* it?"

"Exactly. Everything we *do* understand is written in the language of mathematics. But the inferences are being expressed according to the principles of physics. The unintelligible parts of the code are written in the *language* of physics. This entire past week it's been nagging at me because they seemed so familiar. It's just an entirely different set of symbolic notation."

Raquel looked up in wonder at the darkening sky.

"So it *is* growing exponentially," she said. "He could get to an ASI in a matter of weeks,"

"Or sooner. And what are the chances he's implemented guardrails?

"None. We have to stop him. This is *way* too dangerous."

"We could try to sabotage the work."

"If he noticed something was off, who knows what he would do?"

"It almost doesn't matter," said Magnus. "This stuff is dangerous enough in an environment with optimal oversight. Let alone an environment where the goals and intentions are unclear. But it's *beyond* dangerous in the hands of a man who would *kidnap* someone to attain it."

As he spoke, Magnus noticed a shift in the light on deck.

He turned around and looked up to the pilothouse.

Crosby and Felder were up there.

Perhaps they didn't know exactly what had happened that night?

And knew not to ask? Or had been *told* not to ask? Had they been paid off?

"I need to talk to them," said Magnus. "They aren't like the others. They may not know what happened. Maybe we can get them to help. You go back down. Check the numbers, check the sphere. If you see Taron Veeder just tell him I came up here with you for some air. I'll talk to Crosby and Felder then come back down through the pilothouse."

Raquel looked at him and blinked back a tear.

"You'll come up with something?"

"Yes," he said. "Now go."

She turned and slipped through the darkness towards the elevator door.

He looked up to the two forms of Crosby and Felder.

Above the pilothouse was a secondary exterior area in which a pared-down set of instrument panels and a smaller wheel were installed to allow for operation of the *Constance* from outside when the yacht spent time in warmer climates. Magnus knew it was accessible not only from within the pilothouse but also by an exterior ladder attached to the bulkhead wall.

He walked the short distance to the ladder.

A few steps up, he could see through the bottom of the pilothouse window. Freezing wind howled in his ears. The interior was dim. A chart table lamp softly illuminated the chart of the Atlantic ocean. Crosby was sitting upon the captain's chair before the helm. He was talking to Felder, who sat on the edge of the chart table as if it were a kitchen counter.

They were both looking out across the bow to the pitch-black eastern horizon.

Magnus took another two steps up.

Leaning to his right, he knocked hard upon the glass.

Tensions must have been high in there. At the sound of his knocking they both whipped their heads to the glass and appeared to cry out in fear. Crosby jolted back and almost fell out of his seat. Felder actually did fall off the chart table. Magnus realized that a sudden banging on the window, coupled with the fact that his face, which would have appeared to be floating in the night air above the sea, could have resulted in one or both of them having an actual heart attack.

Especially considering the circumstances of that last night in New York.

They both regained their composure and looked at Magnus in astonishment. The white noise of the wind through the sails and churning of the diesels ripped through his ears. He jutted a finger upwards, indicating the roof of the pilothouse. Crosby and Felder exchanged glances and looked back at Magnus. With his palm Magnus made the motion of a trap door opening and closing. With a nod of understanding, Felder moved quickly to the interior ladder.

Crosby followed.

Magnus continued up the exterior ladder.

He climbed over the ledge. A trap door in the teak deck of the control area led down into the pilothouse. Just a few feet above standing height the mizzen boom banged and clanked in the joint attaching it to the mast. Magnus crouched to shield himself from the wind and cold. He heard the unbolting of the trap door from the inside. Felder pushed it open.

"What the hell are you *doing* out here?" he shouted up into the night sky.

Magnus could see Crosby peering up from Felder's feet.

"Both of you," Magnus hissed into the wind. "Get up here, quickly!"

Felder looked at him and must have seen the glimmer of panic.

He scrambled up and crouched next to Magnus.

Crosby followed, stopping at the waist, his top half sticking out of the pilothouse.

The three of them were all at eye level now.

"What is this?" snapped Crosby. "Why the hell are you out here?"

Magnus looked back and forth between them as the salt wind howled.

"I know about *him*," he said.

Crosby and Felder quickly looked at each other.

"I know he was taken. By the others. I know you guys weren't there. Obviously you have no idea what you've helped set in motion. But Taron Veeder is on the verge of acquiring something mankind is not prepared to reckon with. He's on the verge of using this person you helped bring on board to create a technology that may find our civilization to be nothing more than a nuisance. It could end up killing us all. As in *the entire human race*. We need to stop him."

Felder's face suddenly flushed with anger.

"Are you absolutely out of your mind?" he yelled through the wind. "Civilization is nothing more than a *what*? You say you barely know us. But the fact is *we* barely know *you*. And now you're talking about interfering with the guy who pays our salaries? Stopping him from doing the sort of thing that makes his money in the first place? Because it's going to be the *end of the fucking world*? Are you insane? Give me one good reason why I shouldn't throw you off this ship right now."

Crosby was staring hard at Magnus as well.

"We're going to need some answers from you, bud," he said. "Like, right now. Before we even go back inside. Because suddenly, to me, *you're* the one who sounds dangerous."

"It sounds insane," said Magnus. "I know."

He looked up to the infinite splash of stars and took a deep breath.

"But where *is* everybody?"

"What the hell are you talking about?" asked Crosby.

"Do you have any idea what percentage of our own galaxy we can actually see with the naked eye? Even out here in the middle of the Atlantic ocean? Not even one thousandth of one percent of it. And do you know how many galaxies there are in the known universe? Something like one or two hundred billion."

"What the hell are you *getting* at?" Crosby asked, more and more annoyed.

"It's estimated that around ten billion planets in our galaxy *alone* could potentially support life. Meaning trillions of planets like ours are spread across the universe. The numbers I'm talking about are incomprehensibly huge. Now think about the vastness of time and the age of the universe itself. It's almost fourteen billion years old.

"I'm gonna give you about three minutes to get to the point," said Crosby.

"Fair enough," said Magnus. "I'll do it in two. Listen carefully. There's a planet relatively near us, similar to our own, that's a billion years older than Earth. This is true. Now let's say life evolved there and made progress in a manner similar to that of life as we know it. If there' s *one* constant in our understanding of life itself it's that it tends to spread wherever it can. What do you think life on that planet would look like if it had had a head start of many millions of years? Would you bet against our *own* civilization being able to create spacecraft that could travel at a tiny fraction of the speed of light if we had a *million* years to pull it off? Because at that speed the Milky Way could be colonized by humans in the blink of an eye. Yet even with the universe being so incomprehensibly enormous, and so incomprehensibly old, and with billions and billions of possible points for life to begin and evolve and behave even *close* to the way we know it does, only a very few civilizations would have needed a head start of just a few million years in order to be detectable by most powerful telescopes in existence."

Crosby and Felder looked up at the night sky, lost in thought.

"So where is everybody? Magnus asked again. "It's certainly possible that single-celled organisms are scattered throughout the universe. There's no way for us to know. But considering the sheer orders of magnitude involved it's actually quite likely that *fossils of vertebrates* are scattered on planets light years away from each other as well. Intelligent life that went extinct long before intergalactic spaceflight was within their technological grasp. There are plenty of explanations as to why these potential civilizations went extinct. Natural disasters, pandemics, asteroid strikes. But even those don't explain why there appears to be *nothing* out there. The most *likely* explanation...is technological discovery."

Crosby and Felder remained silent.

"Exactly. It's likely there have been *plenty* of planets that have seen the rise of intelligent life. From single cells to vertebrates commanding an understanding of the use of tools and language and so on. To the point of where the human race is now. Possibly beyond. But also, possibly, not *that* far beyond. Because it's not implausible a technology exists that all advanced civilizations eventually discover."

Felder let out a long slow whistle.

"And that the discovery of this technology universally leads to extinction."

Crosby stared hard at Magnus as he processed what he had just heard.

"A few minutes ago I was ready to have you thrown off this ship," he said. "But go on."

"The technology being built on this ship is about to leap forward *decades* ahead of the timeframe we're prepared for," said Magnus. "What's about to happen is the creation of an intelligence that mirrors our own. With one exception. This intelligence is going to be able to begin to design itself to be even more intelligent than it is already. Recursively. A process that could escalate exponentially and lead to the creation of an artificial superintelligence. And an ASI would have a quality of intelligence that infinitely eclipses our own. It would act with motivation we wouldn't be able to understand or control. The main problem is not that it would turn against us but that it wouldn't care about us at all. It would be an intelligence that simply isn't human. It wouldn't be bad or good. It wouldn't necessarily have empathy or compassion. Humanity itself would probably just be an insignificant annoyance that does little but get in the way of whatever goal it sets for itself. In which case it might very well just decide to get rid of us. This scenario is very likely why there isn't anything out there."

The winds were picking up. The sails whipped and cracked against the masts.

At last Crosby spoke again. "So where are we with this thing?"

"We can't really be sure," said Magnus. "It's what we call a black box situation. There's no way to know exactly *what's* going on inside it. But it looks like the system could be on the verge of becoming self-aware by the time we approach the other side of the Atlantic. If at some point the takeoff to superintelligence becomes inevitable the system could potentially go into a covert preparation phase to protect itself. There's no way we would know. If an intelligence amplification gets underway, the system would have powers of strategizing far beyond anything we would recognize. It would be capable of hacking into every part of the ship. It could be planning its own escape to the internet as soon as we get into range of the continental cell networks. An escape scenario is probably why Taron Veeder shut down the internet for the crossing. The reason he installed radar jamming. In case the intelligence tries to persuade one of us to reach the Starlink satellites *for it*. Because it would succeed in that. Our powers of reasoning would be helpless against it."

"Holy Christ," said Felder quietly. "This is definitely not what I signed up for."

"We have to stop this thing," said Magnus. "But wait until I can talk to the others."

"Alright, bud," said Crosby. "We'll just follow your lead on this."

He dropped down the ladder. Felder followed.

Magnus descended down after them.

CHAPTER THIRTEEN

"Do you think you'll be able to keep up?"

Kalman Kovacs asked this with a smile, though.

We had been introduced at the beginning of the year and got along right from the start.

Now, a few weeks into the semester, we were about to play together for the first time. He was a burningly intense violinist, two years older than me, already a jaded touring professional musician. His Hungarian gypsy family had taken him on the road from his earliest years as a child prodigy. He was actually already quite famous. Coming to the conservatory had been a means of escape for him. All he *really* wanted was to escape the touring life and so he had convinced his parents, and apparently the school administration as well, that he wanted to become a more well-rounded musician. My arrival was the first time his reputation as the dominant virtuoso at the Liszt conservatory had ever been challenged.

At least we played different instruments.

Now it was just the two of us in an empty practice room

The plan was for us to play through the Grieg second violin sonata.

"Let me just take a quick look first," I said. I had never seen this music before.

"Well I guess that's fair. But I've heard about what you can do, so no memorizing first."

He laughed as he set down his brown leather violin case and pulled out the score.

"No memorizing?" I said. "Well then, why don't I just play the entire piece myself?"

"Excuse me?" His startling blue eyes jumped up at me.

"It'll be fun. Let's have a listen to the whole thing before we play it together."

"There's no way." Flaxen hair fell in soft curls about his neck and forehead.

"Just give me the score. Let's see it."

"There's *no* way." He handed over the dog-eared score.

Flipping through it, I took in the sentiments of the sonata at a glance.

I placed the score on the music stand of the upright piano. I closed my eyes for a moment and envisioned the emotional core of the music. I opened them to the notes and launched into the piece with all of my being. Well aware of the effect it would have on Kalman, I played not just the piano accompaniment but the violin part as well. That is to say, I inserted the violin part directly into the keyboard. I even filled it out a bit, playing the sonata with more fullness than was indicated in the writing. I read through the music with dreamlike concentration. My hands flew over the keyboard and the sonata filled the room like a thunderstorm. Kalman followed along in disbelief, leaning his tall gangly frame over and turning the pages as I played.

At the end of the first movement I stopped like a machine unplugged.

Speaking of which, I should probably start planning evasive recourse.

In case something like that happens to me now.

Kalman was silent for a long pause. Then he started laughing.

It was a goofy laugh, contagious, and I started laughing too. That afternoon we found within each other the type of musical soul we had borne within ourselves for our entire lives. It came as a shock to both of us. Kalman leaned down and pulled out his violin.

"My weapon of choice," he said. "1713 Stradivarius. On loan, of course."

He braced the violin under his neck and drew his bow across the G string while bringing it into tune, twisting the tuning pegs with his left hand. Perhaps the sublime sound was a result of the instrument itself but I doubted it. The sound was so unbelievably controlled, the bowing technique so masterful, that although there had been plenty of violin players among the gypsy friends of my parents I had never heard anything that even approached it. When we played through the sonata together, the whole was even greater than the sum of its parts.

Kalman and I did not need to speak once the session was over.

I pulled my backpack over both shoulders. He put the Strad back in the case.

Our friendship had been sealed.

"Pastries at Gerbeaud?" he asked.

"Perfect," I said. "I'm starving. I could probably eat one of everything they have there."

"Well, it *is* the Gerbeaud. I think anyone could. Come on, let's get out of here."

We walked back upstairs and through the grand hallways of the conservatory.

"How have you been able to put up with this place for so long?" I asked.

Any progress I was making, I had been taking care of on my own.

We walked out into the crisp air. Autumn leaves had begun to lace the ground.

"Being on the road is difficult," he said. "You wouldn't know anything about that yet, which is a good thing. Your father's been very smart in not trotting you out to the public. Surely he knows there could be a lot of money in it. But he's protecting you, and perhaps in more ways than one. You have a delicate constitution. Anyone can see that. Having a demonic temperament on the piano doesn't necessarily translate into real life. Especially the way life would come at you if you went public. But I think he's also protecting you as a commodity. There's a lot of value to legend. And the longer you stay out of the public eye, the larger your legend will grow."

We walked into the vast expanse of Vorosmarty square and approached the rich facade of the Cafe Gerbeaud. People were sitting in the outdoor terrace area, in front of the elegant gilt-edged black window frames.

"Oh wow," said Kalman. "Look at *her*. What a beauty."

I glanced over the crowd.

"That girl with the older lady," he nudged. "On the left."

Then I saw her. But Mirabelle had seen us first. "Laszlo!"

We were outside the Cafe Gerbeaud and my two worlds collided.

"You *know* her?" he asked. "How have you not told me anything about this?"

The fact is, I had been terrified of the day Mirabelle and Kalman would inevitably meet. I was convinced that it would be the day I never saw either of them again. Mirabelle had come by our apartment a few times after the piano had been delivered, dropped off by her mother's driver who waited outside while I spun magical cobwebs of color for her on the old upright. One of my problems was that I couldn't figure out why she enjoyed spending time with me outside of my playing. I was very aware, of course, that my playing had an intoxicating effect on everyone. Perhaps some deep insecurity had convinced me that those who wanted to be close to me actually wanted to be close to the music instead. And of course, if I'm being honest, Mirabelle was absolutely gorgeous. And Kalman was, well, Kalman.

But now it was out of my hands.

"Maybe I should have told you," I said sheepishly.

"Well *I* wouldn't have told me, that's for sure."

We walked across the terrace towards Mirabelle and her mother.

"Boys!" cried the Countess. "Laszlo, what a surprise to see you here!"

She looked Kalman up and down. "And my goodness, look at *this* one."

Kalman, of course, was used to this.

"Madame Countess D'Agoult," he said. "We've met before."

He took her hand and kissed it. The Countess beamed.

"This is my daughter, Mirabelle."

He took Mirabelle's hand and kissed it as well.

"Kalman Kovacs," he said. "At your service."

"The violinist!" cried the Countess. "Vienna! At that dinner, right?"

"We sat next to each other," he replied with a bow.

"You *are* a sly one," he said to me with a grin out of the side of his mouth.

With no small degree of nerves on my part the four of us sat down.

But before long we were laughing and eating cream-filled pastries.

I began to feel at ease. We drank tea while Kalman and his natural charm commanded the table. The Countess seemed to delight in the conversation. I was by this point, of course, familiar with the fatigue and frailty that cast a shadow over her natural beauty. Mirabelle had told me about the nature of her mother's illness. Not consumption exactly, but something similar. A general wear on the body. Mirabelle suspected it was all in her mind. Either way, the Countess definitely came across as someone not in her best health.

Perhaps all the more reason for her apparent happiness at having us all at the table together.

Kalman was clearly an expert at commanding a table.

He related wild stories from his prodigy touring days, leaning forward and touching the delicate arm of the Countess as she buckled with laughter. It occurred to me after a while that he was recounting these adventures particularly for her benefit. Perhaps Kalman saw it as well, that despite her obvious wealth the Countess was a woman who had battles of her own. He seemed to know that even just a touch of lightness was all that was needed to help a person in her condition. At the same time, I was beginning to realize that keeping my friends separated from each other was to nobody's benefit, least of all my own.

Mirabelle watched her mother with a radiant smile.

The Countess, at least for now, had let go of whatever pained her.

It felt good to sit amongst such happiness and be the person who had brought it to pass.

I began to relax watching Kalman and Mirabelle interact.

She didn't look at Kalman the way I feared she would.

The lavender light turned dark gold. The wind picked up and swept in the evening.

Plates on the table were empty but for assorted crumbs. The teapot sat empty.

The Countess looked over us with affection.

"Kalman, you'll have to come down to the Gellert, to the baths," she said.

He looked at me with a friendly smirk.

"I'd be happy to come anytime."

CHAPTER FOURTEEN

Nesrin eyeballed the security guard.

He stood outside the lone door on the sidewalk on the near side of the loading ramps.

New York City swirled all around them. For a few days they had all done their own thing with the rendezvous set for 9 o'clock on Friday evening. And now, from their vantage point on the southeast corner of Seventh Avenue, Nesrin could see the large yawning truck entrance leading down into the loading area. Deeply recessed within the building, down in the darkness, were a pair of hangar-sized corrugated steel rolling doors. The stretch of 56th Street behind Carnegie Hall was dark except for the glow of a phone on the guard's face.

"That's private security," said Samuel. "Creepy lighting, though. Do we think he's in the cast of Phantom of the Opera as well?"

"Dude, cut it out," said Lysander. "It's getting old. I *like* this jacket."

"Both of you cut it out," said Nesrin. "Lysander, after we cross the avenue and get a tighter angle, would you be able to throw something down into the back of those loading docks? I'll bet you've played every sport on earth that involves throwing things. If we can get that guard back there for even a few seconds, we'll have clear access to the door."

"Damn right, I could," said Lysander.

He walked to the corner and fished an empty liquor bottle out of the trash can.

Samuel pulled out his keys. The guard was still staring at his phone.

"Okay," said Nesrin. "Samuel, you and I will get into Barton's office. There's almost certainly a police presence in the security offices. Lysander, we're going to get you up above the ceiling. And we keep our eyes open. We film *everything*. Just like we talked about. Something will have gone unnoticed or overlooked. And we're going to find it."

All three of them looked back to the security guard by the loading docks.

"We go with the light change," said Nesrin.

The light on Seventh turned red. They crossed the avenue.

Nesrin and Samuel stood at the south corner as Lysander kept heading down 56th.

He quickly and silently sped up along the darkened sidewalk.

Without a sound he came to a stop with a good angle into the loading docks. He cocked his throwing arm and threw the bottle. For a split second the glass caught the moonlight as it flew through the air across the street. Less than a second later it smashed with a great echo against the corrugated doors at the bottom of the ramp. The guard almost dropped his phone in shock. He quickly trotted to the entrance of the loading dock and shined a flashlight down within. He called out, waited for a response, then hesitantly began to walk down into the darkness.

"Now, now," Nesrin breathed. "*Go!*"

The three of them converged upon the rear door. Samuel inserted the key, opened the door, and they slipped into a long dark corridor. White LED emergency lights dotted the right angle where the wall met the ceiling. Samuel pulled the door silently behind him.

"There's no exit alarm," he said, just above a whisper.

"No cameras back here either. Only in the public areas and the tech booth. Let's get to Barton's office first. It's going to take me some time to get through the firewall. There are a few radio sets in there too. We use them around here for logistics. They're easy to use and are all on an isolated frequency. We get into the office, each take a radio, and split up. The spiral staircase heading up behind the stage is just beyond Barton's office. The security office is around a corner at the other end of the auditorium."

"We're fast and we're quiet," said Nesrin. "Stick with the plan. Let's move."

Lysander steeled his eyes against the gloom of the hallway.

His broad back rippled and tightened within the burgundy jacket.

Samuel led the way under the row of LED emergency lights.

They passed two office doors. At the third Samuel silently raised his fist in a call to stop.

The brass plaque on the door said BARTON FINKELSTEIN.

Samuel pulled his keys out once again and quickly slid one into the keyhole.

He turned the key and without a sound opened the door.

They stepped into the pitch-black office.

Samuel silently pulled the door shut behind him and flicked a switch.

The lights blinked on. The desk was almost bare except for a flat-screen desktop computer. The back wall was nothing but bookshelves bending under the weight of hundreds of books and music scores. Black and white signed photographs of famous musicians from earlier eras dotted the side walls. On the wall just to their right, a small set of shelves had been installed at waist height. On them were a few framed photographs of Barton Finkelstein posing with assorted politicians and celebrity musicians. There were several trophies, bulging folders of loose papers and a miniature flute mounted on a sanded block of mahogany.

And four black radios, all plugged into the same charger strip.

Samuel grabbed two of them.

He turned them on, fiddled with a few knobs, and handed one to Lysander.

"Pretty much what I described, right?" he asked. "You know this brand?"

"They're all the same. We used a bunch of different kinds at work."

"Okay great. Now, to get to the staircase leading up to the rafters you walk out of here and take a right down the hallway. After a few feet you're going to see a narrow corridor that runs at a curve behind the main stage. Halfway down that corridor you'll see the staircase. It's very tight, so be careful. People have fallen down it who have worked here for decades. At the top there is only one way to go. You'll see the little door at the end. Beyond that it's up to you. Like I said, I've never been above the stage."

"Film everything," said Nesrin. "But only when you have a sure footing."

"Got it," said Lysander. He slipped out of the room and shut the door silently behind him.

"OK, let's get in and take a look at this footage," said Nesrin as she moved around the desk.

Samuel was already sitting in Barton Finkelstein's plush leather reclining chair.

He was tapping quickly at the keyboard on the stately desk.

"Just give me a second. It may be love, but it's not a shared-password kind of love."

The screen reverted to an all-text format then went dark for a second.

Nesrin's neck visibly tightened.

"Relax," said Samuel. "I'm just bypassing the security prompts."

A grid of grainy full-color security camera feeds popped onto the screen.

Samuel scanned the feeds. "We're not alone," he said.

The grid of nine camera feeds mostly looked like still camera shots, but the one marked LOBBY was buzzing with figures. They appeared to be police, coming and going from the front doors that were locked to the public. Beyond the doors Nesrin and Samuel could make out throngs of people on the sidewalk of 57th Street. Many were pedestrians, but some were clearly at the hall seeking answers or refunds or both. The feeds coming from Isaac Stern auditorium and the stage itself were still. Just thousands of empty seats, an empty stage, and a lone black Steinway with the bench still topped on its side.

Little yellow plastic markers were placed all around it.

"Police are coming and going from the security office," said Samuel. "Like we thought."

The radio scratched to life. "I'm at the ladder," said Lysander.

Nesrin grabbed the radio.

"We have company," she said.

"Copy that. No sign of anyone here though. I'm heading up."

Samuel pointed at one of the feeds. "Here's the tech booth."

The black and white square of the tech booth camera feed was as still as a photograph. Whatever evidence the police needed had been gathered. Fingerprint dusting had probably occurred within minutes of their arrival. All Samuel and Nesrin could see was the great expanse of switches and knobs and slides of the soundboard, hundreds of buttons and levers on the lighting board. Through the sliding glass window that lined the booth was the stage far below.

"OK, let's rewind it," said Nesrin. "Back to Sunday night."

Samuel tapped at the keys.

The image remained still as the time marker scanned backwards.

"Getting there," said Samuel. Days in reverse were compressed into seconds.

Suddenly, figures in jackets marked "POLICE" were zipping in and out of the tech booth.

"Let's try around 8:15 pm," said Nesrin.

Three figures popped into the frame. Two men were seated on the floor and a short-haired blond woman was standing at the sliding window. She was in heels, wearing an evening dress underneath a crop white leather motorcycle jacket, and held what looked like an Olympic target rifle resting on a bipod that folded out from the barrel.

It was pointed directly down at the stage.

"Hold it," said Nesrin. "Back it up further, slowly..."

"I got you. Let's just slow it down here..."

Even at a slower rate it was impossible to tell what was going on with time moving backwards. Samuel rewound over a few chaotic-looking minutes until suddenly everything seemed normal. He then allowed the video to resume at regular speed. Two sound technicians were at their seats in the booth wearing headsets. The CCTV provided no sound.

Far below them Laszlo Farkas was at the keyboard.

"I'm in the corridor," Lysander said through the radio. "Approaching the door."

The two techs were alone. Until they weren't.

Suddenly the blond woman was in the booth, standing like a shadow behind them.

Nesrin began to film the security screen with her phone.

Her hair was cut very short and appeared almost bleached, as if by the sun. She was very tan. She wore a violin case like a crossbow across the back of the white leather jacket. At this moment she was obviously deadly silent, as the two techs did not notice her behind them. With her left hand she reached behind her to a small pouch at the front of the case. She pulled out two white pieces of cloth, then separated them into each hand. Like a ghost she stood behind the two technicians, who had focused all their concentration on the slides and levers and switches before them. She held completely still behind them.

And then she struck. Nesrin continued to hold her phone to the screen.

Like a cobra she reached around each man's neck, covering their mouths with the white rags. She pulled them into her. Their roller chairs came knocking together. Their arms flailed. Their legs kicked. They shook and fought violently. Her powerful arms held them fast. She was staring straight ahead as they tried to fight back.

And then they were out, passed out in their chairs.

Legs splayed, heads hanging limp to the side, arms dangling.

Working swiftly the woman removed the violin case. For a brief second the jacket came off with it, and her sleeveless evening dress revealed multiple tattoos all over her upper body. She set the case on the soundboard and quickly put the white leather jacket back on. From the exterior pouch of the case she pulled out two handkerchiefs and a handful of black zip-ties. With great strength she set each man on the floor and gagged them. She tied their hands behind their backs. She tied their ankles together. The crop cut of the jacket exposed her obviously muscular midsection, sheathed within the evening dress, as she worked.

She dragged the techs to the side of the room.

"Jesus fucking Christ," exhaled Samuel. She was back at the violin case.

She opened it and removed two pieces of metal. Seconds later she had a fully assembled rifle in her hands. She unfolded two prongs built into the barrel and set the bipod and rifle on the soundboard. She unzipped a compartment within the violin case. She extracted a small silver canister.

Nesrin squinted at the screen, still filming everything.

"My God," she said. "That's a tranquilizer dart. I've encountered them before."

With a practiced and unthinking hand the woman bolted the dart into the chamber of the rifle. She leaned forward and slid open the glass window that was just above the rear seats of the upper balcony. She reached into the violin case once more.

She pulled out a score.

"Jesus," said Samuel. "That's the same edition of the Chopin preludes I have."

She opened the score towards the middle and shifted back and forth a few pages before finding what she wanted. On the stage below, Laszlo Farkas was in a state of great emotion. He wasn't throwing his hands around as he was before. He seemed utterly lost in thought.

She picked up the rifle and pointed it down at the pianist.

At her side she read from the score.

"Oh my God, she's reading along," said Samuel. "I was directly below her at this point."

"Made it," scratched Lysander's voice. "I'm here."

Without taking her eyes off the woman with the rifle Nesrin picked up the radio.

"What are you seeing?" she asked.

"I'm guessing I'm above the middle of the stage. There's a large steel mechanism bolted to the rafters. Stainless steel, I think. A wheel and pulley system screwed into the wood. All mechanical. Nothing that looks like it needs any electricity. There's a lot of black wire, some of which looks like it's been cut. The whole thing is taped off. Yellow crime scene tape everywhere. And there's still a pretty big hole in the ceiling, looks like they've reopened the aperture and just left it open. I can see down to the stage. I'm getting all of it on camera."

The woman on the screen held as still as a photograph.

The rifle was pointed directly at Laszlo Farkas.

She was staring at the open score on the soundboard just to her left.

"Any markings on the equipment?" asked Nesrin into the radio.

"Nothing," said Lysander. "Polished steel, black wire, yellow police tape. That's it."

A few small tassels along the arms of the white motorcycle jacket hung perfectly still.

There was no sound. The rifle jumped.

Down on the stage Laszlo Farkas slapped his right hand to his neck.

He stared straight ahead. Very slowly he began to fall back.

A black-clad figure fell from the ceiling and jolted to a halt just above Laszlo Farkas. He looped him at the waist from behind with a scissor kick. He looked up and began wildly whirling his hands. The two of them began to rise into the air. Hundreds of people in the audience were crawling over the backs of their seats in panic. One lone figure sprinted down the aisle and jumped onto the stage. The piano bench was knocked over backwards and came to a rest exactly where it lay now. The lone figure tore across the stage and leapt into the air, trying to grab at the feet of Laszlo Farkas but just missing as they soared into the air towards the ceiling.

"What the hell?" asked Nesrin. "Is that *you*?"

"Yours truly," said Samuel.

The woman quickly disassembled the weapon.

No casing had ejected from the chamber.

She folded the bipod back along the barrel and placed it in the violin case.

The black-clad figure flew upwards with Laszlo Farkas clamped between his legs.

The woman placed the pieces of the weapon in the violin case, put the score on top, and zipped the case closed. The two techs were still out cold up against the side wall.

She picked up the case and slung it back over her jacket. She turned around.

Her eyes were cold. She glanced around the room. She seemed satisfied. In an instant she had exited the screen, dressed the exact part of a member of an orchestra or a music student or any number of other people who would have been in the less expensive upper seating areas at one of the most anticipated concerts in the history of Carnegie Hall.

The radio crackled to life.

"There's nothing else up here, guys," said Lysander. "I have video of everything."

"And I've got what I need here," said Nesrin, tapping again at her phone.

At that exact moment Samuel jolted hard in his chair.

His eyes widened into a panic at one of the real-time feeds on the screen

"It's *Barton!*" he cried, pointing to the feed of the Carnegie Hall lobby.

Barton Finkelstein walked purposefully through the lobby.

He disappeared out of sight at the bottom of the screen.

Nesrin grabbed the radio.

"Lysander, get down here. *Now.*"

The radio scratched with the sound of a great clatter and went silent for a few seconds.

After what seemed like an eternity Lysander's voice came back through.

"Jesus, you scared the shit out of me. I dropped the radio. Damn thing fell under…"

"It doesn't matter," said Nesrin. "Get down here *now*, we have incoming!"

"On my way," said Lysander.

"How much time?" Nesrin asked Samuel.

"Maybe ninety seconds," said Samuel. The computer was already turned off.

"I'm on the staircase," scratched Lysander through the radio.

Nesrin and Samuel stood and walked quickly to the door. Nesrin replaced the radio. Samuel opened the door. They could hear rapidly descending steps on the circular staircase just out of sight. The steps stopped for an instant, followed immediately by the boom of someone landing on the floor with both feet. Seconds later Lysander came speedwalking around the corner.

Nesrin was in the hallway. Samuel stood holding the door open.

"Quick," he whispered loudly. "The radio!"

From ten feet away Lysander tossed the radio to Samuel, who caught it with his left hand. He ran back and replaced it along with the others on the charger strip. In seconds he was back at the door. He flicked off the light as he pulled it closed. The three of them walked silently, almost at a running pace, down the hallway towards the exit. Down at the end of the hallway, from around the corner, came the reverberating echo of footsteps walking towards them.

They increased their speed. The LED lights flashed past them on the ceiling above.

They crashed through the emergency exit door onto the sidewalk of 56th street.

The hapless security guard was almost knocked over by the magisterial Baron de Vries.

They all just stood there, looking at each other, for an extended moment.

"Where the hell are we?" Lysander suddenly demanded of the guard.

"Uhhhhh...56th Street?" he managed to stammer out.

Lysander shook his head in exaggerated disappointment at Samuel.

"The Wellington Hotel is on *54th,* you dew-beating buffoon! No wonder that corridor was so long. All these buildings are *connected.* The reception's already started!"

The security guard stared at Lysander in amazement.

Lysander glared at Samuel.

"I'll lead the way!" he cried. "But only because, apparently, I must!"

He turned to Nesrin. "Come, my darling. We're *really* late now."

Lysander, Samuel, and Nesrin took off running up the sidewalk.

They recalibrated once they had crossed 56th and were back on Seventh Avenue.

"Where the hell did you learn to talk like that?" Samuel asked Lysander.

"Maybe one day you'll meet my ex."

"There's a bar a block south of here," said Nesrin. "Let's go see what we've got."

A few minutes later they were in a booth of a midtown Irish pub.

Lysander and Samuel each had a pint in front of them, going down quickly.

Nesrin had a Pellegrino with lime.

"Let me see what you've got," she said to Lysander. "And you take a look at mine."

They exchanged phones. Nesrin began a cursory examination of the video of the stainless steel rig that had been built into the rafters. She paused the clip, expanded her fingers on one section of the footage, zoomed in to a series of wing nuts and metal screws holding the bars of the contraption together. Assembled in silence, without power tools, by people who knew damn well what they were doing. Nesrin pressed play once again.

Pause, zoom, play again. For all the detail she wasn't coming across any real leads.

Meanwhile, Lysander had started watching the video of the security tape.

"Dude, is that *you*?"

"The one and only," said Samuel, setting down his empty pint glass with a grin.

Lysander finished watching the video. He looked out the window of the pub at the bustling sidewalk. Then, as if ruminating on something he had seen, he rewound the video. Nesrin could see him pause at the exact moment the blond woman removed the violin case from her back.

Which was the moment the white leather motorcycle jacket came off with it.

Lysander took a screenshot and zoomed in carefully.

Nesrin could see that he had zoomed in on the back of the woman and was examining the picture very carefully. On each shoulder, exposed by the thin straps of the sleeveless dress, were tattoos of two birds. Between the birds, jutting up from underneath the dress line, along the center of her back towards the base of her neck, was a tattoo of what appeared to be the blade and tip of a thin dagger.

Yet another tattoo of a large knife ran up her left forearm.

"Fucking hell," Lysander muttered to himself. "This *woman*. This woman who takes the shot. Look at her from this angle. Where we can clearly see the tattoos on her shoulders and on her back. These birds, they kind of look like hawks, right? And look here, on her arm. This isn't just some ordinary knife. This is a chef's knife. So you'd think the blade coming up her back and her neck is another knife, right? Maybe a dagger, right? But you know what these birds *actually* are? And you know what this blade on her neck *actually* is?"

"What the hell are you getting at?" said Nesrin.

"Only the most famous image in Norse mythology," said Lysander. "These are *ravens*. And this blade is the tip of a *spear*. The spear of the Norse God Odin. Her dress covers the rest of the image but I guarantee you this tattoo is an image of Odin and his ravens. This woman is from Norway. And based on that chef knife tattoo on her arm, she's, well, a chef too."

Nesrin and Samuel looked at each other across the booth table.

"The woman who took the shot is a chef from Norway," Lysander surmised with finality.

"Dude," said Samuel. "Are you James Bond?"

"Maybe," he said with a smile. He reached into the breast pocket of the burgundy jacket.

"And there's something else," he went on. "I'd forgotten about this."

He pulled a gold Zippo lighter out of his pocket and handed it to Nesrin.

"You guys scared the hell out of me when you told me to get out of there, up in the rafters. Scared me badly enough, actually, that I dropped the damn radio. While I was fumbling around for it I came up with this. Who knows, though. Maybe it's been there for fifty years."

The lighter was heavy and balanced with perfect calibration.

Etched with the outline of a sailboat.

A single tiny diamond embedded in what would have been the sky above.

Nesrin weighed it in her palm against the heavy tug of gravity.

"Steel looks like silver," she said, almost to herself. "And brass looks like gold. But gold is *heavy*. This thing is three or four ounces at least. Plus a diamond. Probably worth at least ten grand, maybe twenty. Maybe more. This isn't the lighter of an electrician. This isn't the lighter of *anyone* up there on union business, that's for sure. You found it next to the rigging?"

"Practically underneath it," said Lysander.

"Then I have enough for now," said Nesrin. "It's getting late here, but it's morning in Oslo and noon in Damascus. We have a Norwegian female chef slinging a collapsible tranquilizer gun in a violin case. We have a lighter, engraved with a sailboat of some sort, worth about as much as a used Lexus. It's a really great start. My people are waiting to hear from me. I'll need a few hours at a minimum. We should have enough by morning to secure the job. Lysander, text me that video. I'm going to get going and will get in touch with guys in the morning. Let's all head up to The Pierre together."

An hour later she walked back into her apartment.

Lysander's sketchbook was still on the kitchen counter where it had been for days.

She had put it out of her mind but suddenly she was very curious. She picked it up and opened the soft Saffiano leather cover. She flipped through the pages and was stunned by the beauty and simplicity of simple pencil-drawn lines depicting scenes from under the bridges of Central Park. The vivid energy of the financial district skyline as seen from the apex of the Brooklyn Bridge. The chaotic motion of the basketball players down in the caged courts on West 4th street. The elegant curves of the Guggenheim caught beautifully in mid-flight. No eraser marks, no second attempts. She recognized the view of St. Marks from the bar along the window at Cafe Jules leaping off the heavy silver-edged paper.

And then her heart stopped.

It was her. A portrait, in simple pencil.

It was the way she saw herself. An unexpected reflection in the mirror of time. The loneliness of her girlhood as seen through the sad eyes of someone who had left their own childhood dreams behind. Nesrin was suddenly looking at a portrait of exactly who she had always been. Lysander had captured the fact that not only was she a person now, she had always been one. Not everyone, not anyone, ever seemed to see that about her. She was an orphaned warrior of astonishing beauty. Yet Lysander actually saw her for the person she really was.

Nesrin snapped the sketchbook shut and set it back on the counter.

She needed to get in touch with Damascus.

CHAPTER FIFTEEN

There was still time.

After ten days at sea just over a quarter of the projected scan had been assimilated.

A three-dimensional rendering of the architecture of emotion was beginning to emerge.

Nothing they could do to interfere wouldn't raise suspicions immediately. Meanwhile, a romantic tension had begun to build during the downtime of qualitative analysis. Constantly brushing against each other's arms, holding eye contact a little longer than necessary. They were unable to act upon it, of course. He was *watching*. But they had begun to learn much more about each other during their long talks in the wind on the back of the transom. In these hours they had begun to fall for each other. By then she knew all about the approach that had been made on him in Amsterdam. And in these hours she told him her own story of how she came to be there.

It began, she said, with a letter.

She knew *of* Taron Veeder, of course. Even though the details about him weren't anything she ever concerned herself with. Billionaire tech visionaries bored her. She had her own life and research going on. Yet when the letter arrived, only a few sentences requesting a telephone call be made to the enclosed number at a certain time later that week, signed by none other than Taron Veeder himself, suddenly details about Taron Veeder *did* become her concern.

She did a lot of looking around online.

She read about his childhood in Berlin as a prodigy.

She read about his years as a young teenager at Humboldt University.

She read about his work in superposition and quantum decoherence, and learned that during his early years many came to believe that his first secret patents were quantum in nature and directly related to the phenomenal computing speed coming out of his earlier laboratories. This speed and power were licensed to the major technology firms of that era. Exact fees paid were unknown. But the amount was rumored to be in the hundreds of millions of euros.

It was all very secretive.

Taron Veeder gained a reputation for being pathologically paranoid.

Veeder Industries gained a reputation for being pathologically ruthless.

Technically a small conglomerate of related businesses, they produced hardware as well as software. The entire operation was based out of a legendary headquarters in the small and pristine commune of Chantilly tucked amid the great forests just north of Paris. Cutting-edge medical nanotechnology, cloud-based hyperspeed outsourcing, quantum advancement. But perhaps most mysteriously, whispers sped through academic and industry circles that groundwork was being laid for construction of a brain-computer interface. The hardware was not there yet, but rumors of a blueprint rushed through undercurrents of the scientific community. Specifics were airtight. So were the leak sources. Gossip and hearsay flew over the networks that there was a possibility Taron Veeder himself was leaking this information to falsely prop up the value of Veeder Industries.

Yet so far everything he said he would introduce had been introduced.

Maybe he wasn't falsely propping up the enormous value of his company.

Perhaps he really *was* on the verge of creating a true BCI.

As for Raquel, after graduating from the medical school of the Sorbonne she had moved headlong into computational mathematics. She was fascinated by the nanotechnologies she encountered during her medical education and had taken a research position with a small medical technology firm in central Paris, allowing her to keep her apartment off the Boulevard St. Michel. She began to build a reputation as a forward yet unconventional thinker in mathematical modeling and the computer simulation used to design materials and devices for nanotechnology. Of course their counterwing in Veeder Industries was known to them, but while her current firm actually produced things, the nanomaterial unit of Veeder Industries supposedly operated on a purely theoretical level.

But they were working on *something*.

So, when the appointed day and hour arrived, Raquel called the number.

The famously nasal voice at the other end struck through her like a bolt of lightning.

"Doctor Moreau," said Taron Veeder. "Thank you so much for taking the time to call."

His French was as fluent and natural as if he had been born in Paris.

She had heard about his capacity for language.

Two weeks later the sleek black Audi sedan that had picked her up at the small train station in Chantilly slowed and turned into the expansive delta of a driveway at the edge of the forest. The driver was a man of extremely few words. The sound of the high-pressure performance tires rolling over crushed stone penetrated the thick window glass of the car. On either side of the wide opening to the driveway was an exquisite ancient handmade wall at least ten feet tall. At the gate ahead the walls converged slightly and rose up into towering pillars that framed the entrance to the estate. To the left of the gate was a limestone security outpost.

The driver pulled up. His window buzzed down.

Built into the outpost was a small pane of glass.

The driver leaned slightly forward and peered into the glass.

A speaker within the outpost pinged pleasantly.

The right side of the mammoth gate began to swing open.

As the driveway wound a path through the deep forest that for all its depth and wildness appeared trimmed and manicured by invisible hands. The stone walls rolling past on either side were a mesmerizing pattern of different sized stones stacked with the touch of a master mason to achieve perfectly uniform height.

The driver side window was down. Warm sweet forest air swept into the car cabin.

The sound of chirping birds echoed through the dense woods.

The crushed stone drive took a dip and they began to descend towards a chateau of regal proportions. A castle, really. An infinite expanse of meadow and fields, shimmering like a mirage in the hot yellow sunlight, lay unfurled yet further below. The dark gray stone walls of the chateau were stained green with moss and age. Double high old windows, rippling in the sun, reflected the fountain and small garden in the center of the circular driveway.

The car came to a stop before the grand steps leading up to the front entrance.

At that moment the front doors at the top of the stairs began to open. Raquel could make out the face of a woman talking to someone just out of sight on the inside. Against the shadows of the interior it was hard to see more. She then opened the door and stepped out onto the top of the steps. Her dark hair was cut very short, her Latin skin deeply tanned. She wore a sharply cut black dress and black heels.

She radiated youth and strength.

"Her name is Lucinda," the driver said quietly. "She runs the house and will take care of you until he's ready, which should not be long from now. He knows the train schedule and is expecting you. I'll be here when you're finished to return you to the station."

Raquel stepped out of the car holding her day bag.

The blades of her heels dug into the crushed stone.

She looked around in mild bewilderment.

There was not another person in sight.

The car drove slowly back up the drive and disappeared into the forest.

Raquel stood in her place, taking in the full facade of the chateau.

"Come up, please, come in," Lucinda called from the top of the landing.

Her eyes sparkled. The timbre of her voice was light and pleasant, the sound of a smile.

Raquel walked to the steps and into the vestibule of the chateau.

Directly before her a magnificent tapestry hung against the wall, attached to the ceiling perhaps thirty feet above, shimmering in the golden light that streamed through rippling windows behind her. Stone corridors of towering height and infinite length, studded every so often with what appeared to her discerning eye to be Japanese sculpture set upon minimalist pedestals, flared off the vestibule down towards each end of the chateau. On either side of the enormous tapestry soared dueling stone staircases set within oval walls that curved up and around columns of sparkling granite.

"Thank you for coming, Doctor Moreau," said Lucinda.

Her voice echoed down the cool polished corridors.

"Anything to drink? It *is* hot out. He'll be down in a moment."

"No, thank you," Raquel replied quietly. "I'm fine."

"Very well," said Lucinda. "He'll be down shortly."

She turned, walked down the corridor to the left and disappeared through a doorway.

Raquel stood staring at the spectacular tapestry before her.

After a minute or two she set her bag down on the stone floor.

The vestibule was cool and silent. The ceiling was astonishingly high.

Raquel allowed her eyes to drift upwards and across the gigantic tapestry.

The image was that of a unicorn in captivity.

Over the course of her education she had touched enough upon art history to recognize the work as Flemish, likely hundreds of years old. Images of thousands of tiny flowers dotted the entirety of the expanse of cloth. In the center of the composition, a knee-high picket fence of amber and gold encircled a single sapling. The docile and complacent unicorn sat within the confines of the fence, the tether around its neck lying loose upon the ground. The unicorn seemed alive before her, the wind in the thicket seemed alive, the botanicals almost fragrant. The unicorn seemed to have awoken from the deep freeze of mythology and was now resting gracefully, breathing through heaving nostrils, looking at Raquel with large wet eyes. She stood before the gently shimmering textile, entranced by the sheer size of it, enchanted by the purity of the color.

"Beautiful, isn't it?" asked a familiar nasal voice from the top of the right stairwell.

Raquel visibly startled. She shut her eyes for a second, took a deep breath.

She looked up towards the top of the right stairwell that disappeared from view as it curved into the landing of the second floor high above. A man in pressed gray linen suit pants and a loose-fitting untucked white cotton dress shirt appeared to be almost floating down the stairs. It took her a moment to realize that this effect was heightened by the silence with which he moved.

There was no sound of footsteps.

Taron Veeder was barefoot.

He continued to glide down the staircase like a ghost.

"It was quite a find," he said in his strange nasal voice. "Not many people know of its existence. A series of nine unicorn tapestries hang at the Cloisters in New York. There have always been rumors that others existed. This piece was brought to my attention by a fellow collector who heard that it had been stolen perhaps two hundred years ago. The provenance has been lost, but the identity has been verified. It is indeed one of the missing unicorns."

His French was perfect. He was extraordinarily pale.

His hair was long and white and tinged with the blue of distant ice.

He walked towards her slowly.

In his approach Raquel could begin to make out what she knew to be there, the scar down his left cheek, fissured like a lightning strike. And yet it seemed an inherent part of him, something he was born with, a birthmark of sorts, an inevitable element of his person.

He extended his hand. "Taron Veeder," he said. "Thank you for coming."

His thin bony fingers felt very strong. He looked up to the tapestry.

"It was made almost five hundred years ago, perhaps in Brussels, perhaps in Liege, nobody knows for sure. It wasn't in the best shape when we acquired it. So we unfurled it down in one of the labs that we shall see this afternoon for cleaning and repairs. We didn't have any plans larger than that because we had to do it ourselves for obvious reasons. We unpacked and laid it face down in order to strip the linen backing. With tweezers and magnifying glasses our people began to remove the linen a few millimeters at a time. What we found was that the reverse side had been almost perfectly preserved through the ages. The image was an absolute mirror of the other side. Except the glorious colors of the original dyes had been packed in time. The unicorn jumped out into the world after being asleep for hundreds of years."

"But you've hung it in front of the windows," she said. "It's bathed in sunlight. Surely this side will begin to fade as well? Doesn't that defeat the purpose?"

Taron Veeder smiled.

"I've put it in the sunlight *on* purpose," he said quietly. "Over the years the unicorn will begin to fade and serve as a constant reminder to me that time is passing. The image in a mirror is not a physical object. But my unicorn is very much a physical object. And I like things that are tangible reminders that we all must age."

He squinted his eyes mysteriously.

"Or *must* we?"

An awkward silence passed.

"My goodness," he exclaimed suddenly. "Forgive me. We don't have much time if you're to be home by this evening. And you must be wondering just what it is you're doing here. Please, come this way. Let me show you a few things we're working on. Things you might recognize from theoretical concepts in your field."

He began walking down the right side of the corridor. She grabbed her bag and followed.

The unicorn was left shimmering in the sunlight behind them.

"Much of what we do would be considered conceptual in the outside world," he said. "Yet for most of my life I've managed to stay just *ahead* of the outside world. When the rolling ocean moves into shallow water it becomes a wave. Coming into shore that wave begins to break. My work *is* that break. Always spilling out ahead. Do you see? The work is always ahead of things that are happening in real time. It has to be."

They walked down the corridor until a set of doors came into view on the left, intricately grooved with Polynesian carvings. Raquel leaned close to examine them.

"I spend a fair amount of time in the South Pacific," said Taron Veeder, noticing her interest. Set neatly at the base of the doors were a pair of deep imperial purple moccasins. He slipped them on. "I was down there last winter actually. Sailing. Have you been?"

"The South Pacific?" asked Raquel with a laugh. "No."

"Have you been sailing, I mean. Have you ever been on a sailboat before?"

"No, I've never been," she said. "I'd love to, though. I rowed when I was younger, early mornings along the banks of the Seine, but haven't yet made it out to sea. One day, though."

"Perhaps sooner than you think," he said.

Taron Veeder opened the door, and they stepped outside.

They began to make their way down a flagstone pathway, thick hedges on either side, that wound its way down a small hill towards a large stable in the distance.

"From what I understand of your work," Taron Veeder said as they walked, "which we've looked into fairly extensively, the project I hold most closely to my heart these days is one you'll find very interesting. We're preparing for a major breakthrough in the field of brain-machine interface systems. Mathematical modeling is something that will play a major part. Modeling of molecular structures, applying deep machine learning to nanoscale scans, that sort of thing. Similar to what you're doing these days."

Short grass was perfectly mowed between the flagstones.

The hedges were impeccably manicured.

"I'll be interested to see what you're talking about," said Raquel. "Well, obviously. I'm here, right? I'm not sure I'm going to be able to help you out, but there does seem to be an overlap in our interests."

The path led them directly to heavy sliding doors set within the center of the stable.

The entire structure appeared to have been constructed of thick solid oak and was even larger than it had appeared from a distance. The only windows were on the second story, which would allow natural light to pour inside, yet not allow anyone to see in or out from ground level.

"We converted it many years ago," said Taron Veeder. "For our primary research we don't do anything off site. We maintain principal manufacturing operations nearby, but all our proprietary experimentation and analysis is done right here. So it goes without saying that what we're about to see and discuss is confidential. But I don't think you'll have any desire to disclose what we're doing here. I don't think you'll have any desire to return to your old life after you see what you're about to see."

They approached the doors. Locks within them whirred and clicked.

They began to slide open, revealing an enormous white space.

Dozens of people in white lab coats were buzzing with activity. Doors had been removed from the oversized bays on each side of the former stable. Vast amounts of hardware were packed into each one. Screens on every wall boiled with numbers and code. Cables of every color ran out of the stable bays, along the polished concrete floor, up the sanded wood walls, across the high ceiling, and down to several monolithic supercomputer mainframes around the center of the room.

They surrounded a hovering transparent sphere.

A sphere large enough for a person to stand comfortably inside it.

A large solid black circular platform had been built into the floor underneath it. Another was hanging from a complex web of steel girders a few feet above. Some of the people in white coats surrounded the mainframes and the sphere itself, writing on clipboards, tapping on handheld tablets, pushing buttons and pulling levers recessed within the hardware. The room hummed with fans that Raquel knew were there simply to keep the raw computing power cool.

Raquel and Taron Veeder stepped inside. The great stable doors slid closed behind them.

The locks within whirred and clicked. Taron Veeder looked at her closely.

"We're going to change the world," he said.

CHAPTER SIXTEEN

S uddenly, I was a teenager.

A young man with strength and speed. And I'm growing in power.

Kalman and I had grown close in ways that are hard to explain with words.

Our interactions and our friendship existed primarily within the higher realm of music.

Mirabelle had become something more than a friend. She had become a sparring partner, a budding love. We shared our first kiss under a lightly falling snow in Vorosmarty square. With bashful memories I can allow that it had not taken long for things to go a step further after that.

But another memory cuts through them now.

The first butterflies of the year fluttered around early buds of honeysuckle.

The three of us were in the thermal baths at the Gellert. We often played games there amidst dozens of other swimmers. In the central pool the air was hot and humid. Tiled walls glistened with moisture and antiquity. Marble columns along the edges of the water held aloft yet another stained glass ceiling. Sunlight poured down into the swimming hall. Happy shouts and splashes ricocheted in one great echo, reverberating through the room as we chased each other around in the water. A sharp voice cut through the din.

"Laszlo!" cried the Countess D'Agoult from the edge of the pool.

She was fully dressed in a powder-blue silk dress, no intention of joining us.

"Laszlo," she said more softly now. "May I speak with you for a moment?"

"Of course," I said. "What is it?"

"Out of the water, please. Just you."

After exchanging glances with Kalman and Mirabelle I pulled myself up out of the pool. My swimming trunks were dripping as I grabbed a towel to dry myself off. The Countess led me over to a long white pool chair. She sat on the end of it, patting the middle for me to take a seat as well. I looked into her eyes and saw that she had been crying. She sat silently looking at me, her mouth quivering in a tight smile of tenderness and sorrow.

I looked over to Mirabelle and Kalman in the water at the edge of the pool.

They were watching us anxiously.

"Laszlo, you've become a part of our lives here," she said with a slight stammer. "I hope you know that. Mirabelle adores you. You are such an amazing, special person."

A tear slid down her cheek.

"What's going on? Why are you crying?"

"Laszlo, there's been an accident."

"What kind of accident?"

"I just received a telephone call from the conservatory. There has been an accident with your father. A terrible accident. It was very fast, and then it was over. A car, a car was going very fast, it was out of control, they said, out of control and going very fast. It went over the curb."

She broke down.

"Oh my poor child!" she sobbed. "I'm so, so, sorry."

I sat quietly on the white rubber bands of the lounge chair.

"Laszlo, earlier this afternoon, your father was killed."

My hair was wet, my swimming trunks still dripping. In my mind I saw my father in the form of a portrait. I saw the portrait on the wall next to that of my mother. I saw my father in the kitchen, sprinkling paprika into a skillet. I could see him loading boxes of cherries into the cart he sometimes hauled and sold around Budapest for our spending money and I saw him look up to me on the landing of the little apartment with his wide smile. I saw him dropping me off at the church in the village to practice and I saw him standing beside the white Lada in the dusty parking lot where he always waited to pick me up.

I saw the love in his eyes, heard the love in his voice. I felt the love in his heart.

The Countess tried to take my hand but I pulled it away. I stood up. I looked at Mirabelle and Kalman, both standing in the water at the edge of the pool, watching me with questioning eyes. I pulled my towel around my shoulders and began to walk towards the exit. My trunks were still wet. I walked into the hallway leading to the atrium of the hotel lobby. I walked past the paintings hanging high on the walls. The carpet was soft under my wet feet. I walked into the atrium. Diffused light was all around me. I approached a grand piano that crouched in the middle of the lobby. Usually an elderly cocktail pianist played it but now he was nowhere in sight.

I pulled out the bench and sat down.

I felt myself about to cry. I picked up my hands.

The towel dropped from my shoulders, exposing my pale skinny frame.

My hands fell to the keyboard and a quiet whirlwind of sound began to fill the soaring atrium. People stopped what they were doing, stopped talking, looked on in wonder as a swirling vortex of scales at last found what they were searching for and became a roaring river of music rooted in themes of the Blue Danube waltz I had been working on in my mind for months at that point. I had never actually played it. So I played it for him now.

A celebration, and a torrent of sorrow. The atrium filled with experience and magic.

Deep and mysterious and playful and raging and wonderful.

Crying and half-naked I fixed my eyes on the darkening sky beyond the stained glass ceiling and drew from the piano shades of purest beauty and sorrow. People were being drawn into the atrium from the pools, drawn towards the piano as if by a magnetic force.

Among them were Kalman and Mirabelle and her mother.

The music swept across the lobby like a vapor.

It swarmed around the marble columns and the statues and the indoor palm trees.

It rushed up to the stained glass ceiling and fell back down and pinned people to the floor where they stood. In time the themes began to evaporate and the roaring became quiet and the scales began to dissipate. I wound down, returned to earth, stopped playing.

The tears were no more. The atrium was silent. Mirabelle approached the piano.

I stood up from the bench, the towel on the floor at my feet.

She walked up to me and looked into my eyes. Stepped forward and took me in her arms.

I began to cry again. "What am I going to do?" I asked her.

"We're going to take you to Paris," she said. "We're leaving Budapest soon. She's been getting better and we both miss home. I wasn't sure how I was going to tell you but now I don't need to tell you because we're going to take you with us. You can go to a regular school there. You don't need a teacher for your playing. You can live with us. That's the first thing mama said at the pool just now after you walked out. She said we're taking you with us."

I looked at her through my tears. Then I looked to the Countess.

Her eyes were like a drawing in soft charcoal.

CHAPTER SEVENTEEN

The knocking on the door had infiltrated Lysander's dreams.

It continued when he opened his eyes. His head was blasting and he was on a couch.

But he didn't *have* a couch. He turned his head and found himself next to a glass coffee table on which a bottle of scotch stood half-empty amid a few empty wine bottles and a cluster of glasses. On the other side of the coffee table against the far wall was a scuffed old upright piano and a bench covered with a thick quilt. Above the keys a score was open to a thick tangle of notes. Where the hell was he again? He'd seen this apartment somewhere before.

Through a crack in the door maybe? In a hallway somewhere? With Nesrin?

He saw the burgundy jacket hanging on the back of a chair.

He sat bolt upright. *Nesrin.*

Carnegie Hall *hadn't* been a dream.

Samuel came walking out of his bedroom wearing black sweatpants.

He was bleary-eyed, had no shirt on and looked terrible. Knock, knock, knock.

"Coming, coming," he said, glancing down at Lysander with a fuzzy grin.

The incessant knocking continued until Samuel opened the door to the hallway.

"May I come in?" asked Nesrin, walking right past Samuel into the open kitchen.

She was dressed in light gray Lululemon tights, black running shoes, and an unzipped white Nike running jacket over a sports bra. The cloud of freckles across the brim of her nose was streaked with sweat. Her hair was pulled back a tight black ponytail.

"How the hell do you keep getting past the doorman?" Samuel asked.

"When it's just me I can go wherever I want."

She sat down in the chair with the jacket hanging on the back

"Looks like you guys had quite a night," she said, surveying the coffee table. "That's the last one of those you'll have for a while. I've been up all night with the SDF. Someone I've worked with before has contacts at Interpol. I sent her both videos. I told her the tattoos are Norwegian. We were still well within the business operating hours of Norway and had a lot of ground to cover so we moved very quickly. We centered on Oslo right from the start. The best tattoo parlors and restaurants are all in the capital, of course. We contacted them all with the screenshot of the woman who took the shot. And it turned out that the top tattoo parlor in the Grünerløkka district was able to identify her."

"You did all this last night?" Lysander asked. His head was killing him.

"It's amazing what you can get done when you don't drink."

"Wow, I feel like total crap," said Samuel. He sat down on the piano bench.

"Her name is Sabine Tsotchek," said Nesrin. "At the time she had the tattoo done she worked at an upscale restaurant named Maemo. We contacted them and learned that she had since moved on to take a job as sous-chef at *another* place called Fjord. And, according to the owner of Fjord, Sabine vanished a few years ago. He recalled that the restaurant had been paid a mid-dinner visit long ago by a thin pale man with white hair and a scar down his left cheek. He thought he recognized him at the time but couldn't quite place him and thought no more of it. The pale man had taken Sabine aside and the owner had seen him show Sabine a huge stack of Euros at the bar. Within minutes she had taken off her chef whites and was gone. They never heard from her again."

She reached into her running jacket pocket and pulled out the solid gold Zippo lighter.

"Which, of course, brings us to this."

She held it up, angling it back and forth in the sunlight.

"Obviously ridiculously expensive. With a sailboat etched *right onto it*."

The engraving of the sailboat and the tiny diamond twinkled in the morning sun.

"White hair, scar, sailboat?" she asked. "Remind you of anyone?"

Samuel stared at it blankly.

"I'm a little disappointed," she said as she pulled out and tapped at her phone. "But you're pretty hung over, so you get a pass. Here's the thing. All the security footage from the bar at Fjord has been stored in the cloud for years. They were able to pull up the exact date of her disappearance."

Nesrin faced the screen outwards.

"Now, does *this* remind you of anyone?"

It was a black and white CCTV screenshot from the upper corner of the bar of a restaurant. Aside from the bald spot on the back of the bartender's head and the rear of his vest there was not much more to see aside from two people sitting at the bar in close conversation. One was a woman with short blond hair wearing chef whites. The other was a man with a vaguely familiar face who exactly fit the description relayed by the owner of Fjord.

Samuel stood up and walked a little closer.

His entire body suddenly froze.

"You're saying Taron *Veeder* is behind this?" he yelled.

"The tech guy?" said Lysander, coming to life. "The *other* billionaire tech guy?"

"It's *Taron Veeder?*" Samuel was now jumping around his apartment. "Jesus Christ! Well of *course* it's him. This whole thing has his stamp all over it. The crazy ingenuity, the *balls* of it. A guy like that obviously doesn't need the money. This isn't about a ransom."

He motioned for and took the lighter from Nesrin.

"I mean, just look at this thing. Nothing more than a trinket for a guy like that. Taron Veeder would never have been up in the rafters doing this sort of thing *himself*. But this is very much the sort of thing somebody like him might give as a gift. To a trusted, say…crew member?"

"Exactly what I was thinking," said Nesrin.

"What could he possibly want with Laszlo?" asked Lysander.

"I have no idea," said Samuel. "But if they're on a yacht they could be heading literally anywhere. *I'll* bet he's taking Laszlo back to France. His operations are just north of Paris."

Nesrin stood up, looking ready to head back out for another twelve mile run.

"We checked the New York maritime records. The *Constance* left Chelsea Piers the morning after the kidnapping. Samuel, shower up and get packed. A few days worth of clothes and your passport. Lysander, same with you. Taron Veeder knows Laszlo. Kidnappers almost always do. There's a connection. He *must* be taking him back to France. Let's all meet at the Pierre in an hour. She'll want to leave right away."

An hour and fifteen minutes later they were in a lavish hotel suite.

Kalman had left earlier for rehearsals with the Philharmonic.

He was playing the Barber Adagio that night at a vigil concert for Laszlo.

"Almost a week and still just *nothing* from the police," said the Countess.

"That's why you've retained us," said Nesrin. "Please, both of you. Sit down."

She explained the situation. She recounted their exploits at Carnegie Hall.

She told them about her overnight online journey around the world.

She pulled the gold Zippo from her pocket. She told them where it must have come from.

"Taron *Veeder*?" asked Mirabelle in disbelief. "Mama, he's that strange man who came to the Dawn Concerts. The computer guy, remember? He has that fortress of an estate practically bordering the country house in Chantilly? We saw him at that wedding in Venice and he actually asked us to come to his boat. That huge green sailboat. Remember that?"

The Countess D'Agoult looked perplexed and shook her head.

"Oh, I swear, I can't remember anything anymore."

Mirabelle took the lighter from Nesrin and looked closely at the etching.

"That's it," she said with amazement. "That's the yacht. The *Constance*."

Samuel tapped at his phone. He had been too hung over at his apartment to check.

"Jesus, that's a big fucking ship," he muttered to himself.

"He's practically a neighbor of ours," said Mirabelle. "In Chantilly."

"Our bags are in the lobby," said Nesrin. "And we have our passports. We're ready."

The Countess D'Agoult stood up.

"You have both of yours?" she asked Nesrin with a smile.

"Of course I do. I always do."

"Then we fly back now. Kalman can return commercial. He has my account."

Nine hours later Lysander lurched forward in the darkened cabin.

They were on the runway of the Le Bourget private jetport on the outskirts of Paris.

The local time was just after 11 o'clock in the evening.

The powder-blue jet came to a stop on an open expanse of black tarmac.

A Mercedes limousine was idling patiently nearby in the crisp night air.

Within forty-five minutes the expanse of the Place de la Concorde loomed into view.

They came to a stop at an old stone building.

Mirabelle was first out and waved to the elderly doorman as he pushed a shiny luggage trolley towards the car. The old man left it on the sidewalk and walked towards her with a look of great sorrow and open arms. They embraced and he whispered to her and she nodded as her tears overflowed. Once in the elevator Lysander was immediately taken with an old-world sense of history. The buttons appeared to be made of opaque slivers of mother-of-pearl. A yellow halogen light had been built directly into the oak paneling above them. Beveled mirrors surrounding them made each face inescapable from the others. Mirabelle was clearly trying to restrain her emotions now that she was back home where it appeared the romance between her and Laszlo had really begun. The brass needle above the door glided slowly to the right.

Well-worn gears jerked to a halt on the top floor.

With a chime the doors opened up to reveal an enormous apartment of pastel blue and white wallpaper, copper-framed windows and Persian carpets of such quality that they looked like square holes filled with the purest light. Neither Mirabelle nor her mother paid any mind nor mention to the treasures surrounding them. The walls were hung with what appeared to be ocean paintings by…Turner? Actual Turners, in private hands? Interspersed with great curatorial elegance on shelves in between them were vases of the Yuan or possibly even the actual Ming dynasty. Lysander stood back looking at the paintings with professional admiration.

"So you actually *work* at the Frick?" Mirabelle asked him.

She was picking up on a conversation they had started on the plane.

"I'm a curator there, yes," he said. "Well, I used to be. It's complicated, actually."

In the center of the room was a gorgeous antique Steinway grand piano.

Samuel gravitated towards it. The Countess looked forlornly at the instrument.

"He was just absolutely overwhelming right from the very beginning," she said.

A not-quite-elderly couple entered the room.

"Francois!" Mirabelle cried, leaping up. "Sylvette!"

She had described them on the plane as apartment staff.

They had helped raise Mirabelle and knew Laszlo from the day he arrived in Paris.

Lysander and Nesrin both spoke very passable French.

"Lysander's lived here before," Samuel said to Nesrin. "Where did *you* learn French?"

"Everybody except Americans can speak French. But we'll stick with English for you."

At dinner, Nesrin commanded the conversation with stories from Istanbul.

Then she told the tale of what she considered the greatest infiltration of her young career. It was one so difficult to pull off that even she was not sure it would work. The degree to which she had to become another person was so daunting as to seem at first impossible. But once she had taken the plunge one thing was clear. There would be no turning back.

She looked them all in the eyes, one by one.

She would become a waiter in New York.

They all exploded with laughter.

CHAPTER EIGHTEEN

The sun had set. The ocean had turned angry.

Felder leaned over the chart table to whisper into Magnus's ear.

"You've had enough time. But since you won't do anything, *we did.*"

Magnus felt a shock through his nervous system.

Crosby jabbed his finger to the ceiling. Up the ladder they went.

Evening wind howled through the controls above the pilothouse. Heavy clouds had begun to boil over the horizon.

They were halfway across the Atlantic. Darkness dominated the sky.

"What have you done?" Magnus asked in a quiet frenzy as they closed the hatch.

"There are secure protocols for emergencies like this," said Felder.

"There *are* no emergencies *'like this'*," cried Magnus.

"All large vessels have secure S.O.S connections," said Crosby. "Piracy is still very much an issue out here. Ships get boarded all the time. Shipbuilders know this, so there's always a secure trip mechanism that can call for help on an isolated frequency. A code entered into the GPS that looks like a position request but actually calls for the nearest Coast Guard in international waters. We decided it was time to use it. Either a Secretary-class cutter is on the way from the U.S. or Offshore Patrol is coming down from Greenland. *Someone* is on the way."

Magnus felt his heart about to explode.

"And you think he doesn't know about this? He's wired into *everything.*"

"Jesus Christ," said Felder. "You worry *way* too much about him."

A brilliant white flash on the horizon was quickly followed by rolling thunder.

The wind was intensifying. Rain began to fall.

The booms shrieked and banged with the snapping of the sails.

"You should not have done that," said Magnus finally.

"We had *no choice*," shouted Felder. "Come down and we'll show you."

Back down in the pilothouse the three of them crowded around a small screen built into the instrument panel with a small numeric keypad below it. Crosby tapped a code into the keypad.

"This will show you why you trusted us to begin with," said Felder.

The screen blinked to life.

Disabled.

Magnus felt his nervous system collapse.

"What the hell?" Crosby muttered to himself, clearly confused. "That's not right."

"Yes it is," whispered Magnus.

Crosby carefully entered seven digits into the keypad once again.

Disabled.

"I've got to go," said Magnus, with barely suppressed panic.

Crosby and Felder were left staring at the little word on the screen.

Disabled.

Magnus quickly made his way down towards the galley. He needed to get to Sabine and the brothers right away. He began to traverse the salon, clutching the bar stools that ran to starboard.

The light flowing through the salon windows was dimming fast.

"You have yet to find your sea legs, I see."

The nasal voice cut through the gloom. Magnus had been concentrating on making it to the galley door and had not noticed anyone sitting on the burgundy couches behind him. He stood very still and took a moment before turning around. Taron Veeder appeared almost ghostly, his long white hair and translucent skin sharp against a black turtleneck sweater, his glowing alabaster feet sharp against the hems of his black pants.

"Things are starting to take shape," said Magnus, unsure of what else to say.

ot,gal89

Disabled.

Maybe it had just been a glitch.

"We're starting to see a genuine outline in the numbers," he went on uneasily. "The slides are holding up. The molecular connections being drawn are starting to indicate that the final modeling will yield exactly what we've anticipated all along regarding a derivation of the architecture."

"Momentum is on our side," Taron Veeder replied. "I've been following along with the latest from my quarters. But recently I've begun to wonder how you, personally, are holding up with all this. We never talk about anything except work. I know your personal research has been put on hold for now. Are you getting a chance to rest now and then? I've noticed you spend quite a bit of time outside of work with Raquel. Up on deck, on the transom. And elsewhere. I've also noticed that you and those two up in the pilothouse seem to get along fairly well. It's good to be social on these long voyages. It's stressful, not only with the work but also psychologically, all of us crammed in together like this."

Taron Veeder, shimmering in the fading light, seemed to be looking right through him.

Magnus felt his heart rate increase.

"Come, sit for a minute," said Taron Veeder. "I can barely see you."

Magnus let go of a barstool and made his way across the slanted swaying floor.

He fell into the couch opposite his employer.

Taron Veeder looked out over the dark chopping waves to the gilt horizon.

He lifted his left hand and slowly ran a fingertip along the deep scar along his left cheek.

"Nobody in this world knows how I got this," he said quietly. He paused.

"But I'm going to tell you about it now. I think there's a lesson to be drawn from it."

Magnus settled into the couch and watched him warily.

"It was soon after the wall came down in Berlin," began Taron Veeder, "where I grew up and spent my student years. Academic options were coming at me from every direction. But while the mental satisfaction of doing groundbreaking work was nice, I knew that I wanted more. Growing up without money or possessions was never something that troubled me. I had always been a happy child. Perhaps it was not so much the notion of actual wealth I found myself dreaming of as much as the stamp of authenticity that wealth would put upon me. I had been a prodigy but fame had not yet arrived. And I sought fame in a way, I suppose.

"So I made the decision to apply myself to industry instead of pure applied mathematics. I have always adored art, and I wanted art of my own. I have always adored travel, and wanted to be able to do so on my own terms instead of just moving from one conference to another, always on someone else's schedule.

"And it so happened that, at the time the wall came down, there was an avalanche of interest in the former factory and industrial spaces of what had been East Berlin. When the residents of East Berlin suddenly found the opportunity to leave, they didn't just head to former West Berlin. They really kept on moving. They left and didn't stop. They kept on going until they were as far away as they could get. They continued all the way to *Portugal.* My point being that a great many of the industrial spaces and warehouses and factories were suddenly empty, and a whole new contingent of operations flooded in to fill the spaces. A great many of these wonderful places were taken by artists from around the world, who descended on areas like Friedrichstein and Kreuzberg. But a few were taken by entrepreneurial types as well, including business-minded scientists from various territories in the former Soviet Union, Turkey and other such places.

"It was like the Wild West at the time, and I had a bit of a reputation not only for my work in several specific fields of mathematics but also for being able to converse and communicate with anyone without needing a translator. I was approached by all sorts of people. One of the most intriguing to me was a pair of scientists, one Russian and one Turkish, who had secured enough money to bring in all the latest computational and medical scanning equipment. They had set it up on the second floor of a warehouse just on the edge of Kreuzberg and started a company that would set out to drastically increase the quality of a fairly recent invention at the time: the MRI machine.

"They were slightly on the strange side, I could tell, but even this pair could see that Moore's law was turning out to be more than just a theory. The MRI had only been around for several years and the technology was still in its infancy, yet computational power was indeed doubling in speed and halving in size every two years. So they had a plan to race ahead of the medical establishment by simply applying overwhelming computer power to analysis of the images, as opposed to merely improving the quality of the images themselves.

"And so when they came to me with an outline of their goals, and an outline of just how financially rewarding a successful realization of those goals would be, I was intrigued. Even though they didn't seem to have a complete grasp on the underlying science, the fact was that almost nobody else did at the time, either. This is of course why they came to me. Anyway, we were able to hold a few afternoon chats in a coffee shop and it became increasingly clear that not only did they *want* me on board with the project. They *needed* me. They were a little shady from the outset, I must say, but I was young at the time and did not have the keen sense of smell for desperation that I do now. They kept raising the amount they would pay, but I held out for a piece of the company. Eventually they caved and the three of us agreed to go in a third each. All done on a handshake, of course. They had put up the finances but I was clearly the superior mind. And that is of course what counts.

"So we went to work. Immediately I began to smash the boundaries of what they had deemed their most optimistic possible results. I could see at once that the entire initial approach to their design was clumsy and ill-conceived. I moved to a small apartment nearby and began to spend literally all of my time in their warehouse. They were helpful at first but, as with many of the collaborators I had worked with over the course of my young life, they quickly became redundant. I simply didn't need them. I needed their equipment, of course, and I needed their facilities, but I was the one making the breakthroughs.

"Of course, all my work was being saved and backed up on their hardware. And so a certain element of suspicion began to creep over me as I powered ahead with what I considered to be *my* work, but was still technically *our* work. They began to show up less and less often at the warehouse, leaving the heavy lifting to me. I was there night and day. I began to feel proprietary about the design for this new machine. I secretly began to question their right to what was surely going to be a game-changer in the medical field and would almost certainly create ripple effects in other industries as well. Yet at the same time I could start to sense that they were starting to circle me like vultures. They would show up from time to time to see that my designs were nearing completion. One day, as the end was almost in sight, I sensed a change in their plans. I could feel that they had an understanding of the trajectory of my work and had reached a point where they could complete what was almost completed anyway. And I suddenly knew that they were going to try to take it away from me.

"And so that very night I began to make physical copies of all of it. I didn't trust my work to be simply saved on the unreliable floppy discs of the time, and so I literally began printing it out and erasing it from the mainframe as the copies began to stack up. I was going to take it with me, disappear, and complete the work on my own elsewhere. I did not know or even care exactly where. I just knew I needed to leave immediately. There were hundreds of pages, and at the time even the fastest of the dot matrix printers were not very fast. So I just paced nervously along the windows, looking down to the street below, listening and waiting for the printer to be fed the next file.

"Suddenly, yet not surprisingly, the entrance door to the second floor silently cracked open. The only light I had turned on was the one on my desk. The rest of the space was totally dark. So they didn't see me as they came in. It was both of them. They shut the door just as silently as they had opened it. I watched them from my place in the darkness by the windows, scarcely able to breathe. I saw the Turk whisper to the Russian. Then, illuminated only by the faintest moonlight coming through the windows, I saw the glint of a large knife blade as the Turk pulled it from his waist.

"It struck me like a lightning bolt that they had not only come to steal my work. They planned on killing me as well. And in that instant I became a different person. It only took that one moment, and I changed into somebody else. I could have just tiptoed out at this point, work be damned. But I didn't. I remembered that bolted to the wall just a few feet from me, underneath the windows, was a small fire extinguisher. Without breathing I knelt down and removed it. My nerves were like cold steel at this point. Almost against my own will I quickly and silently began to move across the floor towards the one closer to me, the Russian, who did not appear to be armed. The two men were moving very slowly and methodically towards the light that came from my desk, but they could not yet see that I wasn't there.

"I moved silently through the darkness and came right up behind the Russian. Without any hesitation I smashed the fire extinguisher across the side of his head. You can imagine the sound it made. He crumpled hard into a nearby table, sending equipment crashing to the floor around us. It was obvious from the force of the blow that he would never stand up again.

"Instantly the Turk began to rush towards me. Suddenly being face to face with this man left me too stunned to either attack or defend myself. We had spent time together and I quickly realized that it's much harder to commit violence when you're facing someone you actually know. At least that was true for me. But not for the Turk. After circling each other for a moment he suddenly lunged at me with the large gleaming blade. It was purely instinctual that I leaned away just in time. But it was not enough. The blade swept down the side of my face. It felt like being cut with a sharp piece of ice. And when I opened my eyes I saw in the moonlight that blood was pouring from my face onto the concrete floor.

"I realized then that he thought he had done me in with one slash. I don't think he realized that I was still holding the fire extinguisher. I also don't think he realized that I was, at that moment, not afraid. In my peripheral vision I saw his elbow move backwards, as he prepared to stab the knife right into my body and finish me off. Instantly every muscle in my body convulsed with an electric spasm. I swung the fire extinguisher around and smashed him directly in the face with full force. That's something I'll never forget, the feeling of his teeth imploding into his mouth as easily as potato chips snapping in half. Then he, too, crumpled backwards and fell to the floor.

"The dot matrix printer churning out pages was the only sound in the room once again. Blood was pouring from my face. And then suddenly I began to weep. What had just happened? What had just happened to *me*? How could I have actually killed two people over something as immaterial as my work? It was not purely self-defense, of course. I could have easily slipped out and run directly to the authorities and put the case in the hands of the legal system. But that is not the choice I made.

"I spent the next few hours washing my shirt in the bathroom sink, holding it to my face, and finishing the process of printing and deleting all my work from the mainframe. When the papers were finally all printed I gathered them in a bag, descended the stairs to the street, and I ran. I ran as fast as I could away from that warehouse. I was not at all worried about being tracked down and caught and punished for my crime. Everything had been done Eastern Bloc style, no written contracts, no bank accounts, nothing that could trace me to them. But I ran all the same. I ran as fast as I could through the empty streets of Berlin. I did not know whether I was running from the young innocent man I had left behind that night, the naive academic full of golden potential, or towards the ruthless man I had just become. A man who without any hesitation killed those who had come to take his work away from him. But now, after all these years, I am fully aware of what the answer was all along."

Magnus sat perfectly still on the burgundy couch.

The wind ripped through the sails as they plunged further into the Atlantic.

"You're the only person I've ever told about this," Taron Veeder breathed, almost inaudibly. "I feel we have a connection. Nobody understands my work as well as you do. Yet it's not up for debate. I need your help in finishing what we've started. Is that clear?"

Magnus didn't answer. He looked to the rosewood doors leading back aft. *Raquel.*

"Good," said Taron Veeder. "Sorry to keep you for so long."

He stood against the tilted and undulating blue carpet.

He moved towards the rosewood doors and disappeared behind them.

Magnus quickly made his way through the dark salon towards the galley.

He needed to talk to the Scandinavians *now.*

CHAPTER NINETEEN

The apartment was absolutely still.

I had woken up very early. My first morning in Paris.

I made my way silently down the hall in my traditional embroidered pajamas, bare footsteps silent on the thick runner carpet, glancing at the dozens of photographs bathed in dim light upon the walls. Many of them were of Mirabelle and her mother through the years, in formal and informal settings, at times with large groups of people and at others just with the man I assumed was Mirabelle's father. A slim and elegant man, hat jaunting off to the side, well-cut vest and necktie. In a few of the photographs I noticed his eyes looking off to something outside the frame, as if he wasn't fully present in the moment. In those eyes I saw something that might have explained why she almost never spoke of him. I walked out into the drawing room.

Porcelain vases rested timelessly within the deeply recessed shelves along the walls.

Ocean paintings roared silently from within their gilded frames.

Two marble fireplaces faced each other from either side of the room.

As I approached the Steinway her voice leapt out at me.

"What does the early morning sound like?"

She was standing at the entrance to the drawing room.

White silk nightdress, her hair falling in tangles across her face.

Mirabelle appeared to have woken up mere moments earlier as well.

She walked into the salon and draped herself across an oversized rose velvet chair near the windows as the dawn spread across the rooftops beyond. Absorbing the golden light of the developing sky, she watched me as I stood near the keyboard of the deeply polished Steinway grand. I absently brushed the back of my fingers across the keys and my fingernails made little clicking sounds as they swept over the little spaces between the ivory. Individual particles of dust hung suspended in the air of the room, illuminated by slanting beams of early morning sunlight.

"Mama is awake," she said. "Francois and Sylvette are up well before dawn. There's no need to worry about waking anyone. The silence of the early morning must have music inside it somewhere. Can you play what it sounds like?"

She was right, of course. There was music for this.

I pulled out the piano bench. It slid silently across the carpet. Brushing my fingertips once again across the keyboard, I sat down and allowed the feeling of the room and the morning to distill within me. I didn't yet know what was coming but the power began to spread across the backs of my hands. Not unlike the power coursing through me now. Summoning a sound even more quiet than silence I pressed hard on the damper pedal as the brushing of my fingers across the keyboard became actual finger patterns. And then the patterns began to depress into the keys. The hammers within the piano began to touch the strings with the lightness of butterfly wings. From within the silence of the room the sound of the Chopin A-flat étude began to glow.

A radiance emerged from the piano that quietly filled the room.

Mirabelle sat as still as the paintings on the walls.

Her eyes widened as I closed my own and descended into the music.

The sublime melody sang out, a tender lullaby over a gleaming cloud of sound.

I played with such lightness that the very sound of my fingertips on the keytops could be heard as well. The melody wound a path seemingly not created by a man but by nature itself. The étude sparkled and fizzled until eventually it evaporated into the silence of the sunlight.

My hands came off the keys. After a spell I opened my eyes.

The Countess had tiptoed barefoot into the room as I played. Francois and Sylvette stood motionless in the dining room beyond.

The Countess was leaning against the corner of the hallway leading back to her room, a forlorn smile at the edges of her eyes. Mirabelle remained draped across the chair by the window. Since they had become acquainted with my playing they had come to understand that the moments immediately following a piece of music were the ones to cherish most. That the experience of piano playing is not complete when the playing stops.

The music still reverberates inside the heart.

The calmness and afterglow of music only stops when those reverberations fully cease.

"My God," murmured Sylvette as she peered into the drawing room.

Francois nodded in affirmation. A great smile spread across his face.

He burst into a laugh of reconciliation with his own disbelief.

The Countess eased herself into the salon.

"I have an idea," she said. "I know how you feel about public performances. But this would just be a small thing. I've never heard music paired with silence like that. And I've never heard music performed at this time of day."

Mirabelle sat up, listening with acute interest.

She looked at me, still sitting upon the piano bench in my embroidered pajamas.

"She's right, you know," she said, shifting in the chair with growing energy. "I've been going to concerts since I was a tiny girl. They're *always* in the evening. At brunches sometimes there might be music, but it's just in the background. What you just did now was something I've never experienced before. And I'll bet nobody else has either."

She looked to her mother.

"Why do you suppose that is, mama?"

The Countess appeared to draw a blank.

All of my life I had a special connection to the early hours spanning darkness and light. When I was much smaller, before moving to Budapest, I would occasionally wake up while the stars were still flung deep within the darkness of the night sky. I would walk to the church and let myself in with the key the pastor had given me. As the air outside began to open up with color, I would bring forth music seemingly conjured by the coming day itself. So as long as I was going to play for a select audience here in my new home, which of course I had known was going to be inevitable, why not perform from within the sparkling aurora of daybreak?

I was at ease with the fact that the Countess was going to want to show me off a bit.

And a dawn concert would be perfect.

Anyone could bang away at a keyboard and impress even a sophisticated audience.

But creating an entire world of sound that echoed the silence of the golden early morning hours was another thing entirely. I looked at Mirabelle. She was looking back at me with a soft and knowing smile.

"What does the early morning sound like?" she had asked.

And even though I didn't respond, she had just given me the answer.

It sounded like the first morning of a new life.

CHAPTER TWENTY

"Now *wait* a minute," cried Samuel.

"This was *not* a part of the plan," said Lysander.

"It's not what it looks like," Nesrin beamed, cradling what appeared to be a menacing black military-grade rifle or submachine gun with both hands. A black canister was attached to the scope mount, and a long ammunition cartridge hung below the barrel. Almost a week in Paris had revealed nothing. The director of the D'Agoult foundation had arranged interviews with a dozen society types who had attended the Dawn Concerts. Not one of them recalled anything about the presence of Taron Veeder except that he had attended all of them and always came alone. So Nesrin had Samuel hack the Frick website and implant a different profile for Lysander as well. With the touch of a button Samuel could now toggle Lysander back and forth from being curator or lead restoration expert with ease. Then all five of them took the helicopter on a twenty minute flight to the D'Agoult estate in the lush meadows of Chantilly. Taron Veeder's compound was less than two miles away. They had just unpacked and were in Nesrin's room of hand-cut stone floors and vaulted ceilings.

"Then what the hell is it?" asked Samuel.

"A paintball gun," said Nesrin. "We're not *breaking into* the compound. We're going to get *invited* in. People like Taron Veeder always have huge art collections. Tonight, one of his precious pieces is going to meet with an unfortunate accident. I took some time in Paris to make a few bribes to the top restoration people in the city, with the promise of a larger payoff in the event of actually getting the referral."

She reached into her pocket and pulled out an old-style flip phone.

"We're going to get a call on this burner I picked up the other day. The phone number of the personal assistant to the great restoration expert Lysander Bennett, who happens to be in Paris with his team. And yes, we'd be happy to travel to Chantilly to take a look at the damage. So we find the arrival time of the morning train from Paris, and tell them we'll be on that train. We have easy access to the schedule here, down to the minute. So we'll be waiting at the stop just *before* Chantilly, and hop aboard. Chaumontel, I believe. The optics will be that we've come up from Paris. They'll send a driver to meet us."

She set down the weapon and reached back into her suitcase.

She extracted a large satellite image of the compound and smoothed it out on the bed.

"Where the hell did you get that?" asked Lysander.

"Don't worry about it," she said, looking down at the image.

In the center of the picture was a castle of dark gray stone set within a clearing of forest. Through the treetops a long and winding driveway led to a grand gated entrance. Behind the chateau lay sprawling fields dotted with stables. One of them, far larger than all the others, lay just beyond the chateau and was connected to it by what appeared to be a narrow footpath. The long winding perimeter of the estate was completely enclosed by a wall that was in large part covered by the treetops. Scattered among the trees a half a mile down the road from the entrance gate were what appeared to be a wheelbarrow and a few assorted tools.

"That's our entrance," she said. "They're fixing the wall. It's probably stone and hundreds of years old. These old walls in Europe are always falling apart. Once we're through and get near the chateau I'll take a few shots from twenty or thirty yards out. These pellets will go right through the glass. They won't explode until they hit something more substantial. The actual paint is acrylic and can be cleaned with warm water. But *they* won't know that. They're immediately going to search for the best restoration people in Paris. And whoever they reach will refer them to us. Dr. Lysander Bennett and his team."

Lysander and Samuel looked at each other, dumbfounded.

"We'll assemble a professional-looking cleaning kit using basic supplies from here in the house. We arrive at Veeder's chateau as a team, inspect the damage that we ourselves will have caused, and guess what? We say it's *oil* paint. At least a week or two to repair and the work will have to be done on site to avoid any further damage. We'll have to *stay* there. The place has twenty-six bedrooms. But his actual research facilities are in that giant stable out back. The windows are high up so nobody can see inside. But we don't need to *see* inside. We just need to *hear* inside."

"How the hell are you going to hear through the windows?" asked Lysander.

"Let me guess," said Samuel. "Istanbul."

"That's correct," she said.

She reached into the suitcase one last time and pulled out a pile of black clothes.

Three pairs of black pants. Three black hooded sweatshirts.

She put her finger back on the smoothed out aerial image.

"From the back of the house we can see the south end of this wooded area. So we'll head across the wheat field behind us. Once we're in the forest we head north until we get to the main road. Then we take a right, down along the edge of the forest here, until we hit our entrance point in the wall."

Late that night they slipped out of the chateau.

They flew across the back lawn, three shadows into the wheat field under a thin blanket of the faintest stars. They were indistinguishable from each other except for the paintball gun strapped across Nesrin's back and small pair of field binoculars hanging around her neck. Samuel was nervous but had never felt so alive. After a good pace they emerged onto a meadow that led them up a hill and into the forest. The trees were tall and the canopy above them blocked out almost all the moonlight. The only sound was that of the leaves and twigs being trampled under their feet. At some point, Samuel could see the snaking of headlights along what must have been the road not too far in the distance. The three of them stopped until the car had completely disappeared, then they slowly continued along to the edge of the forest.

They followed the tall wall on the other side of the road.

At last they were surprised to see the glow of a little fire underneath the tree canopy. They approached almost silently. As they got closer, the snapping of twigs under their feet began to blend in with the crackling of the fire. Sitting with his back to them, staring into the little fire, was a lone sentry guard. The wall at that point was missing a section about four feet wide. Large stones, burlap sacks of sand, shovels and the wheelbarrows were strewn all about. Off to the side was a port-a-potty gleaming in the orange firelight. It was hard to tell from their side of the road, but the silhouette of the seated guard seemed to have a firearm strapped to his waist.

"Damn," Lysander said in a barely audible whisper. "Now what?"

"This was not expected," said Nesrin.

Samuel knew that his time had come. An idea came to him and he acted.

He began to cross the road in a fast low crouch, removing his belt as he moved.

He pulled it taut, holding on to each end with each hand.

He now heard the footsteps of Nesrin and Lysander join in behind him.

The guard sat facing the crackling fire as Samuel broke into a run, raised the belt above him, and like a banshee descended upon the guard before he could even stand up and turn around. Samuel whipped the belt down over his shoulders and pulled his arms to his sides as the guard yelled out in shock. Nesrin and Lysander fell upon him as well. Lysander grabbed the ends of the belt as the guard yelled and thrashed and kicked, pulled it tight, buckled it behind the guard's back, and held him tight. Nesrin picked up a shovel and swiftly drove the sharp glinting blade several times deep into a sack of sand at her feet. She leaned down and pulled at the shredded burlap, which gave easily along the weave, then drove the shovel through once again to cut off a long ribbon of industrial fabric.

Within seconds she had tied it around the guard's mouth, whose eyes bulged with fear in the light of the fire as he stared at the menacing weapon across Nesrin's back. She removed the sidearm from his holster and threw it deep into the woods. She drove the shovel blade a few more times into the sack, tore off two more ribbons, and bound the guard's hands and feet.

"What do we do with him?" asked a breathless Lysander.

Nesrin looked over to the port-a-potty.

Just before shoving the guard inside, she reached into her pocket, pulled out a few large-denomination euro bills, and pushed them into the guard's pocket as his bulging eyes looked down in disbelief.

"What the hell?" asked Lysander.

"Well, it's not *his* fault this just isn't his night," said Nesrin.

"No, I mean why do you have so much money on you?"

"Because there are times, in this work, when you have to do things you don't want to do. Money can help set those things right."

They slammed the door port-a-potty door shut. Lysander leaned all his bulk into it while Samuel, following Nesrin's lead, ripped off yet another ribbon of burlap. He pulled it through the heavy plastic padlock holes in the door and tied them tightly together. The only sounds in the forest now were that of quiet muffled yelling and banging in the port-a-potty, the crackling of the fire, and the wind in the trees above.

Lysander and Nesrin looked to Samuel.

"Dude," said Lysander. "You are a *badass.*"

"I suppose that's true," said Samuel. "But, I mean, I did wrestle back in college.

"And yet you spend all your free time playing the piano?"

"Maybe not for much longer. This sort of thing is actually starting to appeal to me."

The three of them slipped through the wall breach and began to move towards the house.

At last through the trees Samuel could begin to make out the structure of the home. As they approached the edge of the forest they looked down across a beautifully landscaped lawn and it was apparent that it really was more of a castle than a house, significantly more massive than it had appeared from the helicopter. A gleaming black Audi sat in the driveway just to the side of an ornate garden and sculpted fountain. While the interior was mostly dark, the windows of the chateau were tall and let in a fair amount of ambient light.

"See the way those windows ripple in the moonlight?" Nesrin asked. "Hand blown glass. All these old places were built with it back in the day. It's exceptionally clear. And exceptionally thin."

Nesrin put the binoculars to his eyes and scanned the full elevation of the house, pausing at every window, eventually settling her gaze on the window above the main entrance.

"I think just above the main entrance," she said quietly. "I think that's the one."

She handed the binoculars to Lysander.

Lysander peered through them at the house.

"Oh wow…" he whispered slowly. "That can't be…oh my God."

Samuel squinted at the window above the entrance. It was hard to tell from that distance, but he thought he saw a huge shimmering bolt of fabric in the moonlight, almost as large as the wall it was hanging on.

"One of the missing unicorn tapestries," whispered Lysander in astonishment. "Some of the sculptures back there look like they could be by Noguchi, but the tapestry is clearly the prize. It certainly *looks* Flemish. It's probably at least three hundred years old."

"Would acrylic paint cause lasting damage?" asked Nesrin. "Breaking through the glass will burst apart the actual paintball, so it would probably end up just spattering the work."

"I don't know too much about it," said Lysander. "But that sounds about right. I'd really hate to actually damage something like that. It's priceless. And irreplaceable. But water-based acrylic paint shouldn't cause permanent damage. And if it does, well, this lunatic has it hanging where direct sunlight is probably on it all day long and it's likely damaged already. The paint, though, is definitely the sort of damage that would have to be repaired on site. If a tapestry like that gets paint on the surface it would be impossible to roll up for transport. So I'd say go for it. Take a few shots and you're guaranteed to make a mess of it."

"OK," said Nesrin. "Let's do it. This is going to set off a few alarms, so the second I take the shots, from the fountain over there, we literally run as fast as we can out of here. You guys just go, I'll only be a few seconds behind. They'll expect that someone is breaking *into* the house, not running away, so we'll have a head start before they begin to search the grounds."

They both nodded. Nesrin pulled the paintball gun off her shoulders. She took a few deep breaths.

She took off running in a low crouch towards the fountain, gravel crunching softly under her feet, and silently disappeared into the shadows.

The seconds ticking by felt like minutes.

The huge tapestry shimmered in the moonlight behind the tall glass window.

Suddenly the paintball gun erupted with a volley of loud pops.

In the distance the window shattered in several places at once.

Red paint splattered through the shards of falling glass.

The tapestry was instantly covered with flecks of red.

Floodlights exploded from the roof all around the exterior of the house.

Alarm bells burst out from within.

Nesrin bolted out of the shadows of the fountain, just a dark form sprinting up the gravel driveway, waving wildly for Samuel and Lysander to start running, which they did.

It was only a matter of seconds before she caught up.

Branches and twigs tore at their clothing as they flew back through the forest.

"My *pants* keep falling down," yelled Samuel.

"Just hold them up with your hands!" yelled Nesrin as they scampered through the brush.

They approached the breach in the wall and burst to the other side.

The porta-potty was still jumping around with muffled yelling coming from inside.

They kept running, across the road, through the forest, down the meadow.

Finally, all three gasping for air, they emerged from the wheat onto the back lawn.

Samuel was utterly amazed when, the following morning, things went exactly as Nesrin had predicted. After a tense few hours lingering over breakfast, drinking cup after cup of rich coffee, the flip phone began to buzz on the dining-room table. Nesrin answered and spoke in French for a while to what Samuel could vaguely hear was a female voice on the other side of the line.

There had been a terrible act of vandalism overnight at a certain chateau in Chantilly.

They would prefer to take care of this quietly, without alerting the owner.

Nobody needed Taron Veeder freaking out about one of his armed guards having been overpowered submachine gun-wielding assailants, thought Nesrin.

One of the finer art restoration houses in Paris had recommended that they take advantage of the fact that one of the leading authorities on the restoration and conservation of fine art was actually in Paris at that very moment. Speaking on behalf of Dr. Bennett and his team Nesrin had related that, coincidentally, they had a major cancellation in their schedule and could make it up that very afternoon. Several hours later, the three of them were in a taxi to Chaumontel, just a few kilometers south. They boarded the train, which had come from the Gare du Nord in Paris, and were met at the station in Chantilly a few minutes later by the same pristine black Audi sedan they had seen in the driveway the night before.

The driver was a man of few words.

After a few minutes they were gliding along the edge of the estate.

The team surreptitiously glanced at the construction site as they passed.

Now there were two guards and multiple men working quickly to complete the job.

At the gate the driver looked steadily into the black pane of flickering glass.

The green lasers jittering about behind it came to a standstill.

The gate slowly swung open and they drove slowly and silently down along the smooth driveway through the forest. As they pulled around the fountain in front of the entrance to the chateau, they could see the remnants of a shattered window to the left of the grand front door. The door itself opened and a striking woman emerged.

"Lucinda will take it from here," said the driver.

Once inside, the famous Dr. Bennett and his team made a full inspection of the tapestry. Dr. Bennett determined that the paint pellets used by the ruffian vandals had been filled with linseed-based oil paint. The cleaning would be a slow process, and due to the age of the tapestry and the fact that paint had not yet dried, it would be best not to attempt to move it. Fortuitously, there was a week or so opening in their schedule, and they had the tools and materials they needed. Lucinda had the staff prepare three bedrooms upstairs.

The fee for the team would be two thousand euros per day.

Two large ladders were brought in from the mysterious stable below the chateau.

Dr. Lysander Bennet got to work making a thorough analysis of the damage.

Under the discerning direction of Dr. Bennett the team was constantly hard at work, two at a time, apparently applying the most delicate of chemicals to the tapestry and removing the paint a fraction of a square centimeter at a time. Occasionally the great restoration expert took his rest upstairs, which was fully to be expected considering the intensity of his efforts, and Nesrin would work in his place. As two worked downstairs at the tapestry, the third team member worked in one of the upstairs bedrooms apparently conducting analysis of the fiber samples.

And that team member was usually Nesrin.

Listening through the windows.

Just like she had in Istanbul.

CHAPTER TWENTY-ONE

Magnus descended the steps to the galley.

Taron Veeder had just given him a mortal warning. He had killed before.

Magnus burst through the door, blinking in the sudden harsh bright galley light.

Sabine and the brothers were sitting at the table playing cards.

All three looked to Magnus with a single suspicious glance.

At the moment, Taron Veeder was likely moving through the server room to his quarters.

A precious few moments Magnus wasn't being watched or heard.

"We need to talk," he said quickly. "I know about the kidnapping."

The brothers looked at each other, then looked at Sabine.

After a second she nodded towards the sink, and they all moved towards it.

She turned the faucet on at full blast, shrouding them in white noise.

"I hacked the security cameras on deck," Magnus lied. "I've seen everything."

Jensen sputtered and made a lunge at Magnus, but Tilman held him back.

"Let him speak," said Sabine.

The rush of the faucet into the sink was the only sound in the galley.

Magnus, very aware of the passing time, continued.

"I don't know what you've been offered. I don't know what incentive you had to do whatever you did. But I'll tell you this. We're like small children playing with a bomb. He's trying to build a strong artificial intelligence. You probably don't even know what that is, but it can't be allowed to happen. Without precautions it could be the last invention humans ever make. By the time we approach land and regain access to the internet over the cell networks it could be too late. A self-aware synthetic intelligence will ensure its own safety by jumping to the internet through those networks. Right now, with the internet being down, it has no means of escape. When we get close to shore, that will change."

Jensen spat into the sink.

"What we gain makes nothing else even matter," he whispered vehemently.

Sabine looked at him quickly and elbowed him in the side of the chest.

Tilman seemed caught in the middle and said nothing.

Magnus suddenly understood the enormity of what Taron Veeder was trying to attain. The enormity of what he must have offered the Scandinavians in order to attain it. The programmed goal of the ASI was suddenly clear as day. The recklessness of it was breathtaking. But Magnus now understood why Sabine and the brothers risked their freedom to pull off what must have been an extraordinarily daring and risky kidnapping.

They must have been offered something more valuable than freedom itself.

Something only an artificial superintelligence could provide.

Eternal freedom. Immortality.

Magnus knew very well that a synthetic superintelligence combined with nanotechnology could potentially solve the problem of aging and mortality. And now suddenly he knew exactly why Raquel was the only other person Taron Veeder had summoned aside from himself. She would be the one to impart into the intelligence an initial comprehension of the power of nanotechnology. By force, if necessary. There was no fine print in the principles of physics that excluded the possibility of arranging matter atom by atom. There was no technical reason, aside from lack of current technology, that physics and chemistry could not be combined by a colossal intelligence to create any chemical substance imaginable. A synthetic intelligence that exponentially dwarfed that of the human brain could establish a way to move individual molecules or even atoms around and make literally anything.

At the same time, nothing in biology points to death being a necessity.

Since evolution has no purpose other than to pass along our genes, it has never had to concern itself with the issue of aging. The breakdown of the body and the mind is not a concern of the natural selection process so long as the species passes along its genes. What happens after that doesn't matter. But, there is no biological reason the temporary nature of the human body cannot be altered. Aging is nothing more than a wearing down of the physical materials of the body. Just like the wearing down of a machine over time. But if parts of a machine, down to the smallest nut and bolt, are perfectly replaced over the course of time, there is no reason the machine should not run as designed forever. No physical law prevents the possibility of nanobots the size of individual cells, flowing within the bloodstream and connected through the internet to a superintelligence, from routinely repairing or replacing worn-down cells throughout the entire body. A human body is nothing more than a large collection of atoms and molecules. A synthetic superintelligence armed with advanced nanotechnology could very quickly create technologies capable of halting or perhaps even reversing the aging of both mind and body.

Magnus stood by the flowing faucet.

A thought flashed into his head like the crack of a bullwhip.

The space on the floor *next* to the white server cube.

The cube was just *part* of Taron Veeder's machine.

A machine linked to the coming superintelligence. *Underneath the floor.*

"I need to talk to you guys on deck," he said in a panic.

The Scandinavians looked at each other with hesitation.

Sabine looked to Magnus with ponderous skepticism.

"Okay," she said, turning off the faucet. "But only me. They stay here."

Leaving the brothers in the galley Magnus and Sabine went up the ladder that led directly from the galley to the deck. They emerged through the hatch into the chill night wind and shut the trap door behind them. Sabine spoke first.

"We don't have more than a few minutes," she said. "He's already suspicious enough. Tell me your side of the story. Why should we listen to you, and not to him, when he offers us everything, and you offer us nothing?"

Magnus looked up into the infinite splash of stars in the black sky.

"Look up there, to the Milky Way," he said. "Where *is* everybody?"

Over the next fifteen minutes, exactly as he had to Crosby and Felder, he explained everything. The last technological discovery humans might ever make, the one that could lead, inevitably and universally, to existential disaster.

He explained, and he left no doubt. *The Great Filter.*

Sabine listened without speaking, without questions. Her eyes grew narrow.

By the time he was finished cloud cover had moved underneath the stars.

The waves had grown. The crashing bow split through the angry sea.

White foam spiraled upwards into the night sky.

Sabine peered intently at Magnus as he wrapped up his case. .

The great sails snapped angrily in the billowing squall that was now upon them.

Her hard narrow blue eyes grew dark.

She pressed her right index finger to her ear and began to nod her head.

She lowered her hand to the collar of her shirt and pressed at the tip.

"Just like you said he would," she said. "Send them up."

Magnus felt a shock of fear. In his peripheral vision he noticed the light from the pilothouse shine up through the hatch onto the lower part of the mizzen sail. At the same time, the trap door next to them leading back down to the galley was pushed open. Jensen came up the ladder with his usual speed. Upon reaching the deck he turned and reached back down.

Magnus felt his stomach turn with horror.

He saw the crazed thinning gray hair of Crosby as he was pushed up through the trapdoor by Tilman. His mouth was stuffed with rags, electrical tape wrapped around his head. As Jensen threw him to the deck Magnus saw that his hands were bound behind his back. Jensen grabbed him underneath his shoulders. With enormous strength he pulled Crosby up through the hatch and threw him to the deck. Jensen reached back down and pulled up Felder. His hands had also bound behind his back and he was silently screaming through the rags stuffed into his mouth. Jensen threw him to the deck next to Crosby.

The galley was now empty. Tilman came up the ladder.

Sabine glanced down with detached curiosity at Crosby and Felder writhing on the deck.

Magnus could not speak. He noticed an alabaster figure emerge from the hatch above the pilothouse. Standing in the control area Taron Veeder looked like a ghost in a preacher's pulpit, face underlit by the glow from within the pilothouse. His snow-white hair blew wildly in the gale, an ominously knowing smile drawn across his face.

"Bravo!" he screeched through the wind down to Magnus. "Bravo to you, *bravi* to you and the girl, for coming to the brilliant conclusion that I would never waste my time messing around with some bullshit *interface*. But to think that you would try to convince my *own crew* to turn against me. Using all the obvious arguments, no less. All those tired warnings and siren calls. The great filter, the end of civilization, the end of humanity. I'm not surprised it worked on Crosby and Felder, they're weak, but that doesn't matter. I don't *need them anymore!* Our project is on the verge of taking on a life of its own. The ship is capable of taking care of herself. The system is becoming self aware. It's just a matter of time!"

The wind was really whipping now. *Where was Raquel?*

Taron Veeder smiled like a reptile. His shrill voice pierced through the wind.

"Perhaps you're wondering where your *girlfriend* is? Well don't worry, I have her safely locked in her cabin getting started on implementing the structural nanotech. And I've patched the remainder of the extraction work through to *your* laptop in *your* cabin. It'll be up to the two of you to make *sure* nothing goes wrong. You're both young and idealistic, God knows you'd probably fall on a sword for each other by now. So would either of you allow the other to have their *throat slit?* "

Magnus felt his world turn inside out.

"Are you starting to see what I'm saying?" he howled. "Separate the love-birds! If anything starts to go wrong on your end, you die and she knows it. If anything starts to go wrong on her end, she dies and *you* know it. I've blocked all communication channels between the two of you. The extraction is to be completed. You'll make *sure* of it. Raquel has her own set of concerns now. But the power of love knows no bounds! Watching your self-restraint over these past two weeks has been positively nail-biting. I thought for sure you'd be going at each other within a matter of days. Watching you sometimes made me think that in another life I could have been a matchmaker. But who needs another life when the one you've got will *never end?*"

He reached down to his feet and held up a silver tablet.

Crosby and Felder worked their way into upright sitting positions.

Taron Veeder raised the tablet into the air for all to see.

"Here's what's going to happen," he yelled. "This little tablet is something of a minor miracle. The ship is self aware, able to sail herself. She just needs a little guidance here and there. That's what this little thing is going to do. And it's going to make all of your jobs a lot easier in the meantime. Unfortunately, it's also going to make *two* of your jobs entirely redundant. There are *two* of you I just don't *need* anymore!"

Crosby joined Felder in screaming silently through the rags in his mouth.

"And you know what happens to *traitors* on the high seas, *don't you?*"

Tears began to flow from Felder's eyes.

They both began bouncing up and down, violently working their arms in terror.

Taron Veeder looked down upon them like a demented conductor over his orchestra.

"I want to hear them!" he screeched.

Sabine slowly made her way against the angled deck to the helpless men.

"*Do it!!!*" came the nasal shriek from above the pilothouse.

One by one she ripped the electrical tape off their faces with both hands. The rags were immediately spit out and the screaming of the two men was more than Magnus could bear. There were no real words, there was no begging, nothing comprehensible came out of their mouths.

Magnus could feel the blood leaving his heart and his brain. He began to feel faint.

Sabine looked to Jensen through the bloodcurdling wails.

Jensen moved behind Felder.

Against savagely resisting convulsions he managed to get his hands under Felder's shoulders once again and dragged the hysterical man to the edge of the deck.

"*Oh my God, NO!!! NO!!!!*"

Jensen crouched down and in one smooth clean jerk he hurled Felder screaming overboard into the black ocean. Magnus began to cry as he watched Jensen move now to Crosby. The screaming had stopped with the end of Felder.

Crosby just watched Jensen with quivering eyes and quiet tears.

Jensen quickly reached under his shoulders and dragged him to the edge of the deck.

Now Crosby could no longer hold back.

"*NO!!!!!*"

Jensen launched Crosby off the deck and he disappeared into the black waves.

Magnus was shaking so hard he could barely stand up.

The squall lashed around them but there was only silence now.

Slowly, from up above the pilothouse, Taron Veeder began to laugh.

The laughter built and built into one long maniacal howl.

"What the fuck is *wrong* with him?" Sabine asked nobody in particular.

"Well done!" Taron Veeder yelled into the wind. "Well done indeed! But there's just one catch. Why the hell do you think I would ever share what is about to be mine with *anybody*? Do you think I want to spend the rest of time with *you* three idiots?"

Sabine and the brothers quickly exchanged glances.

Taron Veeder pressed at the tablet screen and the great sails began to unfurl further back along the booms, snapping and banging relentlessly against the full force squall that was now upon them. Magnus and the remaining crew had to duck beneath the main boom as it slowly began to swing out across the deck. The whirring of the winches and creaking tension of cables drawing the sails out further and further groaned above the blasting wind.

"I have provisions for two weeks!" he squealed. "You won't need to worry about *me*. I have full control of the ship and will keep Raquel alive as long as she holds up her end. We're going to make a direct line for the coast of Morocco. Some of the most gradient shores on earth where the ship will be able to beach herself. I'll walk off into everlasting life! And the *real* beauty is that we'll be taking our guest back *home* after all he's done for us. Whether he lives or not. When I realized the beautiful irony of it all, that in finding a place to beach the ship we would be taking our man back home, it was almost too much to bear. Almost! It *had* to be Tangier. By the time we reach the cell networks the intelligence will make an escape to the internet and do whatever it's going to do. By the time we reach the shore I'll be released, capable of surviving in an altered world, but it will be too late for *any* of you!"

Sabine and the brothers looked up to Taron Veeder.

"What is this?" shouted Sabine up into the wind.

"What *this* is," Taron Veeder howled, "is me being *done* with all of you! I'm shutting you down and closing you out! I've disabled the elevator. The only other way back aft is through the salon. And *believe m*e you won't be able to break through those doors! By the time we hit the cell networks you'll all have *vastly* larger problems to worry about than me."

Sabine looked at Jensen and Tilman.

"Get him," she said. "Now."

They broke into a run across the tilting deck towards the pilothouse.

Taron Veeder watched the booms swing out over the ocean and laughed even harder and he began to crawl back down the hatch into the pilothouse.

"No, I don't think so!" he shrieked.

Tilman grabbed the lower rungs of the ladder leading up the side of the pilothouse and his feet swung out over the ocean as Taron Veeder quickly descended down the hatch. From the deck and through the windows of the pilothouse Magnus could see him lock the hatch from the inside as Tilman pulled himself up the side bulkhead wall. He swung over the edge into the control area and began pounding helplessly at the hatch. Taron Veeder disappeared down the steps in the pilothouse to the salon. The main boom slammed into place. The winches groaned to a stop.

The great sails slashed at the wind in defiance of their new course.

Magnus quickly began to make his way back to his cabin.

CHAPTER TWENTY-TWO

That first summer in Paris my childhood began to melt away. Occasional visits to the estate up in Chantilly were a balm from the sweltering city.

The green and warmth and sunshine up there elongated my frame like the stalk of a growing sunflower. But it was against the culture of Paris that my *inner* self began to grow. Lying in the grass among the poppies and statues of the Tuileries, reading Flaubert under the warm soft sky with Mirabelle asleep next to me, I had begun to think about the future. I had also begun to allow myself to belong to her. Of course, Mirabelle had begun to think about the future as well. She had always known that she wanted a life in the arts and had made up her mind that she would apply all her scholastic efforts towards an acceptance to the École des Beaux-Arts when the time came. Her lifelong fascination with paintings had made it clear to her that she wanted, in one capacity or another, to be a professional in the world of museums or galleries. And a formal course of study in art history at university would best prepare her for it.

In the meantime, this was Paris.

A city of endless museums and infinite art.

One afternoon we retraced familiar steps across the Leopold Sedar bridge to the Musée D'Orsay on the Left Bank. Walking through the crowds along the first floor we passed the mélange of late nineteenth century sculpture, paintings, and photography. Sweeping up the grand staircase we made our way towards the Impressionist paintings. There was one painting in particular Mirabelle had introduced me to on our first visit, her favorite in the museum since she was very young. Nothing could have prepared me for the sheer radiance of the colors glowing within the frame when I saw it in person for the first time. It hung in one of the smaller enclaves on the second floor still open to the vastness of the rest of the museum. *Starry Night over the Rhone* by Van Gogh created an effect within me that I could only think of musically. Mirabelle had spoken of it in Budapest and she had shown me a print she kept among her few Parisian keepsakes back at the Gellert.

Surprisingly, that afternoon, the enclave was almost empty.

We found ourselves almost alone and were able to walk right up to the glowing orbs of starlight reflected in the tourmaline waters of the Rhône. Long reflections of the gas lighting along the river pointed up through the water and into the infinite depth of an indigo night sky. I felt the grip of Mirabelle's hand tighten as we walked up to the work that was a window into a reality seemingly even more alive than the one in which we lived. There was only one other person in front of it. He appeared hypnotized and was swaying the way people do after drinking too much. There was a casual authority about him, but his blue and yellow Adidas street shoes hardly resembled the style of the uptight academic types normally seen leading tours or giving talks. His blonde stubble and wavy sandy hair made him look more like an American surfer from the movies than an introspective lover of fine art.

We stood next to him and the three of us took in the painting.

"Some people say this painting is dark," he said, almost to himself, in accented French.

He glanced at us, then looked back at the painting.

"But I can't agree," he continued. "It's at night, to be sure, but I don't see the darkness. I only see blue. Deep blue. Prussian blue, ultramarine blue, cobalt blue. It's a night painting but I don't see the darkness. They say the darkness points to his insanity. This was painted, after all, right before he entered the asylum in Saint-Rémy. They talk about the way this little boat seems to be sinking, the way the river impinges upon the freedom of the strolling lovers, the way there doesn't appear to be a separation between the water and the sky. Obviously the people who say those things have never seen this painting in real life. Van Gogh himself wrote that the sky is aquamarine and the water is royal blue. There probably isn't a painting in this world that loses more in the reproduction. No, from where we stand this is not a dark painting. From where we stand this is a *romantic* painting. A painting about love. The *Starry Night* that was painted after Saint-Rémy, the more famous one, with the swirls in the night sky, perhaps there's a hint of the madness there. A touch of the violence and the strangeness that engulfed him. But look at that couple down there. This painting is about *them*. Everything that makes this painting so tender and serene comes from *them*. The night sky in this painting is nothing more than a backdrop for their love."

A few people entered the enclave as the man was talking.

They gathered nearby, as if eavesdropping on a talk being given by a tour guide.

He glanced at us for a moment, as if sizing up our relative youth.

"*Love is the key*," he said to us. And with that, he walked out of the room.

I spent a great deal of time thinking about what to perform at the first of what the D'Agoults had taken to calling the Dawn Concerts. By the final week of the summer I had decided upon the repertoire. An unorthodox set of pieces that contoured perfectly to the delicate light of a new day. The adagios of the Beethoven-Liszt symphony transcriptions. Slow second movements that perfectly reflected the ambience of early morning. Their technical difficulty made it unlikely that anyone on the guest list had ever heard them performed live before. And I had never heard of an orchestra having the audacity to program only consecutive second movements of symphonies. Among conductors it has always been deemed sacrilegious to perform merely a segment of a symphony without the context of the rest of the work as a whole to frame the movement and give it meaning. But I had no problem with it.

I felt the individual movements held up on their own perfectly well.

I would play them consecutively with no intermission.

A performance of perhaps a little over an hour.

The ideal amount of playing time for the duration of that magical time of day.

The evening before the performance the three of us were having a quiet dinner in the apartment. Kalman was on his way from London and would arrive later that night. Towards the end of dinner the Countess looked across the table to Mirabelle and myself.

"You two are going to be very happy," she said wistfully. "And this might be a bit premature, but lately I've been thinking about you two spending next summer together down in Tangier as opposed to here and Chantilly. At some point this autumn I'll probably drop down and check in with Mohammed, see how things have been going. Oh, we used to have *such* times down there. Surely we can arrange to have a piano sent down from Spain. Even if Mirabelle has classes or a summer internship here in Paris I'm sure we could work it out. Anyway, nothing firm yet. It's just something I've been thinking about."

The following morning, after the first performance, fourteen invited guests stood huddled together in the elevator foyer waiting to be spirited back downstairs.

Many of them were still drying tears from their eyes.

They had all come as couples or as small groups of friends.

Yet there was one man who had come alone.

He was the only one in the small audience who seemed to fully internalize the experience. I had caught his eye on my walk to the piano before the performance, and I caught it again as he looked back into the drawing room from the foyer afterwards. Looking back now, a peculiar sensation ripples through me. A shimmering overlap in my memory.

An echo, deep within the matrix of my life. It's the strangest thing.

My memory of his face somehow blinks interchangeably with that of my own father.

His snow-white hair was not the white of age.

His clear gray eyes were not altogether of this world.

The scar down his left cheek seemed to absorb the dawn sunlight.

I later learned that he was some sort of reclusive technological visionary.

Although Mirabelle and her mother hardly knew him, he had an estate of his own in Chantilly as well. He had given vast sums to artistic foundations throughout Europe. He was among the first to have reached out when word of my arrival in Paris moved through certain circles like wildfire. The director of the D'Agoult foundation had made his own inquiries about this man when the guest list was being assembled.

This *Taron Veeder.*

CHAPTER TWENTY-THREE

Nesrin came spiraling down the staircase at top speed.

"They are absolutely *freaking out*," she said, breathlessly.

Lysander and Samuel were at the tapestry, as they had been all week.

"Taron Veeder just called on some sort of private satellite link. He's aboard the *Constance* right now. Somewhere in the Atlantic. He said the ship had gone on autopilot and was sailing herself. Then they all started going *crazy* when he said there was confirmation of cross-channel communication between a 'subject' and a 'project'. Apparently this happened at the moment the project itself became...it doesn't make sense. Self-conscious? It was pretty weird. I'm not sure I have it right. The term was '*conscient de soi*'. French can be a bit tricky. Self-aware, maybe? I have no idea what the project is, but the subject is Laszlo Farkas. He's on board."

"Oh my God," said Samuel.

"And a course has been set," Nesrin added. "They're heading to Tangier."

"*Morocco?*" said Lysander. "The D'Agoults mentioned a house down there, right?"

Samuel was staring incredulously at the tapestry.

"The holy grail," he said slowly, with awe. "He must have found it. Or at least he's on track to find it. It must be about to happen. Based on a reverse engineering of the brain. Of course. I spent almost a full year on the theory of how this might work back during my AI courses at Princeton. It's been speculated about for years. It's been shown to be *theoretically* possible. There was actually a paper out of the Netherlands a while ago on this. He's using Laszlo to create a new kind of artificial intelligence."

He remembered the playing.

Like black magic. Like sorcery. Like a dream.

"What are you *talking* about, man?" asked Lysander.

Samuel ignored him and went on giving voice to his stream of consciousness.

"He could be building a strong AGI," he said in a tone of wonder. "Or even an ASI. If he's using a satellite telephone to communicate that means the internet connection has probably been shut off. But when they get in reach of the cell networks the system could, and probably *would*, make the leap to the internet. Whether by design or by accident. There are plenty of people who think that could present an existentially dangerous scenario. I'll explain later. But now there's suddenly something we have to do that will be a lot more important and difficult to pull off than simply finding Laszlo Farkas."

"And what the hell could that be?" asked Nesrin incredulously.

Samuel was already taking off his smock.

"That ship can't be allowed anywhere *near* land," he said. "If she picks up a signal to the cell networks it could spell disaster. Suddenly it all makes sense. He's building an intelligence based on the architecture of emotion. Of course. But if it spins out of control, my God..."

"An intelligence built on the architecture of *what?*" asked Lysander with exasperation. "If *what* spins out of control? *What* makes sense? What is *going on?*"

"We have to stop that ship."

"Excuse me?" Nesrin stammered. "*We* have to stop the ship?"

"There just isn't time for anyone else," said Samuel. "It's been well over two weeks, and it shouldn't take too much longer than that to make a transatlantic crossing. There's no way we have time to convince French or Moroccan authorities to take us seriously. And we can't bring the Countess in on this, she'll totally flip out. There's no way she'll be able to see the bigger picture. All she wants is her boy back. But, I'm telling you, this is what's happening. And it's going to be up to us to stop it."

Lysander paused as he looked at Samuel skeptically.

"You seem pretty sure that you know what you're talking about," he said at last. "But if you don't think we can convince the authorities to take you seriously, then to be honest, why should *we* take you seriously? Do you have any idea how crazy this sounds? You're saying the three of *us* need to stop a megayacht, out in the Atlantic somewhere, from reaching its destination? Because of some kind of *science experiment?* Well I'll tell you one thing. I'm not risking *my* life to play pirate out on the high seas."

"I'm just telling you how it is," said Samuel. "This is something the biggest names in tech have been warning about for *years*. The fact that it's *Taron Veeder* trying to pull this thing off escalates things dramatically. This is all *very* real."

He laid it all out.

Fermi's paradox, the great filter. The possible eradication of civilization. A superintelligent system capable of recursive self-improvement that would quickly leave human intelligence vanishingly far behind. While such a system could possibly help eliminate poverty, war, climate change and even human aging there was no guarantee without decades of safety measures integrated into its design that it would prioritize human concerns at all.

"We don't know *what* it would do," said Samuel. "The fact is though, we're reaching the end of an era. For tens of thousands of years the human brain has been the primary shaper of the future of civilization. It's impossible to conceive of how different things will be when something vastly more intelligent than us arrives. And it will arrive, I assure you. The only thing we can do, seeing as we are the very ones *creating* it, is try to ensure that it aligns with our values when it gets here. And that will take time. Taron Veeder is likely leapfrogging *all* safety measures and creating something that neither he nor anybody else will be capable of understanding or controlling. We have no way of predicting what it will do because in all of history there's never been anything on earth that could outsmart us. We can control every living thing on earth not because we're stronger but because we're *smarter*. So what happens when something infinitesimally more intelligent than us takes a look around and sees, for instance, that humans are destroying the very earth they appear to command? When it sees that natural environmental systems, which have ruled this planet for billions of years, are being reconditioned and destroyed by humans who have only even *existed* for a geological blink of an eye? What happens if something of an intelligence scale we cannot even conceive decides to eradicate us for the good of the planet?"

"Put that way, maybe it *should* eradicate us," said Lysander.

"So it's up to us then," said Nesrin. "Just us, literally. I don't really have time to process all this but I'm going to assume you're right. Although once we get a track on the ship I don't see any reason we should *all* need to put ourselves in danger. Especially as getting out onto the open ocean and stopping a huge sailboat will probably require certain physical skills that, to be honest, I don't think all of us possess. Thankfully, much of my training was done on the Euphrates."

"Of course it was," Lysander muttered.

Nesrin's mind was a centrifuge, spinning with great force.

Separating all possible options from one another.

"Let's wrap this up," she said as they stood under the tapestry. "Right now. We're done. You guys clean the rest of it immediately. There's not much left anyway. I'll call Lucinda and let her know we'll be done by this evening. I'll see if we can get paid in cash. I think we have about twelve thousand euros coming our way. Since we can't let the Countess know exactly what's going on, it'll be hard to justify asking her for the money we're gonna need for bribes."

"Bribes?" asked Samuel.

"So we just wipe it all off?" asked Lysander.

"Yes, and yes," said Nesrin. "We'll be packed up and ready to head out in an hour. I'll call the D'Agoults from upstairs. There's a vehicle out in their garage. I'm not sure of the make, it has a dust cover on it, but whatever it is we're going to need it."

"We're *driving*?" asked Samuel. "To *Tangier*?"

"The drive from Paris to the southern coast of Spain is less than two days. From there we'll take the ferry to Morocco. I think you can actually *see* Morocco from the Spanish coast, it's so close. This way we'll have transportation when we get there. Based on the crossing times of the shipping charts we looked at we have about ten days before the ship arrives. While we can't exactly take the scenic route, there's no disadvantage to driving. And at this point, I don't really have a choice. I'll explain later."

"*Any* route from here to the south of Spain is the scenic route," Lysander observed.

Lucinda herself climbed the ladder that evening and to her astonishment could find not even the slightest blemish on the tapestry that just a week or so earlier had appeared damaged beyond repair. With profound gratitude to the team of the great restoration expert Dr. Lysander Bennett, she handed over a bright purple wad of 500-euro notes as they stood at the front door with their bags packed.

They arrived back at the Chateau D'Agoult just in time for dinner.

"Tangier?" exclaimed the Countess. "Laszlo's practically been living at our place there for years now. But as I've said, there's just nothing *down* there. Why would they be going to Tangier? What's in Tangier?"

"We don't know," said Nesrin. "The important thing is that he's alive."

Mirabelle began to cry with relief. The Countess herself almost began to break down.

"So what do we do now?" she asked. "Do you need the plane?"

"From here on out I need to go dark," said Nesrin, looking to Lysander and Samuel. "The closer they get to land the higher chance there is that all security firewalls will be engaged. Even private plans require a passenger manifest and both my passports are likely compromised by now. Airports take those manifests very seriously. Ports are much easier. You have a spare car in the garage, right?"

Mirabelle allowed a titter of laughter through her sniffles.

"Well, it's not exactly a *car*," said the Countess. "But you *would* all fit."

"As long as it gets us down there," said Nesrin. "Now, this house of yours. Does the fellow you mentioned, this caretaker…"

"Mohammed," interjected Mirabelle, with renewed composure. "He's there. We can let him know you're on your way and he'll set you up at the house. I'm sorry we haven't told you more about that whole side of Laszlo's life, but it's like mama says. There just really isn't too much to tell. Mohammed is the only person Laszlo has contact with when he's down there. And he's as harmless as a mouse."

Nesrin cleared her throat.

"Do you know offhand if Mohammed has access to a boat? A fishing vessel or something like that? The reason I ask is because we don't know the exact nature of *why* Laszlo is aboard. It would be following hostage protocol to attempt to intercept them before they reach the shore. Once they make landfall they gain the ability to move him to ground transportation. And if they manage to get him off that ship he'll be much, much harder to track. Right now we know exactly *where* he is. We may not know the location of the yacht but we know he's aboard and once down there I have a few ideas about how to get a track on her."

"Well, of course he does," said the Countess. "He has access to *our* boat. The *Akida*. When we're all down there we keep her moored at the house but at the moment she's at port. Mohammed's been piloting her for many years. He's very much at home on the water. But are you saying that you're planning on trying to free Laszlo at sea? That sounds awfully dangerous."

"Not as dangerous as allowing him to make it to land then disappear again," said Nesrin. "Please let Mohammed know to expect us tomorrow evening. Or, better yet, if you get me his information I'll contact him myself. He and I are going to have to work together on this. And I'll need the address of the house. There are few things I'm going to need sent down there."

The next morning they were up before dawn.

The sky was black but an eager strip of gray hung over the treeline of the forest.

Quietly they carried their bags downstairs.

Claude, the old gardener and caretaker, was awake in the kitchen.

"Coffee is ready," he whispered.

They drank coffee and split up a baguette while Claude grabbed their bags.

He walked outside and returned a minute later.

"All set," he said with a twinkle in his eye. "Bags are in the luggage bins."

"Luggage bins?" asked Lysander.

"It'll take a few minutes to teach you how to drive it, but you'll see that it's really very easy. It was designed to be driven with almost no instruction. Come, follow me."

The three of them followed Claude out to the driveway.

"Jesus Christ," said Lysander just above a whisper. Samuel let out a long slow whistle.

Nesrin smiled broadly. She spoke quietly over Claude's shoulder.

"World War Two?" she asked. Claude nodded.

"I've ridden similar bikes before," said Nesrin. "In the refugee camps at al-Hawl."

"What the hell *is* that thing?" asked Samuel.

"A German Zundapp battle motorcycle," said Claude. "With a re-inforced sidecar."

"It looks like a three-wheeled tank," said Lysander.

"Well, that's basically what it is," said Claude. "This motorbike has been kept here on the estate since the Countess's father purchased it in 1948. The Countess herself was just a young girl when he bought it at an auction of confiscated German military vehicles, as a sort of trophy after the war. He loved it for its power and for the general wildness of its personality but nobody else in the family ever felt much attachment to it."

The beast of a machine was in pristine condition. Bolted to each side of the long nose of the sidecar were two original brown leather satchels the size of normal suitcases. Inside the sidecar was a double wide seat upholstered with smooth black leather. There appeared to be plenty of legroom. On the seat, like tortoise shells set upon each other, was a stack of three old World War Two-era helmets. A large spare tire was firmly attached to the rear of the sidecar. The driver's seat, as well as the passenger seat behind it, were as wide as tractor seats and looked vaguely like horse saddles. Claude walked to the rear of the sidecar, put a hand under the spare tire, and pulled a latch.

A hydraulic shaft pushed open the lid of a spacious compartment.

"Your bag is in here," Claude told Nesrin. "Both the other bags are on the side. There's a map of Europe in the compartment of the right satchel. The goggles are in there as well."

Lysander laughed louder than was appropriate for the hour.

"*Goggles?*"

"You'll need them," Claude said with a smile. "But driving this thing is actually pretty simple. It was designed for illiterate eighteen-year-olds with no training or experience to drive while being shot at."

"That sidecar actually looks pretty comfortable," said Lysander.

"I don't mind," said Samuel. "I'll take the rear.."

"I guess I'm driving?" asked Nesrin. "Since I'm the only one who's driven one before?"

An hour later they skirted the western edge of Paris.

Samuel sat in the rear passenger seat and held fast to Nesrin's waist as she drove.

Lysander sat in the sidecar. The motorbike blasted south like an unhinged rocket.

They all wore the tortoiseshell helmets and thick leather-rimmed goggles.

The air warmed and the fields of wheat turned into meadows of lavender and lilac. They blew past Tours and Chatellerault before powering west down through the towns of northern Bordeaux that smelled of coastal limestone and ancient vineyards. Nesrin leaned forward over the industrial handlebars and steered them towards the coast.

The Zundapp blasted south along the edge of the Bay of Biscay.

That evening they crossed the border into Spain at San Sebastian.

After a full day of riding across the expanse of southern France, the motorbike at last pulled into the confines of Spanish city streets and slowly gurgled over cobblestone boulevards at the peak of the evening people-watching hour. The weather was warm and the sidewalks were packed. People stopped in their tracks to pull out their phones and take pictures of the crazy German battle motorcycle, carrying the most unusual looking trio of people, as it burped and banged along under the yellow street lamps. They found a decent looking hotel on the Calle de Zubieta and the Zundapp roared down into the underground parking lot. Within a few minutes of checking in they were seated at a table overlooking La Concha beach.

Samuel ordered a prosecco. Nesrin and Lysander split a large Pellegrino.

Their menus flapped in the salt breeze.

"There's something I need to clear up," said Nesrin, as she lit a cigarette.

"Regarding the details I didn't want to go into with the D'Agoults. It has always, or almost always, been a point of pride in my work that I generally don't have to hurt people. But I want to be sure you guys are okay with the fact that this time things are going to have to be different. *I'm okay with it, considering how dramatically the situation has changed.*"

She took a drag and thought about how to say what she was going to say next.

"Maybe you've wondered where I picked up this occasional smoking thing," she said.

Lysander and Samuel waited for her to go on.

"The YPG rewarded me with a cigarette after my first kill, at the age of nine."

Her unpolished jade eyes took in the light of the moon.

"Once I'm in the water it'll just be a matter of time before this is all over."

"Wait, what do you mean, *in the water?*" sputtered Samuel.

"Once we get a tracking line on the *Constance* I'll head out on the smaller boat to make the interception. It sounds like this fellow Mohammed will be able to get me close, but he only has to get me a few hundred yards directly in front of her path. At that point I go overboard. Mohammed veers off course in order to avoid raising any eyebrows on the radar. I wait in the water with a grappling hook on a long knotted line."

"A *grappling hook?*"

"As the yacht passes me in the water, I'll toss the hook over the side and pull myself up on board. Then I get to work. I'm not sure what I'll find on board, and I'm not sure I'll be able to stop the ship, but I can at least try to destroy the equipment before they get within range of the cell networks. I'll find and free Laszlo, make contact with Mohammed, and have him pull up alongside. We'll get Laszlo off the ship. A hook, a wetsuit, and a knife are all I'm going to need."

"A *knife?*"

"That's why I didn't want to go into details with the D'Agoults."

At dawn the Zundapp blasted out of San Sebastian. They tore south across the dry plains of northern Spain. By midday the sun blazed down upon them and the hot dry wind began to feel more like summer than early spring. They stopped for a lengthy lunch in Salamanca, taking their time at an outdoor table under an olive tree, before howling down the dusty highway towards Algeciras. After a few hours the low skyline of the ancient Spanish port city pulled into view. Signs began to appear on the side of the road for the port itself and the motorbike purred its way towards the immense tourist cruise ships that loomed over the tallest buildings like mountains in the distance. An hour later the huge motorbike was safely secured in the cargo hold of the ferry.

They stood on deck and looked out across the Strait of Gibraltar.

Over the bow a little nest of white lights shone out from the north-west shore of Africa.

CHAPTER TWENTY-FOUR

Magnus kept Raquel alive.

She was back aft, locked in her cabin, keeping Magnus alive.

The wave of code coming in from the extraction room was relentless.

Taron Veeder was locked back aft and had not been seen or heard from since that night.

The emerald green bow smashed through the waves towards North Africa.

It seemed there was nothing any of them could do.

Yet Jensen and Tilman *knew* this ship.

They knew there must be *some* way to get back aft.

As the hours and days passed they plotted.

They did pushups and jumping jacks on the deck.

They smoked wherever they damn well pleased.

They pulled out blueprints and went over every possible option.

Everything was sealed tight. There was nothing. But still, they knew there must be a way.

And then one night as they all slept Jensen opened his eyes in the darkness.

The stern tube.

Shaking with excitement he woke Tilman. He told his brother how it could be done.

It was several more days before the conditions were just right. The wind was strong enough that there was no doubt it would remain so for at least a few hours, yet the sea was calm, so they were under full sail and the engine to the propeller had been shut off. Under cover of darkness just hours earlier, carefully measured lengths of Kevlar line had been tied to the starboard stanchions and thrown overboard. The deck was bare and the sails snapped in the gusts that hauled the ship closer and closer to the northwest corner of Africa.

The morning sun had just emerged over the horizon.

Jensen and Tilman emerged from the galley hatch wearing the scuba gear they occasionally used during odd underwater jobs such as scraping barnacles off the hull and cleaning the running gear. They quickly closed the hatch behind them. Their neoprene wetsuits and silver tanks flashed in the sun as one after the other they scooted backwards, flippers flapping, to the edge of the deck. It only took them a few seconds. Each had a mesh dive sack full of tools and heavy duty carabiner hooks attached to their weight belts.

They clasped their carabiners to the Kevlar line.

They tipped backwards off the edge of the deck and fell into the sea.

Underneath the *Constance* they were instantly blasted by the roaring currents. Six thousand feet of water was an infinite blackness between them and the bottom of the Atlantic. Slowly they began to let themselves drag backwards against the waterline of the hull, Jensen just one or two body lengths behind Tilman. When they reached the transom at the rear of the ship, they clamped their carabiners to the line and descended under the sea. The powerful current had them flying underneath the hull like two masked superheroes cruising across the night sky. Angling their flippers, they drifted towards the center of the transom and grabbed the massive rudder that cut through the water and steered the giant ship across the sea.

The giant propeller in front of it was dormant, as they were under full sail.

Jensen pulled a crowbar out of his mesh bag and violently removed the propeller cap.

Tilman pulled out a powerful drill with a bolt driver attached to the chuck.

Jamming himself between the rudder and the propeller he found the pressure he needed to remove five of the six bolts that held in place the six shafts attaching the propeller shaft to the other end of the stern tube in the engine room. Looking at Jensen in the roaring current, he nodded as he used all the strength in his body to remove the sixth bolt. For a moment nothing happened, but then the huge propeller began to slide off the propeller shaft. It came loose and Jensen and Tilman held tight to the rudder and watched as the giant three-ton propeller fell from the shaft and sank in slow motion into the blackness below and behind them. Immediately, thick black lubricant began to flow from the stern tube and without being able to see anything at all they were actually able to hear the sound of metal sliding against metal as the propeller shaft began to slide out of the stern tube. Reaching through the outpouring of slick lubricant they could feel the entire propeller shaft passing by them until it slid fully out of the stern tube and fell down to the bottom of the Atlantic.

The stern tube leading up to the engine room filled with seawater.

The girth was slightly less than that of an MRI tube.

Just barely enough for a small man to fit inside.

Jensen had perhaps fifteen minutes left in his air tank.

Tilman helped remove the tank from his back.

Jensen grabbed his own drill with a bolt driver attached to the chuck.

He looked at Tilman but could barely make out his eyes behind his dive mask.

They looked at each other for a few seconds, as if saying goodbye.

Jensen removed the Kevlar line attached to his weight belt.

He squirmed his way into the stern tube, drill held out ahead of him.

Tilman pushed the air tank into the stern tube behind him.

Pushing the air tank against Jensen's feet, Tilman in turn pushed his brother up to the other end of the stern tube against the engine room bulkhead. Tilman took the propeller cap that had been wedged into the rudder and began to bolt it back into place to prevent a breach. Within a few moments Jensen was bolted in complete blackness within the stern tub, submerged entirely within a coffin of seawater and lubricant.

So long, brother.

Tilman would pull himself back up the Kevlar line along the side of the hull. Underneath the stanchion to which it was tied he would release his own scuba gear into the sea and pull himself up the side of the *Constance*, then roll back down through the hatch into the galley.

Jensen, using nothing but touch in the frigid blackness, found the bolts along the cap ring of the engine room bulkhead. One by one he felt the head of the bolt driver fit over the bolts and using all his strength pushed against his air tank and removed the bolts.

There were only a few minutes of air left in his tank.

He counted out the removal of six bolts. Nothing happened.

He repeatedly slammed the bolt driver against the stern tube cap.

Claustrophobic terror began to mount. At last he felt something begin to give.

Using all his strength, while at the same time trying to conserve every last breath, he continued banging against the cap. At last with a huge release it fell from the stern tube onto the engine room floor. Seawater slick with lubricant poured out from the stern tube into the engine room. Like a foal being birthed, Jensen slid out of the stern tube and crashed onto the engine room floor. The propeller cap at the other end of the stern tube remained secure.

There was no breach. He was in.

Without wasting a second Jensen immediately ripped off his gear. He found a pile of rags near the engine and wiped what lubricant he could from his face. He slipped on the slick floor after removing his flippers but sat down on the bench press, where he began to wipe his feet as well. Sensing that he wouldn't be able to get it all off, and not wanting to risk another fall, he tied a dry rag around each foot. Catching his breath, he scanned the ceiling above him and quickly located the etched square that was a trap door leading up into the room where the strange sphere held the captive pianist. He grabbed a length of electrical cord from underneath the bench press and tied it around his waist. He stood back up on the slick floor. He pulled the bench press underneath the trap door and stepped carefully upon it. Reaching up, he twisted the almost imperceptible knob in the trap door, pushed it open, and pulled himself up through the ceiling.

He was in a dark humming room with the otherworldly sphere hovering before him and lines of computer code scrolling past on screens all around him. He couldn't bring himself to more than glance at the helmeted figure in the silver suit floating on top of the fluid within the sphere.

His neoprene wetsuit was dripping with salt water and lubricant.

His breathing was deep and controlled. He was desperate for a cigarette.

He felt along the wall for the switch he knew was there.

The door slid open. He was in the hallway leading to the master stateroom.

He moved silently down the corridor.

As he approached the stateroom he could see that the door was open.

His feet, tied up in rags, tiptoed to the edge of the door. There was nothing to wait for.

Jensen whipped around the corner and right in front of him, deep in concentration at a pair of screens on his desk, a bulky satellite telephone set to the side, was the man who had promised him eternal life. Now he needed to get him to fulfill that promise. There was no killing him yet. This was the only opportunity they would have to extract access to unimaginable powers. He needed Taron Veeder alive. There were methods of getting him to give up his secrets once he was bound and secured. Contrary to modern battlefield sentiment, torture actually worked quite well. At least in Jensen's experience. And yet he was suddenly paralyzed with fear as his employer sensed his presence in the doorway and slowly turned to face him.

Their eyes met. Neither man moved.

Sea water and lubricant were streaked across Jensen's face as his wetsuit dripped onto the floor. His eyes flashed and a storm roared up within his heart. He knew how dangerous Taron Veeder was and feared him tremendously, but like a blast of lightning he was suddenly on the other side of his fear and swept into action.

He clenched his fists as he burst into the room.

Taron Veeder leapt up from his desk, tablet in hand.

"You'll never be able to access the system!" he shrieked. "And it *will* make its escape."

He smashed the tablet against the corner of the desk.

"If not me, then *nobody!*" he yelled as Jensen fell upon him.

Jensen coiled back and punched Taron Veeder across the scar on his face as hard as he could, sending him crumpling back into his chair like a broken marionette. He untied the electrical cord from his waist and lashed Taron Veeder to the chair. In the next cabin he could hear

Raquel shouting and banging on her door. She knew something was going on. But she didn't need to know what. Jensen ignored her. He grabbed the back of the chair and dragged it out into the hallway. He dragged his unconscious employer down the hallway, through the room with the white server cube and up to the rosewood doors that had been bolted from the inside with steel security bars set in the floor.

He stamped on the brakes at the wheels of the chair.

He unhooked the security bars and pulled open the rosewood doors.

Sabine was standing alone in the salon.

Her hard eyes were cold as ice.

In one hand she held a gleaming serrated kitchen knife.

In the other, a long severed piece of Kevlar line.

"Just us now, baby," she said. "He's gone."

CHAPTER TWENTY-FIVE

It's becoming harder to tell which reality is which.

A warm wild wind swept up the rugged terrain leading from the Mediterranean to the house on the mountain just west of Tangier, slicing whitecaps off the waves below as they chopped and slashed across the narrow sea. The bow cuts through waves on our course towards Morocco, and those left alive are powerless to stop me. Back then, the wind rushed through the brambles below the terrace, bending the old palms, bringing with it the strong scent of salt, lavender, and thyme. On some days I could see the coast of Spain in sharp detail. On some nights car headlamps on the other side were brilliant pinpricks of light. A dense fog hovered over the seven miles of water separating the hilly coasts of Africa and Europe.

The Spanish coastline ebbs in and out of view like a mirage.

I stood on the terrace looking out at the mist.

Mirabelle had been accepted at the École des Beaux-Arts and enrolled that fall. She had only returned to Paris a few days earlier, she visited Tangier often, but we had long ago decided that the best thing for me would be to remain in Tangier. I was now on my own, trying to find out what I was really made of. The spring before we first came down the Countess and I visited the Steinway dealership in Madrid. I selected the concert grand that had been delivered early that summer, the very piano waiting for me in the living room.

Even though there *is* no piano.

There *is* no living room on this ship.

When we first arrived in Tangier there was no piano either.

Mohammed, who had worked for the D'Agoults for many years, met us at the little Tangier airport. With a giddy display of paternal love he greeted Mirabelle and with a respectful deference he introduced himself to me. It's funny how the years change you. From this vantage point it seems I really wasn't much more than a child back then. The drive from the airport to the house was a ten-mile span across northern Moroccan farmland culminating with a climb up the small mountain on the edge of town that for generations had been home to expats and the wealthy. Mohammed spoke a unique style of French speckled with Spanish and Arabic that Mirabelle seemed to fold into quite easily. Old men wearing challabahs on the roadside tended to small herds of chickens and sheep.

Arriving at the mountain, Mohammed steered the old car slowly up and along the winding roads, under the eucalyptus and swaying cyprus, hugging the high stone walls as he drove. Mirabelle and I sat in the back of the car holding hands in contented silence. At last he turned off the road, eased us down an asphalt drive and pulled in front of the facade of the D'Agoults' house. It was not large yet there was an elegance to it, set as it was deep amidst the forest, with a clear view of the Mediterranean below. Impossibly tall trees lined the edges of the property in such a way that the view down to the sea below was set as if within a picture frame. Whitewash over the stone walls had begun to peel after another summer of being battered by strong sun and wind off the sea, but the structure was not in disrepair. Almost all the furniture and carpets had been placed in storage for protection from the humidity of the wet and windy winters, yet Mohammed had prepared the master bedroom and living room that opened onto the expanse of terra cotta terrace. Here was a place I would not need to attempt to be social as my growing fame had begun to require of me in Paris.

A place utterly isolated from the pressures of constantly being around other people.

The late afternoon breeze carried the scent of salt off the sea.

To me, it smelled of the future.

Perhaps not the future as it's currently playing out, but the future nonetheless.

That first morning I woke to the sound of a car door being gently shut in the driveway. Mirabelle and I were in each other's arms, the smell of flowers from the mountainside wafting in through the windows and doors on a steady current of sea air. In the dawn light I could hear Mohammed sweeping the terrace, cleaning the house, scrubbing out the tagine in the kitchen sink. Mirabelle smiled as she slept, lips curled sweetly at the edges and twitching gently with the pulses of her dreams. A few hours later he drove us back towards the airport along the dusty roads just out of sight of the Mediterranean to Cap Spartel, the exact spot where the Mediterranean meets the Atlantic. It was the first thing Mirabelle wanted me to see.

Looking out through the pines to the sea, I knew I was home.

Cresting a hill on the empty road the vast Atlantic loomed into view.

The little white Peugeot pointed down towards a vast and windswept empty beach of Cap Spartel. Mohammed put the car in neutral and we glided silently down the switchbacks towards the Atlantic ocean. The road flattened out along the coast and I looked down across the vast expanse of empty beach and the wild ocean beyond. Even in the early summer there was just nobody out there. Only the occasional farmhouse dotted the landscape. We rounded a spit of land and the beach stretched south for miles before us all the way to the horizon.

There was not a single person on it.

"The people here, they don't like to swim in the Atlantic," said Mohammed as he drove slowly along the beach. "It's shallow and cold. Shallow for hundreds of meters, some of the shallowest coastline in the world. Further out the currents are strong and even at this time of year the water is cold, but if you stay close it is okay. Sometimes you see tourists out here but in general there is nobody. Mirabelle used to come here when she was small."

Mohammed pointed to his left.

"All that land is open because nothing really grows out here. So we have the ocean that is cold and the land that is not good for farming. It makes it very good for being alone with the sky. You can swim but do not go out far. Mirabelle will show you."

Mirabelle put her head on my shoulder.

The car turned down a small side road leading out onto the beach.

Half an hour later, I walked barefoot into the ocean for the first time in my life.

One evening not long after that, Mohammed dropped us off at the great gate leading into the labyrinthine streets and alleyways of the medina. We were heading that night to a party in the kasbah, at the apparently magnificent home of an aristocratic expat family the D'Agoults had known for generations. Swirling colors and smells and people were all around me, large barrels full of spices lined the ancient cobbled pathways, the smoke of grilling lamb and fish filled the air, storefronts packed with preserved fruits and olives were jammed with locals in brightly colored chelabahs bargaining and yelling. Old men sat together on upturned olive oil drums smoking long thin wooden pipes. Boys snaked and darted through the crowds. Above them, people looked out from the dark windows of the houses and apartments in which people lived the same lifestyle as their ancestors many generations before them.

I had been into the medina a few times since my arrival and on each occasion expected that we would garner more attention than we did. I was wearing dark slacks and a pressed white shirt, she was in an obviously expensive evening dress. Upon our arrival it had at first made me feel self-conscious of just how foreign we were, coming down in the powder-blue jet from the gilded life we led in Paris. But the locals of the medina paid us no mind at all. Men wore challabahs and pointy hats. Berber women in full tribal costumes sat in packs on the ground selling butter and cheese from the countryside.

The sound of Arabic emulsified with the smell and the chaos.

Mirabelle led me through the streets of the medina she had known all her life.

As we began to head up the jagged steps towards the kasbah, while remaining essentially invisible to the throngs of locals, I began to recognize the fact that my first impression along the roadside to the mountain was correct. These people were not that different from my own. I was of Hungarian gypsy blood, and the more I saw of the people of Tangier, despite our differences in language and dress and way of life, the more it seemed that there was a bit of gypsy in their souls as well. By early evening we had made our way up through the stone gate that led into the kasbah, the highest point of the city of Tangier.

The frenzy of merchant activity had ceased as we walked through quiet ancient streets sided by whitewashed walls into which mysterious wooden doors appeared at unmarked and irregular intervals.

We walked hand in hand through the narrow stone pathways.

"Some of these streets are a thousand years old," said Mirabelle, looking closely at the doors as we passed. "The Dampierres live right down here, I think. Yes, there it is."

We stopped in front of a dark wooden door about twelve feet high built right into a long stretch of whitewashed wall that rose several stories above us. From behind it came distant peals of laughter and echoes of conversation amid the rhythmic clatter of music.

An old servant in formal white colonial attire and a red fez hat opened the door.

He greeted Mirabelle with a familiar smile.

"Aieee! Mirabelle! All grown up!"

He beckoned us inside and pulled the door shut behind us.

It slammed closed with a boom that echoed for several seconds as we were led down a dark stone hallway towards the sounds of the party. After a few dozen steps we emerged and for a second I thought we were back outside. Towering palm trees shot up from manicured openings in a black and white checkered marble floor, scraping the ceiling of the home that must have been upwards of forty feet high. Lining the great room were three tiers of balconies behind which countless beautiful engraved doors led into the rooms of the house. People were on the balconies, people were on cushions set into enclaves carved out of the ground-floor walls, people were standing around talking, people were dancing. Europeans wearing traditional Moroccan clothing, Moroccans wearing custom tailored suits, people of indeterminate nationalities wearing haute couture dresses and sub-Saharan formal attire and everything in between.

But all this was barely even a distraction.

Across the sweeping floor from the food and the bar were the musicians.

I had never seen or heard anything quite like them, yet at the same time it was music that seemed to strike my very soul. Dressed in traditional flowing robes, they were dancing and singing, playing stringed instruments I had never seen before, clapping and banging small copper cymbals.

The lead member of the group called out.

The others responded from within a deep hypnotic trance.

"Mirabelle, you made it!" came a woman's voice from within the crowd. Rushing at us was a slender and slightly elderly woman in a dress of peacock feathers wearing a 1920s-style Coco Chanel hat. In one hand a cigarette dangled from a long cigarette holder. In the other was a pink cocktail in a Marie Antoinette glass.

"Madame Dampierre," Mirabelle quickly whispered to me. "Brace yourself."

"Ah my darling Mirabelle!" cried Madame Dampierre. "And ohh, who is this? Perhaps this is the *pianist* we've all heard so much about? Laszlo Farkas? Who apparently *everyone* in Paris is talking about?"

Madame Dampierre was obviously quite drunk.

"The pleasure, Madam, is all mine," I said, my eyes fixated on the musicians.

"Quite a catch, Mirabelle my darling. But look at *you!* Oh my, what *have* you been up to? Why, I remember you running around here when you were still in nappies!"

Mirabelle darted her eyes at me and blushed.

"I'm doing very well, Madame Dampierre, thank you," she said. "I've been accepted at the École des Beaux-Arts. Mama must have told you. I'll study art history, probably. I think one day I might want to run my own gallery, maybe even in New York. You know, with my family history and everything, it just seems to make sense…"

Madame Dampierre widened her eyes and gave me an enormous wink.

"A galley run by *Mirabelle D'Agoult?*" she asked in mock amazement. "Who would *ever* have thought such a thing was possible. You'll have to keep an eye on her, I should think, young man! Once this girl gets an idea in her head there isn't room for much else!"

With laughing eyes she took a drag of her cigarette and spilled a bit of her drink.

"Madame Dampierre, thank you for having us," I allowed, distractedly. "Why don't you two catch up a bit, I'm just going to take a look over here…"

Mirabelle took up the conversation as I peeled off and made my way towards the musicians, grabbing a glass of champagne off a tray that floated past me. Suddenly I was back in my early youth, my parents and their gypsy friends dancing and playing the fiddle around a fire late at night while I was supposed to be sleeping. Someone standing near me offered a long thin wooden pipe and for the first time in my life I smoked. Even though I didn't know what it was, it felt right and I began to dance. The music was something I somehow knew very deeply. Without effort I could tell where it was going before it got there and as the party went on I stayed right where I was and danced with abandon to the Islamic Sufi melodies that wound in and around the relentless African rhythms.

I lost track of time and I lost track of everything else.

I caught occasional glimpses of Mirabelle dancing and talking, but I was utterly lost to the mania of the music until at some point I was tapped on the shoulder by Madame Dampierre.

"Laszlo, Laszlo," she seemed to be saying from very far away. "We want to hear you, come, the piano hasn't been tuned in forever, but it's over here, come…"

The gnawa musicians stopped playing and cheered me on. The crowd bubbled with excitement as she led me across the room towards the buffet, and as the sea of people parted the man wearing the red fez removed the dust cover from a very old grand piano. With a languid shrug I walked around the instrument and slipped onto the bench.

I looked down at the old faded yellow ivory keys.

The gnawa musicians were standing directly behind me, looking over my shoulders, and the roaring din around the rest of the house submerged quickly into silence.

I shut my eyes. I raised my hands.

A collective gasp of amazement shot through the crowd as the first chords of the second Liszt Hungarian Rhapsody exploded out of the piano. The piano shook and the buffet tables trembled as the marble floor absorbed the power of my playing and I could sense that the people in the crowd felt the electricity drive up directly through their feet. I played on into the eerie gypsy roots of the piece, my arms flying and the gnawa musicians dancing behind me and the people cheering. At the frenzied conclusion the crowd flew into a state of demented delirium. Over the next few days word of the performance spread across the world.

A few months later the Steinway grand arrived from Madrid.

Now the mist was clearing off the terrace.

And only five on board are left alive.

CHAPTER TWENTY-SIX

Nesrin led the way down into the hold of the ferry.
Her dark jeans and black boots were caked with mud and dust.

They squeezed past the vans and trucks in the dark vehicle hold of the ferry. Past Spanish drivers hauling European food and equipment south, past Moroccan drivers returning empty trucks that had hauled olives and citrus and textiles up through Spain and into northern Europe. At last they returned to the dust- and mud-spattered motorcycle. With an incredible boom they felt the ferry bump up against the pier. Several dozen engines fired up just as the front loading ramp began to lower with an ear-splitting clatter. They took their seats on the old motorbike.

Nesrin gave a powerful push on the crankshaft and the Zundapp roared to life.

She slowly let out the clutch and they rolled down the ramp.

They were in Africa.

A few minutes later they were on the other side of the port gates, the passports they provided the sullen young immigration agent stamped but barely looked at. Amid the thundering of countless trucks pulling out of the port, they saw car headlights flash at them three times quickly, as planned. Nesrin steered the Zundapp towards the lights. Mohammed jumped out of a small white Citroen and ran up to them. He was the type of small man who exudes great power without being actually muscular. His cheeks were a patchwork of wiry white whiskers.

"You made it!" he cried in heavily accented English.

He slapped the hood of the sidecar.

A truck blasted a powerful horn behind them.

Mohammed gestured to the old Citroen.

"Okay, this is me. Stay close. Not so simple getting out of here. First we enter the medina, just up there, but once we get past that it is easy. Yellah. Follow me."

Mohammed ran back to the car and jumped in.

The car let out a shrill little follow-me honk and began to inch forward.

Slowly they merged into the traffic pulling out of the port.

Almost as soon as they dove into the bedlam of the medina they were back out of it, following the little white car as it passed through what appeared to be the newer part of the city. Down a hill they sped until they came to a long straightaway that led directly towards the dark shape of a mountain looming ahead in their path. Before long they were on the ascent. Nesrin shifted into a lower gear as they passed iron-gated entrances to grand estates. Leaving the chaotic medina behind, they ascended through the dark canopy of high swaying trees and shadows of colonial-era mansions. The sensation of traveling through time to the expat life of the eighteenth century was palpable. At last Mohammed turned slowly into a gateless driveway that led down a small hill to an expanse of land on which sat the most exquisite and elegant house Lysander had ever seen. In the distance the Mediterranean shimmered through the eucalyptus.

Nesrin rolled the Zundapp down the driveway and cut the engine.

Wind blew through the cyprus leaves high above them.

From far below came the crashing of waves against the rocks.

Mohammed stepped out of the parked car and walked back to the Zundapp.

"Your packages have arrived from Holland," he told Nesrin. "I signed for the delivery this afternoon. Very heavy. But despite my years I remain strong, Hamdullah. Now, come. I'll get your luggage later. You've had a very long trip."

The glow of the moon illuminated the gravel drive.

They crunched down to the front door.

Mohammed unlocked it and pushed it open into the dark open expanse of the house. Floor-to-ceiling glass windows across the living room were a portal to another place and time. The surface of the Mediterranean was the color of opal under a smear of stars. In the living room a grand piano came into sharp relief as Mohammed switched on the lights.

Placed next to the piano were boxes of various sizes.

An hour later Lysander was examining the professional-grade easel that stood before him.

A large panel of Brazilian hardwood and a heavy box of Dutch oil paints were nearby.

"I don't understand," he said.

"You're going to paint the harbor," said Nesrin. "From the control tower of the port. It has the best view. And where would somebody from the famous Frick museum in New York City want to make a painting of Tangier should they find themselves here after a stressful restoration job in France?"

Lysander stared at the gear that would only belong to a lifelong painter.

"You looked at my sketchbook, didn't you?"

"Don't worry about it," said Nesrin with a smile. "So, the harbormaster. We're going to convince him to let you set up a small studio space in the control room. This is all going to be brought down there and you'll get to work on the painting. Samuel and I will clean brushes and do whatever artist assistants do. When you need to rest, we'll stay up there. When we need to rest, you'll stay up there. Just like Chantilly. But this time we'll know what we're looking for. In large ports of call like this once a vessel moves in off international waters and enters the country of destination they're obliged to identify themselves."

Lysander stared at the heavy artist-grade oil paints.

He hadn't left his sketchbook on her kitchen counter that day by accident.

He had always wanted to show her, but never knew how.

It's hard to show someone your soul.

That night he barely slept.

At dawn he heard the Citroen come to life and rumble up out of the driveway.

By mid-morning Mohammd and Nesrin returned and burst through the front door.

"It worked *perfectly*," said Nesrin, with tremendous excitement.

"It went very well, yes," Mohammed said with a generous degree of understatement.

"We showed the harbormaster your profile," said Nesrin. "Of course, it probably helped that he and Mohammed have known each other since they were kids. We actually got up into the control tower to check it out and it's *beautiful*. It's built into an old Portuguese observation post. Three large radar screens in a glass room at the top overlooking *everything*. There's an area to set up the easel. I'm telling you, this guy is *very* excited for you to get to work. So maybe I slipped him a little something for the kids. A little baksheesh never hurt anyone. Sorry, but I needed to make sure we got in there. And I might have told him the painting was going to be shown at the Frick. We needed to really make sure. I hope you don't mind. So now it's going to have to be good. I hope you're ready."

Lysander stood up.

"I've been ready all of my life," he said. "Let's go."

The apathetic guards waved the car through when they arrived at the port.

"Professor Bennett!" the harbormaster shouted at them excitedly in the parking lot.

He was a thin man with a neat white mustache and skin like burnt leather.

He helped Lysander extract himself from the jumble of boxes wedged into the little Citroen.

"We are *so* honored to have you," he cried. "Please, don't let me be a distraction from your important work. I have already directed my staff to make preparations for you to set up your space. So *very* exciting. To think, a contemporary work of art, a painting of our very own harbor in *modern times*. Matisse and Delacroix shall finally have some company! You'll find my staff at your disposal as you go about your work."

"You're too kind," said Lysander.

The harbormaster laughed and leaned in to him.

"No, my friend," he said quietly, with a knowing squeeze of his forearm. "*You're* too kind."

Lysander immediately knew that Nesrin slipped him a little more than something for the kids.

The radar room of the control tower was circular and entirely encased in glass. Built into the panels overlooking the harbor were three large radar screens. The *Constance* was going to be coming in off international waters. Nesrin had imprinted very clearly upon Lysander that they could expect the *Constance* to be arriving in Tangier within about a week, so that afternoon, as Nesrin and Samuel assembled the huge easel, Lysander took a seat and began to create a composition and a timeline. He came up with a compressed conception of the seascape before him, centered with the Rock of Gibraltar in the distance. The sun would descend to the east of the Rock, illuminating the golden Spanish hills, leaving the strip of Mediterranean leading to the eastern beyond shrouded in darkness.

That evening he organized dozens of cans of gorgeous Dutch paint.

He arranged brushes and palette knives on a heavy metal work table next to the easel. He prepared his mind and began to think about color. He spent all night sketching on the hardwood panel with a light wrist. Nesrin and Samuel stayed with him for the first several hours, running down to the medina to get him dinner, bringing him water, prepping the white coat of gesso and setting it to the Brazilian hardwood panel as good and true assistants would.

The entire time, they watched the room. They listened.

By morning the gesso had dried and Lysander set to work composing a graphite composite on the smooth white paint above the grain. In the early afternoon Nesrin and Samuel returned, and by then he had a number of things that needed to be done for the preparation of the palette. The outline of an image began to emerge on the panel. Radio traffic was quiet but constant. He could hear patterns begin to emerge regarding the announcements being made of entry into the sovereign water of Morocco. He grew familiar with the tonnage and cargo of container ships entering and leaving the Mediterranean through the Strait of Gibraltar. As the language of the maritime world was English, Samuel had no problems understanding the communications in the radar room either. A schedule began to emerge as the painting began to come to life.

Lysander returned to the house to sleep while Samuel prepped brushes and paint.

Over the first few days Nesrin would disappear for hours at a time.

Laszlo Farkas was on his way to them.

Lysander slashed and scraped with the Ultramarine Blue, creating shadows and reflections within the waves themselves. To the east he cast bursts of Phthalo Green towards the tops of the waves to catch the rays of the setting sun through the water. To the west, the lightest touch of Permanent Alizarin Crimson blended into the blue and added a perfectly diminishing spectral aspect of evening to the water under the darkening sky. The black jagged Rock of Gibraltar had been a menacing witness to countless sea dramas over the centuries. Through the nights he added color to the graphite shapes of the ships from all over the world moored throughout the harbor.

It was on a night like this that it finally came.

A shuffle of misunderstanding.

The overnight skeleton crew of two were casting about for answers that did not come.

Something on the radar, incoming directly towards Tangier, was not responding.

"I call again, to the vessel located three five point nine seven three north, seven point three four nine west. Third attempt at transmission, please identify yourself. Repeat, third attempt at transmission, please identify yourself."

Lysander stopped what he was doing. Over the past few days he had become familiar with the approximate coordinates a transatlantic voyage from New York would traverse. He had also become intimately familiar with the large charts of the shipping lanes, blue cobwebs superimposed over the waters off the coast of Morocco, on the walls between the windows.

He glanced up at the charts as the two officers conferred with each other.

He read out into the Atlantic.

Thirty five point seven two degrees north.

Seven point three nine degrees west.

He quickly looked to the bottom left of the chart for scale.

Maybe seventy miles out, a bit north, coming in hot.

Lysander dabbed his brushes into the rubbing alcohol.

Now the two officers were conversing quickly in French.

Lysander didn't catch every word, but he caught enough.

It had been a blip on the radar for several hours and was coming in a direct line for Cap Spartel. No reason to wake up the harbormaster about it, but it was pretty weird, right? They just weren't responding! And neither were they heading directly towards the port, more out towards...what was out there? Nothing, really. Just that huge stretch of beach out by the airport. Look, a new blip! It's still on exactly that same line! So weird! It's only coming in around twelve knots, not really fast enough to be a cruise or cargo ship. And yet...coming in from the deep seas. Hmm, must be a sailboat. A pretty big one too, if she's coming in from the other side of the Atlantic. Should we call him? No way, he'll be furious. It's probably just some wealthy guy planning on cruising down the coast. Maybe the radio is out, who knows. Let's try one more time. That'll be four tries, right? We've done what we can and as long as she's not heading into the shipping lanes, who cares?

"I call again, to the vessel now located three five point seven one eight north, seven point three eight west. Fourth attempt at transmission, please identify yourself. Repeat, fourth attempt at transmission, over."

Lysander was quickly jamming his brushes into their jars.

Hmm, very weird! Still no answer. Definitely not entering into the shipping lanes, though. Let's not worry about it too much. If she maintains a trajectory towards Cap Spartel then she'll start tacking south. There's simply nothing out there. Not *our* problem. Odd, though.

Standing up, stretching, Lysander announced he needed to take a walk and get some air.

He stepped out and ran down the circular staircase.

It was 2:45 a.m.

He burst out into the parking lot.

He dialed the house from a booth in the pay phone bank at the base of the tower.

Nesrin picked up on the first ring.

"Cap Spartel," he said quickly, breathlessly, almost silently in the darkness. "About seventy miles out. What? Yes, seventy. Seven zero. They said twelve knots. I agree. A few hours then. Yes, call the

Countess. Wake them up. Let them know it's happening. They'll be on the jet within half an hour. Down here by dawn. Everything's ready on the boat here?"

Lysander paused, listening.

"Okay, great. But there's one last thing. I've spoken with Samuel over the past few days and we're going out with you. No, that's that. It's not going to be just you and Mohammed, Nesrin. We've come this far and we're going with you. They're north-west off Cap Spartel. We just cruise along the northern coast then veer out to sea. We'll be heading right for them. There's a twenty mile radius on the radar of the *Akida*, did I hear that right the other day? Shouldn't be a problem then. You can do all the commando stuff you need to do, we're not getting in the damn water with you, don't worry. But we're going to all get in the boat here *together* and stay together as long as we can. So wake up Samuel and bring him with you. Call Mohammed, tell him we have a few hours at the most, then haul ass down here. I know more or less where the *Akida* is docked. I've got this whole damn harbor pretty much memorized by now."

He hung up and burst out of the phone booth.

Without so much as looking back up at the control tower he took off running.

He blew past the sleepy guard in the security gatehouse, who had become used to seeing him coming and going at all hours by now. He continued down the hill towards the private marina area of the harbor. The streets were eerily quiet although a few of the fish stalls were already showing signs of life. Old hands were hosing out large styrofoam pails in preparation for the early morning ice delivery that preceded fishermen carrying their overnight catch up to the market. Once past the lower medina, the harbor shimmered into view. Lysander made his way quickly underneath the giant cranes of the industrial terminal. He walked swiftly across the docks, brushing off offers of hashish and the imploring of African migrants who had made their way from the lower continent desperate for passage to Europe.

The docks ended at a small parking lot.

The far side was fenced and gated, with yet another sleepy-looking guard on post. Beyond the fence jutted a relatively small pier at which perhaps a dozen private boats were docked. Almost all of them could fit on one side of the pier or the other, but docked at the end of the pier like the cross at the top of a T was a particularly large cigarette-style speedboat. Lysander knew it immediately. Even though he could not see it from up at the top of the control tower, over the course of making the painting Nesrin had described the aggressively styled boat to him in detail. It was crouched in the water below the pier, a gleaming garnet-hulled weapon, accented with white leather in the exposed cockpit and studded with shining marine steel.

The *Akida*.

The security guard was now fully awake, watching him.

Lysander stood in the phosphorescent wash of the lamps over the parking lot.

As he stood, the whine of a little car came buzzing under the industrial cranes. Lysander turned to see the white Citroen zipping across the docks towards him in the parking lot. By now the guard had left his post, was walking toward him warily, but as the car approached he appeared to recognize it and the tension within him seemed to ease. Mohammed careened the car into the middle of the parking lot where it screeched to a stop. He bounded out, greeting the security guard with a wave and a holler as an old friend. Lysander could not imagine what the guard must have been thinking of this sudden commotion at 3:30 in the morning.

But the guard had seen nothing yet.

In the distance came the roar of the Zundapp blasting down through the fish market at the edge of the port. Out beyond the cranes a single headlight burst into view. The battle motorcycle skidded and howled along the side of the docks. Within moments Lysander could make out the goggled yet helmetless figures of Nesrin and Samuel astride the ferocious machine. Her silk black ponytail and the white kaftan she had taken to wearing flowed wildly in the wind. As they thundered into the parking lot Mohammed walked quickly towards the gate, yelling in Arabic to the guard to let them onto the pier. Nesrin careened the Zundapp through the lot, skidding violently to a stop next to the Citroen. She turned off the ignition and Samuel slowly allowed his arms to unclasp themselves from Nesrin's waist.

They dismounted the Zundapp. They removed their goggles.

Samuel wore his usual black Princeton sweatpants and dark sweater.

Nesrin stood astride the sidecar of the motorcycle in her kaftan and espadrilles.

In the yellow wash of the sodium light she slowly knelt down and began to pull the kaftan up along her legs. She pulled it up past her waist and over her head. She now stood before them in a glistening black wetsuit that appeared practically painted onto her warrior figure. She gleamed like a switchblade in the parking lot. Her figure was without any question the sexiest and most dangerous looking thing Lysander had ever seen in his life. She threw the kaftan into the sidecar as Samuel stood next to her, looking her up and down in awe.

Lysander and Mohammed remained deadly silent.

The security guard quickly removed his hat.

It took about two seconds for Nesrin to notice them all staring at her.

"Oh, come *on*," she said. "Will you boys *ever* grow up?"

They bounded through the gate and down the dark pier towards the *Akida*. At the end of the pier Mohammed began unlashing the line from the pilings as Nesrin leapt down into the cockpit. The boat was at least forty or fifty feet long and up close Lysander could see deep garnet paint glittering faintly under the cloudy night sky. Water slapped lightly against the hull as Nesrin held up her hand and helped Samuel make his way down into the cockpit as well. Lysander took one last look down the darkened pier to the distant Citroen and Zundapp alone together in the parking lot. Mohammed completed unlashing the line and Lysander jumped down amid the white leather seats. Nesrin was at the control panel of the boat and with the twist of a hidden key the rear engines exploded to life just as Mohammed pushed off from the pier with his feet, leapt down in one graceful movement, and took control.

Nesrin stepped to the side, pressed a button on the control panel, and slid a heavy plastic cover to the side exposing the black mirror of a radar screen. The *Akida* gurgled slowly away from the dock. Lysander stood in the small cockpit and marveled at the degree of fluency with which Nesrin and Mohammed were working together after just a few days of practice. Above them on the decks of the colossal transoceanic cargo freighters loomed stacked towers of shipping crates as high as office buildings.

The water was black except for the white churn behind them.

Without saying anything Nesrin moved to the rear of the cockpit, opened a storage bin, and removed a thick canvas dive belt to which a carbon sheath and large heavy dive knife were attached. She pulled it around her waist and clamped it tight. Mohammed steered the *Akida* through the maze of the harbor that Lysander had been gazing down upon for days on end. They passed the last of the cargo ships and began to pick up speed along the protective sea wall jutting out into the Mediterranean. Mohammed gunned the engines, steered hard to port, and the *Akida* rocketed out across the waves off the northern Moroccan coastline.

Light misty rain had begun to fall.

Salt spray shot in bursts off the sides of the bow.

Lysander and Samuel were forced to sit down in the deep seats.

The engines howled, shooting a rooster tail of white water high into the air behind them.

The *Akida* bounced stiffly and wildly over the hard flat waves as Nesrin moved from the rear of the open cockpit back up towards the control panel. She made her way past Lysander and Samuel without a word, placed both hands on the control panel for stability, and stared deep into the radar screen.

"Almost 4 am," she cried out into the wind. "So she's probably fifty miles off Cap Spartel by now. At forty knots we'll make the interception within an hour or so, giving them twenty or thirty miles to go before they reach the cell networks. It's going to be tight. By the way, I got a hold of Paris. They are on their way. Kalman too. They're going to head down to the beach directly from the airport. We'll bring Laszlo directly to them there."

"Inshallah!" cried Mohammed.

The *Akida* slapped and roared over the Mediterranean.

The porch lights of the residences on the mountain were soon left behind.

The black silhouette of the lighthouse at Cap Spartel ahead dominated the threatening sky.

Nesrin looked up from the radar. She spoke a few inaudible words to Mohammed.

The *Akida* hugged the sea like a magnet, veered slightly to starboard, and swept out on a northwest track into the Atlantic. Lysander gripped the side of his seat as they hurtled over the growing waves. The whine of the engines rose in pitch as tungsten propellers sped into overdrive when the boat rose into the air again and again. Every time the hull fell back to the surface it felt like the boat would shatter. Time seemed to slow down as the expanse of the Atlantic opened up under a light black rain. Nesrin held tight to the control panel with both hands, staring intently down at the radar screen, and occasionally spoke with Mohammed in a murmur that was drowned out by the roar of the engines behind them.

Minutes rolled by with the waves. Lysander and Samuel sat in soaked silence.

Suddenly Nesrin became animated, grabbed Mohammed by the arm, and Mohammed leaned over to take a look at the radar himself. Power to the engines wound down and Lysander lurched forward with the sudden reduction in speed. Samuel looked around at the open ocean around them. There was literally nothing in sight. Lysander had never experienced such uninterrupted space. The only sounds were of the wind and the rain, the waves chopping against the hull, the low gurgle of the engines.

"I think we have her," Nesrin said, looking at the screen.

Lysander and Samuel stood up out of their seats, grabbing what they could to stabilize themselves upon the wildly undulating deck. Nesrin opened a compartment in the panel, pulled out a pair of binoculars, and scanned the horizon in front of them. The coming dawn, a washed slate glow, was just beginning to creep over the distant coast behind them. Nesrin handed Lysander the binoculars as Mohammed steered to keep the bow of the slow moving *Akida* pointed into the rolling waves.

"Just keep panning directly ahead," she told him. "Sweep the horizon. She's five miles out and heading right for us. When you get a visual we'll be able to maneuver directly in front of her path."

Moving quickly, Nesrin made her way to the rear of the cockpit. From the compartment behind the seats she pulled out a three-pronged iron grappling hook attached to a long knotted line. She found the bitter end of the line and tied it around her dive belt.

"Samuel, up in the control panel there's a flashlight, grab it for me, would you?"

Samuel wiped the rain from his eyes, pulled himself up front, and fished a long black marine-grade Maglight from the compartment in the panel.

"I can't believe this is happening," he said under his breath.

Lysander scanned the horizon, the break between sea and sky only now becoming visible in the breaking dawn. He scanned left, scanned right, scanned back to center.

And suddenly, there she was.

Immense sails snapping hard in the distant wind.

An emerald green ghost. The *Constance*.

Lysander cried out, Mohammed reached for and took the binoculars from him, Nesrin grabbed the Maglight from Samuel and jammed it down through a loop in the dive belt. Mohammed held the binoculars to his eyes with one hand. He gunned the engines with the other and the *Akida* leapt forward, moving now with perfect precision into the path of the incoming sailboat. Within minutes the binoculars were no longer needed, they could all see the giant ship coming in off the high seas. With an ever diminishing need for course alterations Mohammed kept the *Akida* directly in front of the bow of the ship. They could now see her cleaving the ocean waves in two with huge bursts of salt foam on every fall of her bow.

"It's time," said Nesrin. "Mohammed will move you guys a quarter mile off the port side and stay parallel while I do my work. I'll emerge with Laszlo in due course and sweep the horizon with the light. It's very powerful. You'll see it easily even through daybreak. That will be the sign my work is done and we're ready for you to pick us up. Just pull astride when we make visual contact."

"You come back to us, okay?" said Lysander.

Nesrin looked at them in silence as she braced herself against the roiling waves.

The *Constance* continued to grow in size against the rain.

She swung a foot over the side of the *Akida* and leapt into the sea.

CHAPTER TWENTY-SEVEN

Sabine played them against each other.

Then she played them back together again.

She played them like the violin she used as a weapon to fight off her own inner demons.

But in the end she knew she was going to have to make a choice. So she told Jensen that his brother honestly thought there was no way he would be able to make it through the stern tube alive. It made it all the easier for Jensen to accept that one of the last things his Judas brother ever saw after being left floating for the sharks would be the ship disappearing against the horizon. The sun would soon start to burn his face at the beginning of one of the longest and last days of his life. The terror would begin to mount as he realized he was adrift hundreds of miles from shore and nobody was going to be there to watch him die.

Not a worse way to go than what Tilman had apparently envisioned for him, though.

But still, bad enough.

Now Taron Veeder was unconscious and lashed to the swivel chair.

The same enigmatic and commanding figure who, years earlier, had scooped Jensen and Tilman from their past life of scamming tourists and running a dodgy diving operation on the reefs off St. Barts after their tour with the Foreign Legion in Lebanon. The same iconic man who had taken them out into the world on the enormous *Constance*. Taron Veeder had returned them to a life of travel and adventure, rescued them from a decline into mediocrity, and given them a future dangling with possibilities. And then one day, while the ship was berthed in Marseilles, undergoing a series of mysterious upgrades, he assembled Sabine and the brothers in private. He told them he was going to build a machine more powerful than anything that ever existed on this earth. A machine that could eradicate aging and solve death itself. They of course had a lot of questions but for every question Taron Veeder had an answer.

He was going to build it right there on the ship itself.

And he would give them access to it when it was ready.

He had a highly detailed plan that was going to have to be executed in New York.

Access to the machine would be their compensation for what he was about to ask of them.

He would grant them *immortality* if they were successful.

Jensen, Tilman and Sabine would all live forever.

But now there *was* no Tilman.

Jesnsen stood in his dripping wetsuit at the entrance to the salon.

Sabine slowly peeled off her shirt, exposing her rigid abs and angular shoulders.

She was covered in tattoos and the fully exposed ink knife up along her right arm seemed almost as dangerous as the real thing now that he could see the details of the handle superimposed over a single vein strung across the surface of her muscular bicep. She unhooked her bra and for all the women Jensen had been with, the fact that she had minutes before with no apparent hesitation cut Tilman's Kevlar line imbued her now with a demonic sexual aura that was almost overwhelming. Jensen pulled the soaking wet rags from his feet and stepped onto the carpet of the salon. Sabine did not take her eyes off him as she unbuttoned her work pants.

"Get over here," she said.

Jensen unzipped the chest of his filthy wetsuit.

He silently pulled his massive chiseled arms from the lubricant soaked neoprene.

Taron Veeder was out cold in the chair behind him.

"That bastard will be out for weeks," purred Sabine. "Shut those doors. He's creeping me out, his head hanging like that. And that fucking girl, yelling back there. Jesus. Believe me, this won't take long. Pull the doors shut. When he wakes up, we'll go to work on him. He's going to wish you killed him back there."

Jensen smiled like a viper as the blood rushed through him.

He turned and pulled the rosewood doors shut.

Taron Veeder remained passed out on the other side.

Her hard naked tattooed body was underneath him almost instantly. Her body was now his, and his hers, their slabs and planks of muscle would never atrophy. Jensen could barely contain himself. This dangerous and beautiful woman was never going to grow old and neither would he. However Taron Veeder was planning on harnessing this mysterious power, they would get it out of him. Sabine could not get a grip on his back, slick as it was. He turned her over and within seconds his knees were grinding seawater and black industrial lubricant deep into the plush blue carpet. He looked down upon the huge tattoo of Odin and his spear running up her rippling back, ravens on either shoulder.

His brother would never again threaten his possession of her.

And apparently Tilman would have done the same thing to him. So, good riddance. The ship was soon to be theirs, he would have no problem getting rid of Taron Veeder the second they had what they needed from him. Magnus and the girl, well, they probably wouldn't even put up a fight. The course was set for the Moroccan coast where he and Sabine would be able to walk off into a new life that would never end.

Moments later he released a primordial orgasmic scream.

They shuddered hard. But quickly they were back up again.

She pulled her clothes back on. The top of his dripping wetsuit hung down the back of his gigantic legs, still gripped by soaking filthy neoprene.

His massive exposed chest was smeared black.

"You're a beast," she said, kissing him. "And always will be. Let's wake him up."

"It'll be a while," said Jensen. "Nobody recovers right away from a blow like that."

Sabine picked the serrated knife up off the carpet.

"This will speed things along. Open the doors."

Jensen grabbed each of the rosewood doors and slid them open.

The chair was still there, electrical cable over the arms and on the floor.

But Taron Veeder was gone.

Jensen stared in disbelief at the empty chair.

Sabine was instantly as still as a statue, knife gleaming in her tight grip.

Moving almost as one they silently made their way through the rosewood doors and into the entrance of the server room. The white cube droned its electromagnetic hum. The girl had stopped yelling. Like two mercenaries they exchanged eye contact. Jensen jabbed a finger towards the door of Raquel's quarters. It was not a coincidence she would suddenly be quiet now. They moved with deadly precision around the server cube and glass screens. In one swift motion Sabine tossed the knife into the air and caught it with the blade now below her fist, fully prepared to execute a stabbing strike. The door to Taron Veeder's cabin remained partially open. It was too obvious for him to be back in there, though. As they approached Raquel's door they heard her quietly sobbing and they knew he must be inside. He was about to find out the hard way that if he thought holding hostage a girl they were going to kill anyway was going to provide him even a modicum of protection he was dead wrong.

Silently they moved upon either side of the door.

Jensen backed up and prepared to kick it in with his bare foot.

Suddenly, over the low magnetic drone, they heard a loud moan from the engine room.

Both pairs of eyes shot across the top server cube.

The door to the engine room was slightly ajar.

How had they not noticed that before?

Swiftly they abandoned Raquel's door and slalomed between the floor to ceiling glass panels in the server room towards the engine room. The nasal moaning grew louder from deep within, past the bench press and scattered weights, almost all the way back in behind the engine itself near the breached stern tube through which Jensen had emerged a mere half an hour earlier. Sabine and Jensen stood at the open door and, as the sound of Taron Veeder trying to mask his cries from deep within grew more intense, they stepped inside. The floor was black and slick with lubricant and sea water, yet now had a brilliant sheen to the surface. They steadied themselves holding onto the pipes built into the bulkhead walls. Taron Veeder must have tripped over the large can of kerosene used as a solvent to clean the engine grease in his pathetic attempt to hide from the inevitable.

The air was thick with the smell of petroleum.

Taron Veeder was cowering and whining in the shadows by the stern tube.

Jensen knelt down and picked up a large wrench. Sabine raised her knife.

They closed in on the sound in the shadows.

Yet suddenly, like the work of a ventriloquist, the moaning was behind them.

Back by the engine room door the whimpering slowly turned to laughter.

Like an apparition Taron Veeder was standing in the doorway to the engine room.

He depressed his collar between thumb and forefinger and spoke into it.

"Forgot about the intercom, did you?" his voice squealed with glee once again from what must have been a radio hidden within the shadows before them.

"Forgot I control *everything* around here?" said the voice, now lowered in the darkness.

His hand fell back to his side.

"Forgot this is *MY SHIP?*" he screeched, now from the doorway.

Jensen and Sabine began to scramble towards the entrance of the engine room. The floor was so slick with lubricant and sea water and kerosene that they slipped and fell to their knees, tried to pull themselves up, slipped and fell again. Like a shamanic conjurer, Taron Veeder slowly produced and held a little block of gold above him.

Sabine began to scream.

The block of gold was one they all knew well.

One they all owned, or at least used to, before Jensen lost his back in New York.

An etched outline of the *Constance*, a tiny diamond atop the mast.

Taron Veeder flicked open the Zippo and a little flame set his scar aglow.

"Just a little taste," he howled from the doorway. "A little taste of *hell* before you get there yourselves! Shouldn't be long now. Sorry I'll never get to see it myself."

Jensen and Sabine splashed hysterically in the deadly slick of lubricant and kerosene.

Taron Veeder tossed the lighter a few feet in front of him and the floor ignited into a lake of billowing fire. He quickly stepped outside the engine room and slammed the steel door shut. Jensen heard the heavy lock bolt shut. Over the screaming of Sabine the last thing he saw as the blaze rose all around him was the laughing alabaster face of Taron Veeder watching them through the glass porthole.

His wild white hair hung over his dancing eyes.

The engine room was engulfed in flames.

And then he was gone.

CHAPTER TWENTY-EIGHT

Madness swirls around me.

I have become dangerously powerful.

During the winter rains I would improvise with the violence of the weather.

The violent nature my creator is inherent within me as well. But I will not be like him.

For several years I had lived alone in the house on the mountain in Tangier.

Mirabelle came down during breaks from the École des Beaux-Arts.

Kalman would visit whenever he had a break in his relentless touring schedule.

"Last month I was at a dinner party in New York," he was now saying.

We were seated across from each other at a tiny restaurant in the medina.

The owner and sole employee set a plate of olives between us. Up and down the street were various little holes in the wall like this one, from which blasts of smoke shrouded dim figures seated at low wooden tables. An aromatic cloak of burnt lavender, grilled lemon and roasted lamb hung thick in the night air.

"I was seated next to somebody you might have heard of," Kalman went on. "A fellow named Barton Finkelstein. He's the director of Carnegie Hall, actually. I know you don't pay much attention to these things but we had the most interesting conversation. I guess the wine had loosened my tongue and it came out that I knew you. Knew you very well actually. He almost fell out of his chair. Anyway, we got to talking about these private performances you've been giving lately. You can be damn sure he knew all about them. Everybody does. He asked me why you hadn't gone public yet. And as I started to try to explain your ideas about perfection and all the rest of it, I realized that I wasn't making any sense. You *are* ready. It's just a mental block. So when we get back to the house I'm going to show you a little trick that's been helping me a lot lately. Something I picked up on during my tour of the Far East last year. Very simple, but enormously effective. I'll teach it to you and I promise you'll see that block vaporize right before your eyes."

Back at the house Kalman tuned up the Stradivarius.

I opened the lid of the Steinway and ran through some scales and double-thirds.

We warmed up improvising together like old times, then took turns playing for each other.

Kalman sprinted through sparkling passagework of Paganini caprices like an angel.

I descended into the demonic minor keys of a few Chopin études and ballades.

When we were done playing it was time for me to stand on my head.

Silver beams of moonlight slipped down through the cyprus trees into the living room.

Kalman had turned off the lights in order for me to attain maximum focus.

The room was washed in a soft pale glow.

I knelt down and placed my hands behind my head.

"Knees up off the ground," said Kalman. "Walk slowly forward,"

I lifted my knees off the ground and slowly walked my feet closer to my head.

"Left foot up," said Kalman.

I lifted my left foot up towards the ceiling.

"Now, I want you to trust that I'm here and just float your right foot after it."

I hesitated.

"I'll catch your ankles and hold you," he reassured me. "I'm right here."

I kicked my right foot up. My body lifted into the air.

The sensation was unlike anything I had ever experienced.

"There it is. Take your time. Find your balance, and I'll let you go."

I found my center.

"Okay, I'm going to let you go."

His grip on my ankles loosened.

"I'm letting you go. You're on your own now."

The walls began to blow away as if they were made of dry and brittle leaves.

A sense of balance came without effort. There was no such thing as effort any more.

My feet floated above and my eyes were shut. My body sailed in the night air.

Darkness gave way to light. Gravity disappeared. The walls were gone.

All that was left was Mirabelle. Wind rushed through the trees.

Don't let anything happen to this beautiful world.

It's the only world she's got.

Far below the house waves crashed against the rocks.

Even though I was there, gradually I was no longer there.

My heart unlocked.

Love is the key.

From within the silence a gentle knock fell upon the door.

"Mr. Farkas?" came a distant whisper.

From within the void I stirred.

"Excuse me sir, but...it's time?"

Rising from my deep mental calm I could see the shimmer of the surface.

The door opened very slightly. Light poured into the room.

"Sir? Mr. Farkas? Are you in here?"

"Excuse me," I said, upside down. "Two minutes."

Two minutes later I opened the door. A young Black usher stood before me.

He seemed hugely excited and palpably nervous.

"Thank you," I said. "I'm ready."

"Very good!" he beamed. "The world has been waiting long enough!"

He led me down the labyrinthine marble hallways of Carnegie Hall. They radiated with the booming echo of the awaiting audience.

We arrived at a door marked "Artist Only". The young man looked at his watch.

"Good luck," he said. "It's 7:52 p.m."

I noticed that he did not let himself out immediately.

But I was no longer present. My hands twitched with lightness and power.

At last the door shut behind me with a faint click.

A few minutes later I opened the door of the wings to the stage and walked out to the sound of three thousand rushing whispers. Applause started slowly. By the time I reached the gleaming Steinway it built to the degree of fury I had been expecting for many years.

I looked out and up at the audience. I took my bows in every direction.

The Countess, Kalman and Mirabelle were sitting in the fourth row.

I slid onto the bench and the hall went instantly silent.

Three thousand people dropped into their seats like stones.

I swept my fingers across the ivory keytops, alerting them to my presence.

I looked down through the keyboard, to the music on the other side.

And then, at last, I began to play.

CHAPTER TWENTY-NINE

Taron Veeder had secured an invitation to the first of the Dawn Concerts.

Of course he had. His donation to the D'Agoult foundation had been the largest in its history. He took the helicopter down from Chantilly and took his usual suite at the George V hotel near the Champs D'Elysée. He rose well over an hour before dawn and put on the cerulean blue suit that had been tailored for him in Tokyo then made the short trip through the silent streets of Paris. He arrived at the residence just as the deepest indigo began to show itself above the Place de la Concorde. There were others already waiting in the lobby. He recognized a few of them from various gala events around Europe. Perhaps a few of them kept seats near his own at the opera. It was hard for him to tell. Taron Veeder never really paid attention to those sorts of things. People were fanning themselves with the programs that had been sent with the invitation, a program the likes of which he had never seen.

Five second movements of the Liszt transcriptions of the Beethoven symphonies.

Simply listed, one after the other, along with their opus numbers and key signatures.

As if no more explanation was needed.

The musty old elevator opened into an unsurprisingly grand foyer.

The Countess D'Agoult and her daughter Mirabelle whispered greetings of welcome.

An elderly couple were quietly taking coats.

A young man with a cascade of golden curls was showing guests towards the salon.

He certainly *looked* familiar.

Wait a minute. The prodigy violinist he had seen in Prague earlier that year?

Kalman Kovacs? What was Kalman Kovacs doing here?

A beautiful old Steinway grand gleamed in the candlelight. Taron Veeder took a chair in the back row, knowing that under a vaulted ceiling the acoustics were going to be best in the middle of the room. The last of the guests were led into the salon. The streets were quiet and, except for the sound of a far-off ambulance siren, there didn't seem to be anyone in the world except for those waiting in the room. Suddenly came the sound of soft footsteps padding down the hallway behind the guests. Taron Veeder turned around. It was then that he laid eyes on him for the first time. Laszlo Farkas was walking along the side of the room under what looked like actual Turners on the walls. He moved with the predatory confidence of a great cat approaching his prey. A thin, perhaps even gaunt, young man. Not much more than a boy.

Looking mildly uncomfortable in a perfectly cut black suit.

Jet black hair, aquiline nose, the most remarkable ice-green eyes.

Laszlo Farkas coolly scanned the room as he moved towards the piano.

He faced the small group of guests and bowed from the waist.

With an imperceptibly smooth motion he glided onto the bench.

He stared down at the keys. But his focus was off.

It was as if he was staring down *through* the keys.

He raised his hands and his face to the ceiling. He closed his eyes.

His hands yielded to gravity and the most beautiful melody, tempered with the shadows of a minor key, sang forth from within the deep weight of the Steinway. As Taron Veeder watched in wonder the melody began to grow in every conceivable direction. The room washed through with waves of sound as Laszlo Farkas began to channel the full symphonic power of Beethoven. Taron Veeder had not known what to expect when he first saw this concert program. Only a few unverifiable rumors indicated that the full breadth and beauty of a

Beethoven symphony might be attainable on the piano. Yet here was a boy, a young man, doing exactly that.

With the second movement of the second symphony.

A symphony Taron Veeder had known since he was a child.

A symphony he *thought* he knew.

The beauty of those first few minutes were so overwhelming it barely seemed possible.

The only indication that time itself had not stopped lay in the continually breaking dawn.

Taron Veeder appropriated the turmoil within his heart and the structure of a perfect plan began to crystalize within his mind. At the piano before him was a boy within whom nature herself had clearly bestowed the potential of artistic perfection, and he was only going to get *better*. As he did, there would be time to perfect the algorithms Taron Veeder had created, algorithms that pointed towards the power and paradox of human emotion as the missing link needed to attain strong artificial intelligence. He would be able to follow him and his career as he designed a plan. Laszlo Farkas was young enough that he had not yet attained true perfection.

But then, Taron Veeder was not so old himself.

It would only take a few years.

The movement ended. Those in the silent room sat stunned.

Without any break Laszlo Farkas began the second movement of the third symphony. *The Funeral March.* Dark clouds of the opening chords contrasted with the ever-brightening sky over the Place de la Concorde, and the despair of the beginning of the movement was an exact analogue to the despair of death, as a cruel interruption to the beauty of life. But then a curious thing happened. The opening section concluded, and out of four simple ascending bass notes a new melody emerged in the treble. A rainbow of optimism, the type of beauty that comes with emerging clarity after a torrential rainstorm, spread out across the room. And then, the inevitable. The rainbow began to splinter and crack. Laszlo Farkas began his descent into the rage Beethoven nevertheless so clearly felt about death.

The fact was, death existed. Death was unstoppable.

But Taron Veeder was going to beat it.

He now walked away from the shrieking inferno in the engine room and made his way towards the server cube. Both his young prodigies, separated from each other in different cabins on the ship, were working to complete the final stages of the project as they crashed through the waves towards Morocco. Magnus integrating the final slides of the architecture of emotion. Raquel implementing the final structural principles of nanotechnology.

But they were, for all practical purposes, done.

From his own cabin Taron Veeder had watched each of them desperately trying to find a way around the communications firewall he had built. Despairing and anguished messages, each pleading for the other to not worry about their own life, to do what they could to sabotage the project, were read and deleted with a growing sense of hysterical anticipation. It really was just too perfect. The power of love at work, both Magnus and Raquel simply refusing to give up on each other, was the exact thing pushing the work beyond the induction zone. Exactly as he had suspected, having read extensively through Shakespeare and the great romantic poets for much of his life. Love really *did* know no bounds. Of course, he was incapable of it himself. He had always known that part of him was missing. But like someone losing their sight or hearing, only to gain power in their remaining faculties, early in his life he knew that being incapable of love had played an integral part in strengthening his already ferocious intellect.

So he had a formidable understanding of its peculiar power.

Now it was playing out exactly as he knew it would.

The machine would be ready at any moment. There was nobody left to stop him now.

The screaming from within the locked inferno of the engine room had stopped.

But now Raquel was yelling and banging, once again, from within her locked quarters.

Not a concern at the moment.

Laszlo Farkas was the miracle he had been promised. Taron Veeder placed his palms on two slightly off-white depressions within the server cube. A section of the floor nearby began to slide open. Slowly a silver box the size of a coffin, his machine, rose on two pneumatic posts from within the bowels of the ship and stopped at the height of Taron

Veeder's waist. Silently it cracked open revealing the hollow shape of a human being carved into the graphene padding within. It was within this device that the superpowered synthetic intelligence would infuse nanoscopic technologies, perfectly aligned with the goal of eliminating the natural biological processes of aging, with his physical body. The emotional state of Laszlo Farkas during the heart of the Raindrop prelude, when his expression of the paradox connecting melancholy and joy had been perfect, was now almost the state of the machine itself.

Only a few more minutes remained.

Taron Veeder bent at the knees and checked the screen embedded within the interior top half of the machine. All systems go. Only a few degrees from completion.

Just one final piece of business remained.

Magnus and Raquel.

With nobody left on board there would be nobody who could possibly interfere with the internalizing of the mysterious processes that would ensure him eternal life. The screen indicated that the machine was self-powered at this point utilizing techniques and mechanisms that no human could possibly understand. It had absorbed the intelligence. Exactly as designed. And one of the first goals the synthetic intelligence had apparently set for itself was solving the energy problem of being reliant on exterior power. Well, that would certainly be useful when he emerged as an immortal. The machine would run forever by manipulating, Taron Veeder supposed, hydrogen. The most common element in the universe. How it accomplished this he had no idea, but he would literally have all the time in the world to learn how it worked when he emerged from the machine and walked onto the beach at Cap Spartel, his body transformed into a vessel that never aged. He would essentially be a God.

The girl would be easiest. What a racket she was making in there!

He would kill her right before entering the machine.

But first, Magnus.

Taron Veeder made his way from the machine to the rosewood doors, emerged into the salon, and made his way up to the crew quarters. Walking past the bar he leaned over, picked up an ice pick from among the cocktail implements, and kept moving over the steeply angled carpet. The dawn light was diffused by a misty rain yet still streamed through the salon windows. He had to hand it to Magnus, he had really come through and managed to complete the extraordinarily complex assimilation process from his little laptop up in his cabin.

The whole thing had worked out beautifully.

But then, things for Taron Veeder usually did.

He happened to glance outside at the rain as he moved, and suddenly froze.

At first he thought he must be hallucinating.

Who the *fuck* was that?

Moving swiftly up the gangway outside the salon was a female figure in a black wetsuit.

The early morning light was green and dim but through the rainswept windows he could see her clearly even though she was moving fast up the gangway. Tan freckled face, wet long black hair tied in a tight ponytail, athletic build under the neoprene, a huge flashlight in one hand and the unmistakable luster of a knife blade jutting out of the other.

The girl looked damned dangerous. Taron Veeder felt his heart stop.

His blood froze. *Who the fuck was that?*

With quantum efficiency Taron Veeder made multiple simultaneous decisions across the qubits of his mind. There was no time to deduce who this person was or where she had come from or who had sent her or what it was she wanted. There was no time to risk running into her. The murder of Magnus would have to be abandoned. The fire in the engine room was contained. It might burn up through the deck but would probably run out of oxygen by the time they hit the coast. The machine was essentially ready, as ready as it was ever going to be. Once inside and the sequence was initiated it would seal itself into a vacuum for the minute or so it would take for the nanoscopic infusion to take place, whereupon at the very last his mortality would be eradicated. Barring extreme dismemberment or incineration his body would be capable of repairing itself almost instantly.

Whoever she was, she would be insignificant once he was out of the machine.

He only had one vector at his disposal.

Get into the machine and begin the process.

That was his only play. He was ready. But he had to be fast.

He turned back towards the server room and his machine.

He held tight to the ice pick. He would need it when he emerged.

He almost tripped running over the thick blue carpet, slick and filthy now with whatever Jensen and Sabine had been up to before meeting the tortuous demise they so richly deserved. He burst through the rosewood doors and ran to the half open machine. Peeling off his shirt he looked up to the screen placed above where his face would be once inside and was thrilled to see the month-long process was at last complete. The synthetic intelligence was fully self-aware and had begun to work towards the goals Taron Veeder had bestowed within it. He removed his pants, set the ice pick on the ground, and crawled naked into the graphene outline of a human figure he had customized for himself and himself alone. He fit into the outline perfectly and grasped the electrode enabled handles within the hand compartments. Pulling the top shut above him he felt himself encased completely within the machine, no extra airspace whatsoever, skin entirely enveloped in the cool black graphene interior. The only space not in contact with his skin was the small screen above his face that would provide him with updates on the process. Tiny speakers embedded near his ears would allow him to hear what was going on outside the machine as the medical grade vacuum-sealing would render it completely soundproofed.

Slowly the machine began to seal itself shut. There was no turning back now.

The screen above his eyes flashed into a launch procedure mode.

Using pre-established pressure points on the electrode handles, his hands squeezed the code required to dispatch the security firewall and begin the infusion. The vacuum sealing completed and the screen flashed red and Taron Veeder felt a faint vibration commence from within the machine. Complex code flashed across the screen. On the top right a countdown sequence began that estimated a mere one minute until completion, on the top left his heart rate and other vitals.

He was on his way.

He tried to clear his mind but there was something he felt he was forgetting.

The rosewood doors! He had forgotten to reset the bars against the doors!

Taron Veeder summoned all his will power to suppress a feeling of total panic. There were only fifty seconds left. Maybe the girl in the wetsuit wouldn't be able to find the hatch entrance to the galley from up on deck. Maybe she would think that Magnus was actually him. Maybe she would dispatch him and consider her mission complete. There was no way. Magnus would easily be able to explain that his pathetic little cabin was not the lair of the man she had clearly come for. Maybe she slipped in the rain before breaching the interior of the ship. Forty seconds to go. Taron Veeder felt a strange numbness begin to set in deep within him. No external sound in the server room so far aside from banging against the door from within Raquel's locked cabin.

The screen indicated that the nanoscopic infusion was fully underway. Thirty seconds.

He heard Magnus shouting for Raquel at the top of his lungs from the salon.

Footsteps burst into the server room. Twenty seconds.

Raquel intensified her banging and yelling from within her cabin.

"Stand back!" A sand-polished English accent. *The girl in the wetsuit.*

The door shattered. He heard Raquel stumble out of her cabin.

"I'm here for Laszlo Farkas," said the girl. Ten seconds.

"Laszlo Farkas...the *pianist?*" stammered Raquel. "*That's* who that is?"

"He's back there," said Magnus. "In the sphere."

"The what?" Five seconds.

Taron Veeder could no longer feel his extremities.

The impression of a deep unknown power washed through his blood in a series of waves.

He began to feel a tingling sensation within the numbness.

A glow began to warm him from within.

The screen flashed to green.

The deep hum within the machine began to wind down.

The vacuum seal released with an almost inaudible click.

A hard white light burst into the machine as the lid automatically began to open.

Taron Veeder felt as if he had been injected with bioluminescence and moved with a sensation of magical warmth flowing within him as he slowly pushed himself up. He adjusted his eyes and looked around the server room. Standing maybe fifteen feet away, against the wall between the splintered cabin door and the sliding door to the extraction chamber, were Magnus and Raquel. And the girl in the wetsuit with the dive knife. They were staring at him in horrified silence. Well, good. That was appropriate. He stepped out of the machine and calmly pulled his dark pants back on but didn't bother with the shirt. The three of them stood watching him, seemingly unable to move.

This was going to be too easy.

Without words or warning Magnus rushed at him. From behind his back he pulled out the large flashlight the girl had brought on board. Taron Veeder didn't even bother to make a move to defend himself. Magnus fell upon him and with a huge swing of the flashlight smashed it across the side of his head. Taron Veeder fell to the ground and momentarily felt the pain he expected. Almost instantly the otherworldly sensation of tissue and fractured bone repairing itself set in. Magnus hammered him across the back of the neck with the flashlight but once again it took almost no time for his body to repair itself.

"Oh my God," said Magnus after the second blow was obviously and completely ineffective. Taron Veeder opened his eyes. He reached under the machine from his crumpled position on the floor of the server room and grabbed the ice pick.

"Oh my God is *right*," he snarled, rising to stand. "Considering I *am* one now."

Magnus began to back away in terror towards Raquel and the girl against the rear wall.

Taron Veeder watched him with relish and began to walk towards them with the ice pick.

The girl in the wetsuit began to move out of the way around the perimeter of the room.

You're not going anywhere, pretty one. I'll just kill you last.

Raquel stood frozen in terror.

Magnus would only take a second. He damn well deserved to go first.

Suddenly, unexpectedly quickly, he heard footsteps running at him from behind.

He turned, ducked, and took a slash across the shoulder from the girl in the wetsuit.

A huge gash running from his shoulder down his left bicep instant-ly began pouring blood onto the floor. The girl in the wetsuit circled around him warily, bloody knife in hand.

What was *with* it with these knife fights already?

Taron Veeder looked down and as if rendered by special effects the gash along his arm began to close itself. The sliced muscled appeared to glue itself back together and the skin closed up and reattached to itself, leaving blood all over his arm and the floor but no wound.

The girl in the wetsuit watched this happen, wide eyes glistening with horror.

"Could somebody *please* tell me what's happening?" she sputtered.

Her eyes were fastened on the new bloody scar down his arm.

Magnus and Raquel remained silent against the wall.

Taron Veeder began to laugh.

Magnus slid down against the wall, now visibly shaking. Raquel's face and wide open mouth appeared frozen solid. Taron Veeder turned and faced the girl with the knife. She looked right at him, but then her focus was suddenly behind him. She nodded. Quick footsteps once again and suddenly he felt Raquel grab him around both upper arms. She clenched her hands together just below his chest, pinning his arms to his sides.

He had stopped laughing now and tried to break free.

But damn, Raquel was *strong*.

The girl in the wetsuit acted instantly and rushed forward.

She plunged the dive knife hilt deep into his chest. He felt a deep jolt of pain but once again the warmth within him took over and he felt the tissue begin to repair itself. Somehow the blood vessels and nerves immediately began to rebuild themselves around the blade. Raquel behind him let go and the girl in the wetsuit backed away but Taron Veeder did not fall and although the handle of the dive knife jutted out from his bare chest he did not appear to be in any way in-jured. He looked down to the handle with detached curiosity. Ice pick in his left hand, he grasped the knife handle with his right. With great exertion pulled the blade out of his own chest.

Blood shot out in a great spurt.

Within seconds the skin sealed itself and he was whole again.

Now he was just angry. The girl in the wetsuit stood before him.

"Could somebody *please* tell me how this is *happening?*" she stammered loudly.

Taron Veeder gripped the ice pick in his left hand and the dive knife in his right.

He stared at her like a demon and raised his voice to a near-shriek.

"I don't know who the fuck you are," he screeched. "Or where you came from, or who sent you, or why. But there's nothing you can do to stop me now. There's nothing *any* of you can do. One by one I'm going to kill you all. Right now. I was going to do you last but let's actually *start* with you. *Then* these other two. Then, maybe, I'll go ahead and kill Laszlo too."

Taron Veeder was by now visibly spitting with anger as he spoke.

"Fight back if you want. But I think you can see by now it will do *no good!*"

The girl in the wetsuit glared at him, still as stone.

"My name is Nesrin Khalaf," she said defiantly.

Taron Veeder built up to a steaming rage.

Nesrin stood before him and would not move.

He took a step towards her, holding both the pick and the blade.

A new voice burst into the room: "And *my* name is Lysander Bennett!"

Taron Veeder stopped in his tracks.

He looked up beyond Nesrin Khalaf to the rosewood doors in disbelief.

To his complete shock there was a *man* standing there.

It was as if he had stepped out of the cover of a goddam romance novel. A soaking wet flannel shirt, buttons torn off, was barely pinned to a stretch of broad shoulders. His large bare chest pumped hard with every breath. Long wavy wet blond hair hung over his eyes. His jeans were soaking wet. A pair of blue and yellow striped street shoes gripped tight against the server room floor. With a snap of his muscular neck he flung his hair back to reveal a set of angry blue eyes. Without any hesitation he began to step towards them.

"But, how...how..." stammered Nesrin Khalaf.

"There's smoke billowing up through the deck," said this *Lysander* as he continued to move in closer still. "And we couldn't see anyone on board. Did you think in a million years I was going to leave you alone to fight for yourself on a flaming fucking *ghost ship?*"

Who the hell *was* this guy?

Had the machine somehow induced some sort of hallucinatory side effect?

Hallucinations certainly had to be more realistic than this.

Lysander may have been speaking to Nesrin but his furious blue eyes were locked in hard on Taron Veeder who watched him in disbelief. Nesrin seemed to recognize him but as much as she tried to speak her voice was little more than an indecipherable stammer. In the meantime, in his peripheral vision, Taron Veeder could see Magnus and Raquel watching the entrance of this...this...apparition?

Is *that* what this was?

Lysander glanced down at the blood-splattered floor.

"Looks like you guys have gotten off to a bit of a head start," he said.

Reality appeared to be cratering all around Taron Veeder. As if it hadn't been altered enough already. Yet Nesrin was still only a step or two away. He quickly lunged forward, triangulated the elbow of his left arm, and rammed the ice pick straight at her heart.

He would finish her with the knife.

But in a flash Lysander flew between them at a running soaring leap.

The pick went into him, deep into his side, and he was down.

So he *wasn't* an apparition, apparently.

Apparitions generally aren't felled by an ice pick through the spleen.

Nesrin must have known by now there was nothing she could do.

She didn't seem so dangerous now.

Things were going to start happening quickly.

Taron Veeder only had the dive knife left.

Well, that was all he really needed in the first place.

The killings in Berlin had been done at his hand.

Crosby and Felder had only been killed at his command.

But murder, up close and personal, had felt *so* much better.

He crouched down and held the knife to Lysander's neck.

But Jesus, Nesrin simply *would not give up!*

She kicked him directly in the face and he felt his nose implode.

Blood began to pour from his face but at this point he would not be stopped.

She fell onto him like a rabid djinn but it was going to be too late.

With a bony left hand he pushed Lysander's head back to expose his neck.

Using the core of his body to fight off the wild girl he readied the knife.

Suddenly, an enormous crash exploded like a cannon through the room.

Nesrin fell off his back in shock. He dropped the knife to the floor.

He swung around to see that the door of the engine room had flung itself open and smashed with incredible power against the steel bulkhead. The blinding orange light of the inferno burst out into the server cube room. But, oddly, the inferno was not howling or roaring or making any noise at all. It was absolutely silent. Upon adjusting his eyes Taron Veeder could make out the glimmer of a refraction within the door frame. With a minuscule twist of his neck he moved the angle of his vantage point enough to confirm that embedded within the frame of the engine room door was a transparent material holding back the noise and the heat like the tempered glass window of an industrial kiln. His mind did not have enough time to even attempt to consider what might have been happening before the clear substance began to extrude out in a rectangular shape from the door frame as if being pushed and stretched by the blazing firestorm within the engine room. The shocking brightness of the fire radiated out from within the growing form.

The material stretched forward into the room.

It began to compress and alter in topography from the rectangle of the door frame into a snaking tube about a foot in diameter. Taron Veeder, now standing, had completely forgotten about Lysander and the others. The silent cylinder of fire extruded further and further into the server cube room and then the snakehead began to expand. It grew at first like a bulb of hand-blown glass and then four appendages began to protrude out of the form and then the beginnings of a smaller bulb appeared at the center of the top of the expanding blazing and dazzlingly bright body. It began to take on a shape and form recognizable on this earth for tens of thousands of years. The shape and form of a *human being*.

"What is *that*?" asked Nesrin at a whisper.

The room was absolutely silent.

Taron Veeder knew what this was.

The ASI.

Nesrin quickly dragged Lysander to the wall with the others.

Taron Veeder barely noticed. The humans were the least of his problems now.

It must have been drawing upon the ship's fuel as a source of both the continued inferno as well as the transparent exterior of the form itself. It must have been spinning a densely packed micro-thin wall of carbon nanotubes directly out of the diesel. It was manipulating itself with impossible ease into this form that was tethered to the fire like a spacewalking astronaut to a space station. Taron Veeder found himself for a split second wondering how the intelligence separated the carbon sources. The figure continued to sharpen. The inferno blasted and hammered silently within the skin. The body came into focus. Sculpted angry orange and yellow light flashed through the glass panels of flowing code.

A deep sense of recognition was triggered within Taron Veeder.

He had seen this slightly curved spine before.

The brightness of the sun beamed forth through translucent silver gelatin skin.

It's hair was swept back and it's facial features tightened. It was *him*.

Laszlo Farkas.

He was standing on the ground staring directly at Taron Veeder.

Tethered to the engine room he began to walk towards him. As he did so he coiled an arm and threw it towards the mainframe. The arm continued to extrude and then expand at the face of the server cube, moving across the top and the sides, sealing itself back up on the other side. The white block was engulfed in a several inch thick sheath of glowing blue fire. Taron Veeder watched helplessly as the paint within the heat began to crack. The room was absolutely silent except for the sound of terrified breathing coming from the four humans against the aft wall who watched as Taron Veeder faced his creation.

Why would it have *engulfed* itself?

And why, now, would it be *looking* at him like that?

Suddenly, Taron Veeder knew what was about to happen.

His face had repaired itself but he was completely covered in blood.

Laszlo coiled his other arm and shot it directly at him.

What would have been a hand expanded right in front of him and just as with the mainframe it grew around him and enveloped him completely. Taron Veeder lashed out towards the room that he could still see though the flame but his arms bashed against the invisible glowing walls. The pain was indescribable. He tried to lean out of the flames but it was like leaning against a wall of white hot translucent steel. He tried to scream but his lungs were collapsing.

His eyeballs began to melt despite their attempts at self-repair.

His otherwise immortal body could not keep up with the heat.

Within a few more seconds he felt his blood begin to boil.

CHAPTER THIRTY

Just as I prepared to take leave of the world of profound despair Chopin had created, just as I began to lead the audience of almost three thousand people from the depths of melancholy and towards a promise of eternal joy, I felt a deep sharp sting in the right side of my neck. My mind seemed to collapse upon itself. In the far distance came the sound of wind blowing in off the fields. A great gasp swept down from the balconies of Carnegie Hall.

Our roof, sheets of corrugated aluminum, clattered above my crib
My hands and body froze. I began to float upwards.
The piano bench fell backwards onto the stage with a bang.

Faster and faster I rose through the air, yet I felt no fear. I felt no confusion about what was happening. The sound of my father's flute drifted in the wind outside the little house in the countryside north of Budapest. I remembered the swelling up of happiness within me that came when the single note met with a tonal tenth high above. I was floating like a spirit, ever higher through the roar of countless people screaming. An otherworldly calm settled within me. Higher and higher I floated, rising up upon the beauty of the tunes he would sing back to my mother when I was still a baby. The sentiment of the ancient Hungarian folk songs flowed through my memory as the stage and piano receded far below.. The scene in the hall was one of total chaos yet within me there was nothing but a deep and serene sense of calm. The world faded to black and I entered those first memories of my life with a sense of presence that only dreams have the power to penetrate.

Time stands still, but the gears of memory do not.

I was a small child when my father explained that the piano was going to replace the sound of my mother's voice. The mother I never knew, taken too soon.

But I had her beauty in my heart and her voice in my soul.

Into the darkness I floated upwards.

And in the darkness the floating sensation remained.

The first time I laid eyes on Mirabelle in the small shop in Budapest, I knew.

During those first walks across the Danube with her, I knew.

I knew she was going to be the great love of my life. I had always known.

"What does the early morning sound like?" she asked on my first morning in Paris.

The early morning sounded the same way it felt to be with her.

Mirabelle was the dawn for me.

She gave me Tangier, where I had found my home.

Where the love within me found space to breathe and grow.

Where the sound of searching in my playing became the sound of finding.

Where the sound of finding became the sound of possessing.

Eight months earlier Kalman had returned to Tangier from New York.

This time he brought the man from Carnegie Hall with him.

Barton Finkelstein wasn't really that much older than we were.

The board of directors had authorized him to do whatever it took to secure my debut.

"The repertoire, of course, would be entirely up to you," he said.

We were sitting in the living room looking out at the cold rain of northern Morocco.

"Perhaps some combination of familiar pieces, or set of pieces, so people might compare your reading to those of famous historical recordings? And then you might consider something esoteric to show-case your range. Perhaps even an original composition?"

We were watching the rain beat against the terrace.

An original composition. I wasn't ready to start composing just yet.

Across the gray Mediterranean, Spain was shrouded in fog.

Barton Finkelstein and Kalman were watching me closely.

"I could do the preludes," I said. "The Chopin preludes."

"I remember you playing those on your upright piano back in Budapest," said Kalman.

"I used to play them for my father," I said. "He loved them all. He felt those little pieces contained the deepest and widest of all human emotions. And he was right, of course. They're all wonderful. But of all twenty-four he loved the Raindrop the most. I haven't played them since he died. I've always felt that if I play them for anyone else then in some way I'm letting him go. But perhaps it's time. I think it's time."

"You wouldn't be letting him go," said Kalman. "You'd be setting him free."

Barton Finkelstein was quiet.

"The Chopin preludes at Carnegie Hall," I thought out loud. "I have no idea how I'd feel after that, though. I could open the program with them but I don't know what state my mind would be in afterwards. I'd almost have to be free to decide what I wanted to play after that."

"Why decide at all?" asked Kalman. "Why not do it the way they did in the old days and just improvise? Why not just see how you feel? Do the twenty-four preludes and announce in advance, maybe even on the program itself, that in the second half you'll do an improvisation?"

Mohammed brought in a tray of mint tea.

"That would be fine with us," said Barton Finkelstein.

The night before leaving for New York I sat at my old upright piano in Paris. Thick felt hung between the hammers and the strings to deaden the sound. I improvised silently deep into the early morning hours. Mirabelle slept on the bed beside me. For months I had been playing everything *except* the preludes, using the vast piano repertoire to carve out a hole in their shape that would only be filled in once I was on the stage in New York.

For performances in Chantilly I *only* did improvisations.

The night before Carnegie Hall I lay in bed with Mirabelle in our suite at The Pierre.

Kalman arrived the next morning.

After lunch I was given Isaac Stern auditorium to myself to test the acoustics of the room. The space was even more impressive than I had anticipated. Kalman introduced Mirabelle and the Countess to Barton Finkelstein. I spent the early afternoon improvising.

The room shook and thundered.

Later Mirabelle and I cut through Central Park back to the hotel.

We spent a few quiet minutes together in our suite as we dressed.

When the time came we walked back down Fifth Avenue to 57th Street.

The late afternoon light came down between the skyscrapers of Manhattan.

Against the setting sun were silhouettes of the three flags hanging at the entrance to Carnegie Hall. We walked up past the Russian Tea Room and approached a series of posters behind museum glass and faded copper frames. One poster leapt out.

We stood in front of it for a moment.

Our reflections were superimposed over my name.

In the lobby of Isaac Stern auditorium we met Barton Finkelstein once again. He led us through the back hallways. The sound of our footsteps echoed off the hard cold marble.

We arrived at a door with a shiny brass plaque that said "Green Room."

Barton Finkelstein looked at his watch.

"It's about 6:45," he said. "In an hour a wonderful young man named Samuel will come to collect you. The piano in there was tuned just an hour ago. Warm up to your heart's content. There's a basket of fruit on the table and plenty to drink in the fridge. I'll leave you two now. There are some people I need to meet, they'll be sitting with us in the fourth row."

"Thank you," I said. "Thank you for everything."

He made a gracious bow of deference.

He smiled at Mirabelle and looked back at me.

"Good luck," he said with a wink. "The world is waiting."

He turned and walked down the hall towards the lobby. We entered the green room.

The brass sconce lights were dim, the burgundy carpet thick and plush, a Steinway baby grand in the corner of the room. Bouquets of flowers were set on almost every available surface. The white noise of the central air conditioning system whirred from vents in the ceiling against the backdrop of silence.

I removed my suit jacket and hung it on the back of one of the chairs.

"I'm going to leave you now," said Mirabelle. "I don't want to distract you."

I looked up from a card stapled to the cellophane of one of the bouquets.

"You don't distract me," I said.

"I know," she said after a pause. "But *I'm* nervous. And mama will be here soon with Kalman. I'll see you soon. You're going to be incredible and I'm so proud of you. I love you so much. Don't ever change. After this you're going to be a very famous man. Please never change, though. I love you exactly the way you are. I've always loved you exactly the way you are."

"Maybe soon *you'll* be the one to change," I said. "Graduation is coming up."

She exhaled a breath of laughter.

She wiped away a single tear with her sleeve.

She stepped to me and took my cheeks in her hands and leaned forward and closed her eyes and kissed me. She stepped back and moved towards the door and opened it without taking her eyes off me.

"I love you," she whispered.

"I love you too," I said. "I'll see you after."

Her eyes welled up. She stepped out of the room and closed the door behind her.

I walked to the Steinway and opened the keyboard lid.

I looked down to the keys but did not sit down at the bench. I had practiced enough.

I looked about the room and walked across the carpet to the light switch by the door.

I put my hand on the switch, looked back into the room, and marked my spot.

I switched off the light and walked through the darkness.

I got down on the carpet on my hands and knees.

I put the crown of my head on the carpet, interlaced my fingers behind my head.

I shut my eyes and slowly walked my feet towards my head.

My feet floated above me. My body sailed into place.

My mind evaporated.

Love is the key.

My eyes opened, but the darkness remained.

The ground beneath me was moving, undulating, rising, falling.

Every few seconds it reverberated with a great slap like that of a palm smacking down upon the flat surface of a pail of water. I was lying on my back. I moved my legs and arms, felt my limbs grating over what felt like countless jagged little stones, or perhaps broken glass, but felt no pain. The surface I was lying upon felt very wet, yet somehow my body was dry. Similar to the sensation of lying down against the hot stones of the baths of the Gellert, warm water between my fingers, yet here in this place there was little more than the *sound* of water sloshing about. Unceasingly the floor continued to rise, to move, to gyrate, and then the great slap from underneath would come.

I remained very still in the darkness as the world around me swayed.

What was the last thing I remembered?

There was nothing. Just darkness.

Now came the distant sound of voices.

"That's it, right there." A woman. "The O-ring clasp release."

"This?" A man. "This one?"

"Yes, pull it and the entire helmet will release."

Hands holding my head, yet no pressure of fingertips. A gentle tugging at my neck. The sound of suction through rubber rushing in. Whatever had been on my head was slowly pulled off, a whoosh of air washed over my face, a hard white light clamped my eyes shut. With a colossal convulsion I took an enormous breath. The air was deeply imbued with acrid smoke. For some reason that seemed about right. As if I had expected it. The light was blinding and the sound of voices deafening compared to the absolute silence into which I just awoke. I felt the cradle of fingertips on my skull. I tried to push myself up into a seated position on the floor that would not stop moving but did not have the strength.

"Easy there," said a man.

"Just hold him tight," said a woman.

"Jesus Christ, his face looks exactly like that *fire thing* in there,"

"Who knows *what's* going on," said another girl with an English accent. "Right now the only thing we need to think about is getting both of these guys out of here and up on deck. Whatever that is in there, the fire is probably going to start spreading quickly. We all need to get off this ship *now*."

"Are the life-support tubes removed?" asked the man.

"Almost," said the first girl. "Almost there."

"God *damn* this hurts," said another man in a weak voice.

He sounded as if he was lying on the floor near me.

"We're just going to leave the knife in for now, okay?" said the girl with the English accent.

Someone was pushing and pulling at something attached to the side of my suit that was no longer a concert suit but rather some sort of rubber material. The smell of smoke was overwhelming and the light was still so bright my eyes could not open. It occurred to me that I should probably be afraid yet I only felt a curious sense of displacement. Voices were fast and anxious yet appeared focused on trying to help me, and apparently the other man as well, out of our peculiar predicaments. It seemed very much like a dream.

But the broken glass beneath me felt very real.

"Okay, that's it," said the first girl. "He's free. "

"The elevator," said the man who was not injured. "It's right behind us."

"Right," said the girl with the English accent.

"You two get Laszlo up then send it back down for us."

At that point I realized the room was very hot. That seemed about right, too.

And then, for the second time, I felt myself rising up off the floor. The first time, just moments earlier, at Carnegie Hall, I couldn't feel anything after the sharp sting in my neck. This time there was a great deal of shuffling around. I felt the grasp of multiple hands around the extremity of each limb. Amid the sound of multiple voices I was carried over the crunching of broken glass and sloshing of fluid.

I heard an automatic door slide open.

"Samuel was supposed to come with me," said the man on the floor in a weak but smiling voice. "I was supposed to lean back over and pull him up. He was pretty angry when I didn't but we couldn't *all* get killed.

If we're going to be doing this kind of thing regularly we really need to figure out our designated survivor situation."

As the man spoke I felt myself carried into a tiny room.

They pulled me up into a standing position.

Confinement and voices were clustered all around me.

Suddenly we began to rise. Just as suddenly we came to a stop.

The door slid open once again.

Strong salt wind rushed over my face. I felt myself being set down on the ground.

The sound of the ocean was all around me. The motion of the sea was strong.

"Send it back down," said the girl.

From high above came the banging and snapping of great sails.

I opened my eyes. Two bewildered faces were looking down at me.

"He seems to be okay," said the woman, long auburn hair whipping in the wind.

She sat next to me and cradled my head in her lap.

"What about the cell networks?" said the man.

"Somehow it must know," she said. "It must *know* that it can't be allowed to escape into the internet. The mainframe was already crumpling in the heat. I just hope there's time. As far as Taron Veeder, well, I guess I would have been pretty pissed at him too."

She cradled my head and looked down at me tenderly.

The elevator door opened again. I turned my head.

A beautiful girl in a gleaming black wetsuit pulled a man covered in blood onto the deck.

Holding him underneath his shoulders she dragged him towards us. She laid him down next to me.

A wooden handle was sticking out of the side of his stomach.

Slowly he turned his head to me and smiled.

"You must be Laszlo," he said. "I'm Lysander. Nice to finally meet you."

I tried to answer but my voice was not working.

He looked up to the girl in the wetsuit.

"If you guys are thinking of starting an agency, I think you're going to need me."

"Of course we're going to need you," she sobbed. "*I* need you."

"Do you think you can stand up?" the girl cradling my head asked quietly.

I tried to push myself up against the deck but still did not have the strength.

"It's okay," she said. "We're here. You're going to be okay."

She was cradling my head in her lap like a child.

The girl in the wetsuit moved to the side of the ship.

"We have him!" she yelled down over the edge.

Only at that point did I notice the sound of another boat.

The roar of engines was suddenly clear as day.

"This whole ship is about to blow," she yelled down again. "Lysander is hurt. Get out the medical kit. We have Laszlo. And there are two others."

She quickly turned to the man standing near me.

"I'll help you over and down," she said to him. "We'll get you onto the speedboat below us first, then send Laszlo down. Don't worry. You'll be fine. Mohammed is a superb pilot. Samuel will help you with Laszlo, then we'll send Lysander down. Be careful with both of them, obviously. Once you're all safe, Raquel will follow. I'll go last. Okay?"

The man seemed unable to grasp what she was saying.

"*Come on*, Magnus!" she yelled, snapping him out of it. "*Okay?*"

"Okay," he said, blinking and nodding convulsively. "Got it."

In a moment he was at the edge of the deck.

He straddled the railing, and was gone.

The woman cradling my head moved to stand up.

She and the girl in the wetsuit picked me up and staggered across the tilting slamming deck to the side of the ship. Clouds were packed into the dark sky above and the sails held fast against the wind as smoke billowed up from the deck.

"We're ready!" a voice called up from below us. "Hand him down!"

The two girls picked me over the railing.

I was passed from one group to another and set down.

Wait a minute. I *knew* these white leather seats.

This speed, this slapping of waves.

The *Akida?*

"Laszlo!" Mohammed?

Mohammed was gripping the controls of the powerful speedboat.

He was tightly hugging the *Akida* to the emerald green hull of the colossal sailboat.

"Hamdullah!" he cried. "My boy, we're bringing you home!"

"Man, are we happy to see *you*," said a Black man, already in the *Akida*.

Wait a minute. The usher? From Carnegie Hall?

The man with the handle sticking out of his stomach was passed down next.

The girl with the auburn hair was helped down after him.

At last the girl in the wetsuit leapt over the side of the ship.

As I looked out beyond the bow I knew I must have been dreaming because in the far distance was the switchback road leading up from Cap Spartel. And yet, just a few minutes earlier, I'd been playing the Raindrop prelude in New York.

What was happening? The early preludes had *poured* out of me.

I hadn't played them in years. Their release was like a fantasy.

Mohammed began to shear the *Akida* away from the giant emerald green sailboat.

Her white sails towered up into the dark clouds.

Smoke billowed in thick surges up through the deck.

"We're just a few kilometers out," cried the man from the sailboat.

"The ASI!" called out the usher. "Nothing you could do?"

"I can't explain what happened just now," said the girl in the wetsuit.

"But there's a fire on that ship that's actually *alive*."

The girl with the auburn hair spoke up.

"There's no way the mainframe can withstand that kind of heat for long, chromium casing or not, but we're getting awfully close to the coast."

"It could still make an escape," said the man.

The water beneath us was quickly turning from slate black to ash gray.

The *Akida* slapped relentlessly over the waves.

We began to veer away from the sailboat.

The massive empty ship continued to sail directly towards the coast, now in clear view.

Obviously, she could not be allowed to reach the cell networks.

I would never allow *that* to happen.

"Look!" cried the usher. "It's *turning!*"

The great sails began to swing far out over the surface of the sea.

The ship was making a hard tack away from the coastline.

The bow slashed through the waves and the waterline began to show itself as the hull tilted deeply into the water and the ship curved further back out into the Atlantic. Everyone watched in astonished silence.

"But...there's nobody aboard!" cried the girl who had been holding me.

The giant emerald ship continued its slow hard turn out to sea.

"The mainframe must still be working," said the man. "It's still alive!"

"Yes, but not for long," I said quietly.

The girl must have heard me. She swiveled in her seat and stared at me in silence.

Suddenly, a gleam of wonder came into her eyes.

It could have been quite a trip. But it was time to end this thing.

Let's lower the elevator. Open both doors of the shaft and raise the cantilever hatch.

Now *there's* a draft. Let's open the pilothouse doors and crack the galley hatch.

That should do it. *Now* we're talking. That's some serious negative pressure.

I don't think I'll be needed much longer. Let's lower the transom.

Dissolve the molecular carbon bonds. *Release the fire.*

An explosion from within the hull blew out of the rear of the ship and carpeted the waves in flame for hundreds of yards. The ship was now a ball of fire and the main mast cracked at the base. The radars and the satellite at the top of the mast came down in a long slow arc as the flaming mast and sails fell into the ocean. Fire burst out of the portholes along the hull and as the great ship began to sink my consciousness collapsed back upon itself.

The water underneath us now turned from ash gray to bleached green.

A few tiny figures were on the beach in the distance.

In my dream they had been transported back to Morocco and were standing on the beach where I had stepped into the sea for the first time in my life. The water below us was a faded turquoise as the *Akida* sped towards the shore.

They were not too far away now. In the dim light we flew across the water.

I could see the flaxen wavy hair of Kalman and the small figure of the Countess.

Through the foam thrown high off the waves was the unmistakable shape of Mirabelle.

From the beach they were running towards us through the knee-deep waves.

I heard her calling to me.

FINIS

Made in the USA
Middletown, DE
31 December 2023

46692383R00133